DRAKE

THE KINGS OF GUARDIAN - BOOK ELEVEN

KRIS MICHAELS

Copyright © 2018 by Kris Michaels

Krismichaelsauthor.com

All rights reserved.

No part of this book may be reproduced in any form or by any electronic or mechanical means, including information storage and retrieval systems, without written permission from the author, except for the use of brief quotations in a book review.

Licensed material is being used for illustrative purposes only and any person depicted in the licensed material is a model. This book is fiction. Names, characters and incidents are the product of the author's imagination or used fictitiously. Any resemblance to any actual persons, living or dead, events, or locations are entirely coincidental.

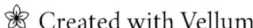 Created with Vellum

CHAPTER 1

*D*rake Simmons leaned against the back of a leather chair in the cabin of Guardian's G6 and seethed as his twin brother Dixon rechecked his go-bag. They'd piloted the aircraft to White Plains, just outside New York City, and touched down not more than thirty minutes ago. Other than what was necessary to successfully pilot the aircraft, they hadn't exchanged a word in hours, but that wasn't uncommon. Today, unlike their normal silent connection that freaked everyone out, they *weren't* communicating. Drake had spent the entire flight banking the coals of the silent rage burning him alive. For the first time in years, the cause of his fury was his brother. Dixon zipped the A-3 bag and glanced over his shoulder at him. Drake averted his eyes.

"I can't leave if you're mad." Dixon turned around and sat on the corner of the G-6's leather couch.

"Good, then you can't leave. I'm pissed enough to keep you here for the rest of your life." Drake crossed his arms and leaned against the bulkhead.

"You know I have to go."

Fuck. He loathed the note of defeat in Dixon's voice. Anger shot through him like a bullet through the muzzle of a gun. "No, I don't. What happened wasn't your fault. He's a fucking criminal and a bastard. They *both* used us."

Dixon shook his head. The emotion in his eyes as they held each other's gaze was easy to recognize. Guilt. "You didn't do what I did."

"Look, none of that shit, *none of it*, was because of you. It could have been me! Instead, he took you. Why? Why did he pick you and not me? Why did he 'love' you and not me? Fuck, his actions weren't the result of 'love,' and you know it! But ask yourself why! Why did he abandon me to that monster? We were children, and we had zero say in anything that went down. What he forced you to do *wasn't* your fault. You cannot be held responsible for making choices that had no right ending. He abused your mind as much as that whore let those men physically abuse me. I can't let you go back into that pit, Dixon." Drake raked his hand through his hair and shook his head. "It took years for you to stop screaming in the middle of the night. *Years*, D. He is a monster, but worse than that, dear old dad would get off on tearing you down simply so he could watch you die. You don't have to go back into that snake pit." His words contained years of anguish and hatred for the motherfuckers that hurt them both. His venom wasn't directed at Dixon. He'd never turn his rage toward his brother, but their parents were fair game. Guardian shouldn't have exploited that connection. He was pissed at Archangel. Hell, he wanted to rage at the entire organization, to the point that he'd even considered just walking away.

Dixon leaned his forearms on his knees and leveled a stare at him. Drake saw the pain and regret Dixon tried to hide. That bastard, their sperm donor, had fucked up Dixon. Their father, the man who was supposed to nurture and protect Dixon, had created a hell-on-earth and abandoned his son in the middle of it. It'd been left to Drake to pull Dixon out. He did it while licking the wounds inflicted on him from his mother. They'd both had to grow up, fast. They'd managed, but... No, he'd never understood how Dixon could willingly go back.

His brother's voice thickened with emotion, "How can I make you understand that I need to do this. *For me.* No other reason. I need to face my demons."

"You mean demon." Drake threw that out there. Their father. The abomination.

Dixon lifted his chin acknowledging Drake's correction before he continued, "Yeah, singular, demon. Guardian is asking me to do no more than they'd ask any other person they employ. I'm the way in. I've been teaching the investigators' course for years now. I know what I'm doing." His eyes flickered with a hint of mischief. "I'm the smarter of the two of us, remember?"

Drake snorted. When they tested before entering college, his brother scored one point higher on the Stanford-Binet Intelligence Scale. He'd scored a 210, and Dixon had scored a 211. They hadn't bothered to retake the test, but some days Drake swore he'd happily sit through the hours of bullshit questions one more time if it would shut his brother up.

"I need your support on this." Dixon looked down at his boots.

Drake took a breath and then another. While he tried to get a grip on his anger, he took the time to truly look at his brother, his other half. The same person, different circumstances. Hell, raised in a different world. The man was going to have to change clothes before he dropped in on dear old fucking Dad. Nothing less than bespoke suits and hand-made shoes would be permitted in that bastard's realm...unless...no.

Drake pushed the thoughts away and cleared his throat. Bile rose at the thoughts that surfaced. He couldn't let Dixon do this. He tried again. "You want my support on this? How can I support you? He fucking broke you. Tell me you don't remember those nights when you couldn't sleep or the depression that almost consumed you. I remember it all, Dix. I was there with you. Every. Fucking. Night. I held you when the dreams wouldn't release you." Drake slumped down in the chair and whispered, "How can I support you when I know what it's going to do to you?" Drake shook his head. "You *can* walk away."

Dixon's eyes fixed on the aircraft's floor. His words were soft, and Drake had to concentrate to hear them. "You weren't there. I still live it over and over. Here." His fingers lifted and tapped his temple. He gave Drake a sad smile. "I'm not that scared kid anymore. I have more training and education than anyone he's ever employed, or for that matter, ever met. I know I can do this and, if I do, I'll make him pay for what he did to them, to her."

Drake just stood there. He didn't share his brother's belief he could have changed the course of history. Dixon's life had been a living hell when they were separated. So was his; he just occupied a different pit. His mother was a conniving, vicious bitch, and he suffered beatings and verbal abuse from her and the human waste that slithered in and out of her bed. As bad as he'd had it, what Dixon suffered had been far worse. He swallowed back the denial and vehemence and corralled them. It was apparent Dixon needed to purge this specter. If Dixon could summon the balls to walk back into a living hell, then the least he could do was match his brother's courage and not dump his fear on Dix. Fuck, he felt like someone was gutting him with a dull spoon. The heartache of letting his brother go...the pain was indescribable and the cost... He popped up and grabbed his brother out of his chair, pulling him into a death grip of a hug. "You'll call me and check in. That isn't up for debate. I'll find you if you're late. Even once." Drake's voice cracked, but he continued, "I can't lose you. I... Damn-it, you're all I have."

Dixon nodded and held him. Words had always been extraneous when they were alone, and a defense mechanism when people were around, even those people they trusted. Their banter was a way to deflect, so people didn't look deeper. What they honestly shared was quiet, solemn communication between two parts that were whole, but not complete without each other. Drake needed his brother to fill fractured places in him that no one else knew existed. All twins shared a bond, but the ties that held *them* together had been forged in the hottest fires and deepest trenches of perdition. They existed without each other, but only thrived when they were together. Their parents had tried to keep them apart and, in doing so, had established a link that could never be broken.

"That's not true. We have a family now, but I know what you mean." Dixon's arms tightened around him until his ribs and lungs protested. "I can't call. You know I can't. Don't come for me.

Stay away from him, from New York. You promise me, dammit."

Drake grabbed a fistful his brother's shirt and tugged on it. "I can't. I can't promise you that. I'll come for you if you get in trouble." Fuck, he couldn't make that promise.

Dixon pushed away and stared at Drake with eyes exact mirrors of his. "If I have to worry about you showing up, I won't be able to concentrate. I can't let him win. You show up only if Guardian approves it. Can you give me that much?"

Drake dipped his head downward.

Dixon saw the minuscule movement. "I'll be back. As soon as it's over, I'll be back."

Drake nodded again and pulled his brother into another hug. Dixon slapped his back once before he pulled away and picked up his A-3 bag. Drake opened the door to the aircraft and dropped the stairs. He grabbed his bag and jerked his head at the opening. Dixon drew a deep breath and blinked several times before he exited the aircraft. They walked side by side until they reached the two pre-positioned SUV's. They were both provided by Guardian. Dixon's wasn't equipped with an armory like Drake's, but the vehicle did have a hidden panic button and

Guardian tracked and monitored the SUV twenty-four seven.

"Say hey to Cliff for me." Dixon threw his bag into the rear of his vehicle and opened the driver's side door.

"I will." Drake opened the rear of his vehicle and slid his bag onto the seat. "Do me a favor? When the time comes, you let that bastard know that he's lucky it was you Guardian chose for this assignment. If they'd chosen me, I'd invent new ways to gut the bastard and slowly let him bleed out for what he did to you."

Dixon lifted an eyebrow. "What makes you think I won't?"

Drake met his brother's stare, and for the first time since Dixon accepted the fucking assignment, Drake saw what he needed to see. The confidence of numerous missions had seeped back into his brother as evidenced by the slight raise of his right eyebrow when he dared Drake to do something better than him. That observation gave him a modicum of peace.

Drake let a small smile spread across his face. He didn't feel it, but he knew it was important to his brother. Dixon returned the favor. They were parting. Neither wanted it, but life demanded it.

He stood at the door of his vehicle and watched as his brother got into his SUV, started the engine and drove out of the hanger. He stood there for a while coming to grips with the fact that his brother was heading south into New York, into danger, and Drake wasn't going with him. The suckage was so strong on so many levels that he let it hit him and then wash by. There was nothing he could do, and he fucking hated it.

So, he did what he came to do—other than fly with Drake to New York. Three days ago, Doctor Heathcliff O'Rourke, their scholastic mentor, and now a tenured professor at MESE, Massachusetts Engineering School of Excellence, had called and asked Dixon and Drake to come and see him. He slipped behind the wheel and started the engine for his three-hour drive via I-84 and I-90 east. As the SUV rumbled to life, he closed his eyes and said a prayer for his brother. Dix was going to need all the help he could get.

Traffic wasn't insane, which was unusual and unfortunately allowed Drake to think. He pushed his worries about his brother to the side and tried to recall when he first realized that Dr. Heathcliff O'Rourke was important to them. The man had guest lectured on robotic engineering at their high school in Louisville when they were juniors. Both he and Dixon were immediately intrigued with the possibilities Dr. O'Rourke's words orchestrated in their minds. A small chuckle escaped him as he remembered how they'd begged, cajoled, harassed, and finally worn down their high school physics teacher until she'd arranged a personal meeting for them. That two-hour meeting had turned into a lifetime mentorship. Drake smiled as he checked his rear-view mirror. His Uncle Bob had removed them from hell, but Cliff had given them purpose and a sense of pride. Cliff was a foster parent to two kids who'd been handed a rough deal, and he understood trauma. Looking back, Drake knew without Cliff, he and Dixon would have never gone to college. Hell, Cliff helped them fill out the college admission forms. Their father made too much money for them to be eligible for student loans, so they applied for every scholarship they could find. They'd shovel shit for the rest of their lives before they'd ask that bastard to give them anything. They funded their own way through college and worked on the horse ranch their uncle managed until they both graduated. Shoveling shit. It was tough, but the accomplishment was theirs and wasn't tainted by their father's influence or money.

Cliff...damn, he hadn't seen the man in over ten years, but they did keep in touch. Until Frank Marshall, Cliff O'Rourke was the closest thing to a father they'd ever had. Their uncle provided them a place to live, but he didn't know what to do with two boys who'd gone through hell. Drake couldn't blame him. The man liked horses, not people, but he'd been there, and for that, they'd always be grateful.

College was where he and Dixon had...well, bloomed, but fuck that was a frilly way to put it. Maybe expanded was a better term. They were able to drop the emotional shields they used to surround themselves. Encouragement from Cliff and timely successes in school gave them the confidence to take small steps towards normality, or at least their version of normal. Each step toward independence fueled the next. Each step forward left their trauma further behind. The momentum of the small victories led to strides of confidence and self-revelation and then to the marathon that they'd been running. If their life was a lock, few people held the keys able to untangle the writhing knot of emotional and physical trauma their parents had bound them together with. Cliff, Gabriel, the Skipper, Chief, Adam, Frank, and Amanda all had keys, and in one way or another, each had opened and freed them from a piece of their past. Except Dixon still carried a locked portion of himself that hadn't been released. Drake drew a deep breath. He forced himself to admit Dixon needed to find that key and purge himself of the past that still haunted him.

Drake pulled into the sleepy town and pointed his SUV straight for the college and the MESE Campus Police Department. He was on official business, and his vehicle had enough firepower to stage a third-world coup, so he was checking in to make sure he followed protocols. He closed an eye at a stop light and considered that last thought. He wasn't *technically* on official business, but he'd be damned if he'd be without his weapons.

He wove through the campus and pulled up in front of the police station. He grabbed his credentials and badge, secured his SUV, and headed into the building. Bright overheads lit the neat reception area. Several people sat in the lobby, students if he had to guess. A clerk sat behind a small window to his right that bore a sign, "Parking Violations". Ahh, yeah. He chuckled to himself. He'd gotten several of those bad boys when he'd attended the University of Louisville. A middle-aged man in uniform looked up from his computer. "Can I help you?" Drake got a once over. He was wearing what he usually wore at the ranch, although the shirt was new. Stuck in the middle of college students wearing shorts, flip flops and t-shirts, the cowboy boots, wide leather belt and boot cut jeans he wore made him stick out like a sore thumb.

"Yes, sir. May I speak to your chief?" Drake walked forward and opened his credential holder, presenting the officer with a face full of badge and identification. The clerk blinked a couple times as he examined the open leather case in front of his face.

"Yeah, hang on." The man exited stage left in one hell of a hurry. Drake glanced up at the television that was streaming a national news network.

The door into the lobby opened again, and a younger man exited. "I'm Chief Reardon." He extended his hand to Drake who shook it.

Drake presented his credentials again and asked, "Sir, may we speak in private?"

"Certainly." Drake followed through the door to the reception area and into an office at the back of the facility.

"What business does Guardian Security have here?" The chief motioned for Drake to sit.

"That's unknown, sir. My goal at this time is to gather information and see if there is anything Guardian should be involved in. Of course, as a courtesy between our agencies, if we believe there is any information you need to know, we will ensure you are read in immediately." The way he'd phrased his response made it seem as if they were investigating a case. Meh... he'd stretched the truth farther than that without it breaking, and the stretch stroked the chief's ego.

The chief let out a big sigh and smiled for the first time. "So just checking in as a courtesy?"

"Affirmative. As a federal agent, you're aware that I'm carrying, and I know you need to know I'm here on official business."

"Where are you going?" The chief leaned forward and grabbed his pen looking up at Drake expectantly.

"Engineering Department."

The chief cocked his head and scribbled something down. "Who are you seeing?"

"Doctor Heathcliff O'Rourke."

The chief lifted his head. "O'Rourke in any trouble?"

Drake shook his head. "He's our complainant."

The chief focused on the paper again and mumbled, "Good. Good." He scribbled a few more words and finished his writing with a flourish. "Present this if you get stopped by anyone."

Drake extended his hand and took the paper from the Chief. After a glance at it, he smiled. "Did you just give me a hall pass?" He couldn't help but laugh. That shit was funny.

The man's brow furrowed. "No, Mr. Simmons, I just gave you a get out of jail free card." The chief stood up and extended his hand again, although his smile was missing this time. Drake ate his laughter and hid his smile as he shook the man's hand and pocketed his hall pass. If he needed a get out of jail free card, he only had to make one call to Guardian.

CHAPTER 2

"Okay, I understand that maybe things are a little too closely connected, but why did you have to call *them*?" Jillian Law sat in the front row of her foster father's lecture hall. It could hold over a hundred people but currently held only two. Herself and Doctor Heathcliff O'Rourke, father by choice, not birth.

"They happen to be federal law enforcement officials." He closed his laptop and leaned back in his chair sliding his hands over his stomach and linking his fingers. "Besides I trust them. If they don't think I need to worry, I'll drop it." He cocked his head at her and narrowed his eyes.

No, he wouldn't, but Jillian appreciated the attempt on his part. She didn't call him on his fib and checked the clock behind her dad's head. "They were supposed to be here by now."

Her father tipped his head back to look at the clock. His long hair flopped over the back of the chair. His t-shirt, blue jeans, and tennis shoes were a far cry from the other professors' garb, but her dad had always marched to the beat of his own drum. He was a hippie from the sixties, living by necessity in the new millennia. Woodstock was his chosen era. Apparently, the creator of the universe hadn't gotten the memo. He made a non-committal noise as he righted himself. "So why the angst about me calling them?" His question got straight to the point. He always did.

She shrugged. "Angst?" She chuckled and shook her head. "No, not really. I agree that the things that have been happening are really weird, but aren't we starting at the top of the pyramid here? Maybe I should talk to some of the local authorities?"

Jillian threw the carrot out there and hoped that Cliff would nibble on it. He gave a noncommittal sound. Her reservations centered on a man she'd crushed on throughout her last two years of high school and into college—a man she just did not want to see. She blushed at the memory of her affection for the brothers in general, but more so for her adolescent and then young adult lust for tall, quiet Drake. Shit, she'd been so in love with him—in the soul-crushing way that only a teenager could fall prey to—desperate and needy, with a side order of hero-worship. She'd never had a problem telling the twins apart. She could see the subtle differences no one else seemed to pick out. Yeah, her first love. The way she'd idolized him was epic, and the poor man didn't even know she existed. Jillian snorted at her own folly.

Her father's eyes cut to her. "What?"

"Nothing. Just thinking about things." She smoothed a shiny veneer over a version of the truth she'd be comfortable sharing with her father. Her blush deepened. God, she really needed to grow up. There was no way either of the twins ever noticed her. At least not in the way she wanted. God knows she tried to get their attention and failed. She cringed internally. Failed wasn't the proper verb. Perhaps bombed, blundered, flopped, crashed...yeah, any of those would better describe her ridiculousness.

Jillian drew a circle with her fingertip on the surface below her hand. Growing up she'd been thin to the point her tormentors called her SG. It was short for skeleton geek. Her glasses were thick and heavy, sliding down her nose. It seemed her index finger's permanent position was between her eyes pushing her glasses back into place. But as a freshman in college, emboldened by a love so deep and fierce, Jillian went shopping. She bought a dress that revealed more skin than she'd ever dared show before. At eighteen, she went to a salon for the first time and had her hair cut and styled. The purpose? There was a Sadie Hawkins dance at the college, and she'd finally built up enough nerve to ask Drake to take her.

Jillian glanced at Cliff who seemed to be fascinated with the toe of his sneaker. She bit the inside of her lip thinking about that day. She knew Dixon and Drake always stopped by her father's office at the University of Louisville after classes, so she'd timed her arrival to coincide. She would wait for her moment and then ask Drake to take her to the dance. It was a perfect plan until Sissy Calhoun literally pushed her aside in the hall and snuggled up to Drake. Jillian was three feet away from him, three feet away from asking the man she adored to go to the dance with her. Everything she'd tried shattered when Sissy said, "Hey Drake, will you take me to the Sadie Hawkins dance?"

She couldn't recall Drake's answer because Sissy slid a hostile glance back toward her like she'd oozed out of some hole in the ground. Hearing what he said wasn't important. One look from that girl had shattered her carefully constructed confidence. The moment crushed her. Absolutely decimated her. She went home and folded the dress carefully before she placed it in the back of the closet and then stood under the shower until it ran cold. There was no way she could compete for Drake's attention with the likes of Sissy. It took months before she gathered enough shards of confidence to back up, strategize and come up with a plan to make Drake notice her. Drake had no problem attracting women. She'd seen the woman who flirted with him on campus, and she lacked the physical blessings to compete with them.

Jillian drew a deep breath and glanced at the clock again. The twins were definitely late. She closed her eyes. No, she couldn't have competed on a physical level with all those women, so she used a weapon most of the other women didn't or couldn't use. She met the twins on an academic level. That's when she discovered her love for science and then fell in love with mechanical engineering. Okay, maybe her initial interest was prompted because the twins were studying in the field, but the journey left a seed, and the seed blossomed into a wonderful career.

A sound from her father stopped her memory-driven stroll down "Remember When Lane". Cliff stood and stretched. Fifty-four-years old and both male and female coeds routinely hit on him. His long brown hair, close-cropped beard, and brilliant smile made him irresistible to just about everyone. The gray he did have only accented his handsome features. Jillian loved the man more than almost anyone on the planet. He'd rescued her and her brother from a life of bouncing from foster home to foster home. Back in Louisville, her brother Matthew had no interest in academia and was happily married with the proverbial two point five kids, dog, and white picket fence. He was an electrician and ran his own business. Matt had struggled at times, but Cliff had always been there for both of them.

The fact that Cliff would always take care of them was why she was squirming on her seat in her father's lecture hall waiting for Dixon and Drake Simmons to walk through those doors.

"When was the last time you talked to them?"

Her father walked over to where she was sitting and leaned against the first row of desktops.

USB ports and electrical outlets for the students' computers and electronics dotted the seating area. She reached over and shut an open pop up port as she spoke so she wouldn't have to look at her father. "I haven't seen or spoken to them since they left to join military." Drake's leaving had left her empty, so she buried her unrequited feelings and got on with her life. She'd gone on to get her master's degree and then her doctorate. Since graduating she'd worked in several positions before she developed and patented technology that three world-wide companies had paid through the nose to use. Now she rented space in one of the best labs in the country and worked for herself.

"Seriously, not once since they left? Huh." Her father glanced at his watch and shook his head.

"Why, when was the last time you talked to them?"

"Three days ago."

Jillian laughed and pushed his arm making him sway. "Stop being so damn literal."

Cliff laughed and rearranged his hip against the sturdy, raised partition. "We talk about three or four times a year. They are living in the Midwest now.

"You never told me you spoke with them so regularly. Why are they living in the Midwest? I thought you said they worked for Guardian Security? Isn't that company headquartered in Washington D.C.?" She recalled every minute detail her father had ever told her about the twins. Rather pathetic, but it was the truth.

Her father tipped his head. "They do. I don't know what they are doing out there in the land of corn and cows, but I think they've lived there for three or four years now." He stroked his closely shaved beard as he spoke. "Shame they didn't pursue their education. They could have made a major impact in the world. I wonder if they know the lives they could have changed."

"Actually, we do make one hell of an impact, but if you ever heard about it, it would mean we'd failed."

Jillian snapped her head toward the door. *Oh. My. God. There was no way.* The twenty-year-old version of her crush shattered and fell at her feet replaced by a very adult lust for the tall, muscular man who sauntered toward them. Cowboy boots, blue jeans, a white long-sleeved shirt, a leather belt and a buckle the size of a salad plate adorned one of the most handsome men she'd ever seen.

Cliff gave a laugh and pushed off the partition, meeting the Greek god halfway. They gripped hands and then hugged. She heard a mumbled greeting between the men before her father turned towards her.

"You remember Jillian?"

Yes, Drake remembered, but that beautiful woman could not be Jillian. There was no way that skinny, bespectacled mouse of a girl was the woman sitting in front of him. Holy shit, the sweet, shy, nerdy teenager with braces and glasses that were too thick and kept sliding down her nose *was not* the woman he was staring at. Couldn't be.

"Silly Jilly?" Surprised, Drake let the nickname slip out.

"Oh, my God. Seriously? That is how you remember me? By the name Sara Jane Mathison and her clique of cheerleading clones coined?"

The woman's face flamed in mortification. The deep rose-colored blush went well with her dark blond hair. Her eyes were huge, brown and beautiful. It was amazing what her old coke bottle thick glasses had hidden.

Drake laughed at her embarrassment and walked over, extending his hand. "Sorry, I wouldn't have recognized you if I passed you in the street. You've changed." He took her hand and smiled at her as he held it. "In the best way possible."

"You, too." Her eyes widened as if her words surprised her. Yep, that was a slip of the tongue. A fresh wave of red climbing her cheeks attested to it. She pulled her hand back, and he released it, reluctantly.

Drake swung his attention back toward Cliff. "Dixon is on an assignment. He sends his regards."

"I'm sorry for asking you to come out here, but I didn't know what else to do." Cliff motioned toward a seat beside Jillian. Drake didn't mind that at all. He was all about getting closer to the woman. He walked behind the partition and was glad that he did. She was wearing a tight skirt with a generous slit that exposed shapely, toned legs. He took in the expanse of skin without lingering, although he'd have loved to take the time to examine every way Silly Jilly had grown.

He sat down and leaned back in his chair. "So,

what has you concerned?" Cliff hadn't gone into specifics on the phone, so he was curious.

"Well, I think someone is trying to kill Jillian."

Cliff's words were no sooner out of his mouth than Jillian piped up, "You're overreacting. Nobody is trying to kill me—"

"Whoa!" Drake leaned forward, his single strongly enunciated word silencing her objection midsentence.

"Let's take this from the top. What's going on?" Jill opened her mouth and Drake immediately put up a finger. "Why don't we let Cliff explain why he's concerned then you can refute any of the allegations he makes after he makes them." He raised an eyebrow and held her chocolate brown gaze for a couple of seconds before she narrowed her eyes and gracefully leaned back into her chair. Ah, Jilly has a temper. Good to know.

As much as he'd wanted to keep his focus on the beautiful revelation next to him, he couldn't. He returned his attention to his mentor and friend. "Present your facts, Cliff."

The man in front of him gave him a quick smile. "You learned well, young grasshopper."

"I had a fantastic mentor." Drake leaned

forward on his forearms and gave Cliff his undivided attention.

Cliff smiled briefly and stroked his beard. "Jillian came out here to do a guest lecture series for my class. Her accomplishments in the networked and interconnected systems of Control Theory are leading the nation, well for that matter, the world."

Drake swung his head toward Jilly. To say he was impressed would be an understatement. "Congratulations. What field, specifically?"

"Sustainable power."

She didn't elaborate, and as intrigued as he was with the field of study, now wasn't the time to ask her to expand. Not that she probably gave a shit, but Drake acknowledged her work and dedication, because, fuck him, to get to that level took determination. "I'm impressed."

She blushed again and glanced toward her father. Cliff held up one finger. "Three days after she arrived, she was nearly run over."

Jillian leaned forward. "Counterpoint. The campus police said the vehicle was stolen and they believed the driver wasn't trying to kill me as much as he was trying to flee the scene of his own crime." She leaned back in her seat and cocked her head at her father. Drake swiveled his head toward Cliff.

"You sprained your wrist." Her father hit the remark across the net, and Drake followed the lob to Jilly.

She lifted up her wrist. An ugly purple bruise trailed from her wrist down the length of her forearm. "I'm fine. It's just a little boo-boo, dad."

"Well, if that's a little boo-boo, I don't want to know what you call an injury," Cliff responded and then held up a second finger stilling Jill's retort.

"Four days after you get here you get a call, from the San Jose police. They told you your apartment had been broken into."

Jillian held up her hand stopping her father. "They also said, as you heard, that there were several break-ins in a five-block radius." She shrugged, "I haven't been home a lot. If someone were looking for an easy target, my apartment would be it." She batted her eyes at him and gave him a smile. The woman was enjoying the debate and Drake could tell Cliff was becoming frustrated with the way she was playing it off.

"That same day, earlier in the morning, you were mugged going across campus to get us coffee. Your computer satchel was stolen."

"There was nothing in my satchel but my driver's license and sixty-five dollars in cash, several old newspapers and my rental car agreement. My computer and tablet were here with you."

"In broad daylight?" Drake asked shifting his gaze between the two.

"Yeah, just before noon. As Dad said, I was heading to the coffee shop across campus. They have great iced coffees and lunch bagels."

"Did you get a look at the guy? Did you call campus security?"

"Dad called security. I gave them my statement. I saw him because I wasn't giving up my bag without a fight. He was older than a typical college student, although he was dressed in jeans and a hoodie as if he was dressing to fit in. He had brown hair, scruff and was built. Muscular. I screamed and fought to draw a crowd. He ripped my bag from my hands." Jilly turned and looked directly at her father. "He's also limping because I kicked his knee. Hard."

Cliff groaned and rubbed the back of his neck. "I know there isn't a lot here Drake, but when we tell you what Jillian has invented, you'll understand why I'm so concerned."

Drake swiveled his gaze from Cliff to Jilly. "Do tell."

"Yeah, okay." She drew a breath as if gathering her thoughts. "I've reached a solution for miniaturizing photovoltaic panels for solar arrays."

Drake's eyes widened at her comment. "You've found a way to shrink huge solar panels into something small?" His brows furrowed. "How?"

"It was a simple idea really. In the current technology, the sun's rays excite electrons in silicon cells using the photons of light from the sun."

"Correct. We've used the technology extensively at the complex where I work." Drake glanced at her, encouraging her to continue.

"Well, as you know there is a significant decrease if the PV panels are not positioned correctly or are shaded. The efficiency of the power transfer is horrendous."

Drake agreed. "From personal experience with our solar arrays, I've determined that if even one cell is shaded our energy gather could drop by fifty percent."

"Right, but that is because the PV panels are massive and interconnected. I've developed a single contained unit, the approximate size of a loaf of bread, that does the work of an entire array. The module follows the sun through its orbit, receiving the most sun possible. As I stated earlier, the massive panels are inefficient. After all, we are only talking photons that excite electrons. Billions of those particles can fit in the space of my fingertip. I've used nanotechnology, some of which is my proprietary tech, to reduce the footprint without marginalizing the energy that can be produced. Additionally, by activating a small charge into the chamber as the reaction occurs, the dynamic of the interchange between the photons and electrons is elongated, creating more energy with less exposure. I can show you the science behind it." She shrugged. "PV74589V-1 is my baby."

"I'd be honored to learn the science behind the project, but you really should think of something shorter to call it."

Jillian let a slow smile spread across her face before she chuckled, "What like Delbert or something?"

"Delbert? Why Delbert?"

Jillian laughed again. "Don't you remember Delbert Pike? He was that kid on campus that—"

Drake's head snapped up when the memory popped into his head. "Oh shit, yeah! Dynamo

Delbert! That kid was on something, I swear he never stopped moving."

Jillian winked at him, and a blush spread across her face. "Perpetual energy."

Drake smiled, the memory of the small man firmly etched into his mind. "A fitting name for a power supply. Have you published, patented, and copyrighted yet?"

"No, I'm working on that now, but I did mention my work to several people who were interested in its applications."

"I'll need a list of names."

"Of course." Jillian rattled off the names and pulled up the email addresses for each from her phone. Drake typed them into his cell as she spoke. "I'm sorry, but I don't know cell phone numbers or physical addresses. All my consulting is done via video conference or over email."

"That's fine." He returned his attention back to Cliff. "You believe her development of this technology has spurred recent events. Are you assuming professional jealousy or corporate espionage?"

"Tell him the rest Jillian." Cliff lifted an eyebrow and stared at his daughter.

She dropped her head and spoke to the desktop. "Obviously one or more of my colleagues have mentioned my project." She lifted her liquid chocolate gaze to him. "I've been approached by numerous automobile manufacturers, and I've had an offer from three entities in the Middle East to outright purchase my research and prototype. One offer was for over five hundred million dollars."

Drake leaned forward and rested his weight on his elbows as he thought. An invention such as hers would cause OPEC to blanch. "You refused." He shifted his eyes to his left, and she shrugged.

"Jillian." Cliff's voice prompted a huge sigh from her.

"Fine. I received three emails since I rejected the offers." She lifted her phone from the desk in front of her and swiped the screen. "I don't know who sent them, but they weren't very nice."

Drake accepted the proffered device and read the first message in the thread. "*Reconsider the offer.*" Non-threatening. Harassment at best. He moved the screen up and read the second. The time stamp was two weeks later. "*Sell or else.*" Drake blinked at the message and shot a glance at Cliff. The man stared back at him. Jilly was doing her best to ignore both of them. Drake pushed the screen up and read the final email. "*Accept or lose everything.*"

"Well, this just moved from a series of unfortunate incidents into a reason to consider personal protection." Drake sat her phone in front of him. "Do you know which offer they were talking about?"

Jillian shook her head and sighed. "I don't have a clue."

Drake tapped his fingers on the counter as he thought. "Where is your invention?"

"San Jose. In a bank safety deposit box. I got a little nervous after the third email, so I put the essential and proprietary mechanisms in a small Faraday case and rented a safety deposit box big enough to hold it. All my research and data are on external hard drives also enclosed inside the case."

Drake smiled at that. Jill was a smart cookie with common sense. A Faraday case would protect the electronics and the hard drive against any static charge. Hell, it would also protect it against an electromagnetic pulse.

"Okay. So, we can do this several ways. The first option, you can take this," he picked up her phone, "to the San Jose Police department." Jilly glanced at her father.

Cliff cleared his throat. "What are the other options?"

Drake drew a deep breath and released it slowly as he considered his words. "The threats could be international, which requires federal law enforcement involvement. The FBI or the CIA depending on the pissing contest and judicial limitations, or you could hire Guardian. We have federal authority and an overseas reach." He needed them to know they had options beyond what he could bring to the table. Although his hand was clearly the winner, he wouldn't make that decision for them.

"Would you be overseeing the case?" Cliff crossed his arms and rocked back on his heels as he waited for an answer.

"I don't work in the field any longer, but I can petition the boss and let him know this is personal." He figured Alpha and even Archangel would get it. He had several people who could hold the complex together while he was gone. One of the best things about Guardian was that no one person was a point of failure. There were always people being trained to fill your position. The mission must go on regardless of the personnel running it.

"What exactly do you do now?" Jillian cocked her head sending her long blond hair off her shoulder. The curls bounced around her in a cascade of gold.

Drake shrugged. "I run the training portion of a complex Guardian maintains."

"Have you ever worked something like this?" Jillian crossed her legs, and it was everything he could do not to drop his eyes to take them in.

"Personal security? Yes and no." He shook his head. "Before I started working at the complex, I was on a highly specialized team that worked overseas. We were the means to ensure people and resources were protected. Normally those missions involved armed conflict. Suffice to say, the training I've received is far beyond the training required to perform personal security details. Whoever is tracking you has no idea what I *am* capable of doing." His tone became ice cold and deadly as he let his meaning flow through his words. "I am a Guardian."

Jillian glanced at her father for a second before she nodded. "Okay, then...I choose Guardian."

Cliff let out a long breath and chuckled, "Thank God. I thought you were going to fight me on this."

Jilly shook her head. "I'll admit this has spooked me enough that I flew across the country to be with my dad under the pretense of a being guest lecturer. While I don't think any of the incidents that have happened here are actually related to the emails, *they* are enough to concern me. The emails may be intimidation tactics, and I really hope they are, but each time I read them..."

Drake heard the emotion in her voice and noticed she blinked back moisture that gathered in her eyes. He got that. At a minimum, she'd been violated by an anonymous mind-fuck, and she was scared.

He reached in his pocket and withdrew his phone. "Well then, let's begin." He hit the number two on his speed dial and put the phone on speaker.

CHAPTER 3

Jillian watched Drake as he folded his arms and leaned over his phone. The muscles in his biceps bulged, testing the tensile strength of the crisp cotton material that tried to confine them.

"Operator Three-Seven-Four."

"This is Alpha-Five. Send me to Alpha."

"One moment, Alpha-Five," the professional voice responded.

Jillian blinked, darted a glance at her father and then whipped her head back to Drake. "Is that like double-oh-seven?" She couldn't hold back the joke.

Drake lifted his eyes to her and shook his head with a seriousness she didn't expect and couldn't ignore. "No. That fictional character isn't as good as we are."

Jillian swallowed hard at his no-nonsense words. "Okay. Noted."

"What's up, D?" A male's voice came through the connection.

"Skipper, you're on speaker. I'm up at MESE with friends. I think we have a situation and they'd like Guardian to help. Specifically, me."

There was a pause before the man replied. "Standby." Drake leaned back in his chair and stared at the phone.

"The line is secure." A woman's voice spoke, and Jillian's eyes jolted from the phone to Drake.

"Hey, Jewell."

"Hey, yourself. What are you doing in the engineering department at MESE?"

Jillian jumped. "How did they know—"

Drake held up a hand. "I have a situation. I have Doctor Heathcliff O'Rourke and his daughter, Jilly, here with me."

Jilly? Jillian sent a glare Drake's direction. *As if.* The sound of a keyboard being manipulated at a tremendous speed filtered through the speaker before the woman came back onto the connection.

"Ah, there we go. It's a pleasure to meet you Doctor O'Rourke and Doctor Law."

Jillian jolted as if she'd been stung by a bee. Her attention swung from Drake to her father and then back to Drake.

"Archangel online."

"Dom Ops online."

Two distinct male voices chimed in before a third spoke, "Okay, D. Fill us in."

"Dr. Law has developed some cutting-edge technology that would, in my opinion, set the world's oil-based economy on its ear. There have been multiple offers for her new tech, up to an offer of five hundred million dollars."

She heard a whistle from one of the men.

"I know, right?" said the woman who spoke earlier.

Drake continued, "She declined and then received three emails. Jewell, can you..."

"Got it. Doctor Law, which account did you receive those on? You have three that I see."

"Umm...my account under Doctor dot law dot-_"

"Got it. Do I have permission to enter your accounts?"

"Uh, yeah, sure. The password is—" Jillian listened to the keyboard in the background.

"Don't need it. Okay, I'm in. Let's see." The keystroke slowed, then a staccato flurry of sound followed by silence. "Yeah, this is interesting. The IP address is different each time. The email account that it came from was made the same day as the emails were sent, no further traffic on any of the accounts. It's a common tactic and impossible to track, especially since we don't have the same IP address. Not the same computer and I'd lay odds they junked the computer they sent it from after it was sent. That's what I'd do, but I'll add these addresses to Godzilla, and if he finds them, we'll know."

"Godzilla?" Jillian snapped her eyes to Drake. What did a movie monster have to do with the threatening emails she'd received?

"Oh, he's a computer program that has become a, I don't know, Centurion maybe. Not only does he defend our systems, but he also runs analytics and searches for me." The woman responded as if defining the system was a routine happening.

"He?" Jillian mouthed the question towards Drake. He smiled and winked at her.

"Okay, all of you have access to the three emails

she received." The constant click of a keyboard working remained the only sound.

"D, while the emails alone aren't serious enough to mandate a PSO presence, everything else, to include the manner in which these emails were sent, is enough for us to justify taking the case. Jared, who do we have available?"

"Sir, they want me to be involved." Drake stared directly at the phone not making eye contact with her.

"Not procedurally sound."

She couldn't tell which man spoke.

Drake leaned forward. "I know. We need to travel to San Jose to retrieve her prototype and research data. I have the G6 here. We could be back at the complex by Monday evening. You can assign someone to run down any leads you find, but before you decide, you need to know there have been other incidents within the last week."

She listened as Drake detailed the two incidents on campus and the break-in at her apartment.

"I don't believe in coincidences." That came from the man with the raspy, gravelly voice. "D, take her to California. Get that tech and get her to the ranch. You see anything suspicious, you hold up, and you call in backup. Who do we have in northern California?"

One of the men spoke, "Six PSO's on assignment. Two forensic accountants. No wait, they are in San Diego."

Another man interrupted. "Delta Team is in San Francisco. I can tell them to move south."

The woman chimed in, "Zane says he has one asset in Oregon."

"Roger, copy all. Drake, do you have a Guardian SUV now?" That was the raspy-voiced man again.

"Yes, sir," Drake responded immediately.

"When will you leave for San Jose?" Drake looked at Jillian and Cliff when the question was posed by one of the many men talking.

"I have my last lecture in," Jillian glanced up at the clock, "twenty minutes. I'm free any time after that."

Drake glanced at the clock. "We'll leave tomorrow morning. I'll need the G6 fueled, and I'll file a flight plan, but I won't drop it until necessary. I can fly without a co-pilot, but that's against regulations. I'll leave that to your determination, either way, we'll be at the airport at nine tomorrow morning. Let me know if you're sending up a co-pilot. Tomorrow's Saturday, so after we land, we'll lay low until Monday morning, get the device and head back to the complex."

"Sounds like a solid plan. Jacob, get with Kannon Starling and find out where our pilots are located. Drake, I take it you were flying back to the complex by yourself?"

"Roger that." He'd be damned if he had a third person tag along when he brought Dixon to New York. Call him a fucking rebel.

"Copy, I'm not sure I'm happy about it, but I get the rationale, and I'll admit I've done it myself. Where are you at with the data mining, Jewell?"

"I'm working the electronic trails. I do not see anything from the offertory emails that would tie to any of the threatening emails that were sent. I'll have my team jump on the video chats and phone calls Dr. Law has had within the last three months. If there is a link to whoever has threatened her located in her past conversations, we'll find it. I'm also pulling any camera data we have from traffic cams around the locations where these emails originated. Long shot, but we've been lucky before."

Raspy voice spoke again. "Jared pull your closest PSO for three days. Whoever else is on the case with them will have to pull double duty while they are gone. They can sleep when the primary sleeps. Get them up to San Jose. My Spidey sense is twitching on this one. I want back up in the area if Drake needs it."

"Got it."

"Let me know about the co-pilot situation," Drake added.

"Will do. Archangel clear."

"Alpha out."

"Dom Ops out."

"Well, looks like they all left the party, D. Do me a favor and don't take any stupid chances, or I'll send Jade to kick your ass." The woman's voice floated clearly across the connection.

Drake threw back his head and laughed. "She wouldn't kick my ass, she loves me."

"If you think that will save you, you're as batshit crazy as she is. Toodles, D. Be good."

Drake hit the side button on his phone and looked up at her. "Well, Silly Jilly, it looks like it's you and me for the foreseeable future."

"Awesome, and my name is Jillian." If she was going to be with him "for the foreseeable future" that nickname thing had to stop. She stood up and smoothed her skirt down around her hips before she brushed past him where he sat. She stopped behind him and whispered in his ear, "Silly Jilly was a nickname given to a teenage girl. Even then I hated it. It made me feel inadequate and was meant to mock me. In case you hadn't noticed, I'm all grown up." She squeezed his shoulders. The rock-solid muscle under her hands sent a small shiver across her skin. She stepped down and walked across the lecture hall floor to her father. Drake's eyes followed her. The heat they held was impossible to believe, and she wouldn't let her romantic imagination out to play. She wrapped her arms around her father's waist and laid her head down on his shoulder. "Thank you." She whispered her gratitude because it was too precious to say aloud.

"I'll always be here for you. Always." He gave her a squeeze before he spoke again. "Let him do his job. Let him keep you safe. I'm trusting him to take care of my baby girl."

She leaned into his soft t-shirt. No matter how crazy the world got, she knew Cliff was a sane and rational port in any storm. Drake, on the other hand, he was a whirlwind. Her schoolgirl crush aside, the man had put his organization into action within ten minutes of hearing about the stupid emails. She'd tried to pretend they hadn't bothered her, but they had. They made her look over her shoulder, made her jump at noises and fear being alone when being alone used to be her solace. If nothing else, finding out who was trying to scare her would relieve the unneeded stress in her life. She'd let Drake do his job. Take her invention to his complex and just...relax. It had been a while since she'd had a vacation.

The door opened, and Jillian pulled away from her father. Early birds were going to be filtering in. She glanced at Drake who'd leaned back in his chair and was scrolling through his phone. "Are you staying for my lecture?"

He lifted his eyes from his phone to hers. The sky-blue orbs reflected his serious demeanor. "Until we figure out what is happening, I'm your shadow. You don't go anywhere without me."

Jillian sucked her bottom lip into her mouth and worried it for a moment while she sorted through the ramifications of *that* comment. Fifteen-year-old Jilly would have been head over heels at the prospect of spending so much time in Drake's company. The Jillian of today, however, found room for caution. She glanced at him from under her lashes. He was well over six feet tall. His muscles couldn't be disguised with clothing. He had thick strawberry blonde hair and a smile that invited sinful thoughts. God, when he used that smile on her, it was like the sun upped the wattage and everything was brighter, clearer, and more vivid. The man was pure sex, wrapped up in cowboy clothes, and tied with a bow of a potential "hero riding in on a white horse to her rescue". A wave of heat bubbled through her. If only her younger self could have seen the man he'd become. Movie star handsome, wicked smart, and sweet suds and soda, he carried a badge.

Oh! Jillian glanced over at him again. Did he have a gun? On him? It was illegal on campus, right? A shiver skated over her skin. Why was the thought of him with a badge and a gun so freaking hot? She needed to temper her attraction. The doors to the lecture hall opened, and a group of five or six students came in, laughing and joking as they found seats. Her father was sitting next to Drake in the front row. She winked at her dad and plugged in her laptop. The final two hours of her lecture and hour-long question and answer period that followed were on tap, and she welcomed the distraction.

CHAPTER 4

*D*rake watched as the last of the students milled around to talk with Jillian. The question and answer session had bled over the regular class hours, but only a few students still lingered. His stomach lamented his lack of food today. He glanced at the clock behind her and stood, stretching the kinks out of his back. He hadn't exercised today, and his body was making sure he knew how displeased it was with him.

Another loud grumble from his gut reminded him the only thing he'd eaten since this morning was a muffin Miss Amanda slipped each of them as they said their goodbyes. He made his way down to the instructor's podium. Cliff was involved with two students by the door. Their conversation appeared animated and congenial. Several of the students who lingered next to Jillian turned as he approached. He read the looks on their faces. Several of the young men puffed up, trying to look more intimidating. The girls, well…they were girls. Batting eyes, coy looks, and blushes. If Dixon were here, the girls would be treated to lively conversation. He, on the other hand, wasn't much on convo. In fact, he hated meeting new people. Dixon had that talent, he didn't. He'd follow D's lead and play to his hand, but if it were left to Drake, he'd end up sitting at the bar, alone.

"Hi. Are you a new professor?" A four-foot-nothing little piece of blonde cheerleader-type female tipped her head back and smiled at him, fluttering her eyelashes. Damn. What was she? Eighteen? Drake lifted an eyebrow at her and glanced at Jillian. The imp. She hid a smile behind her hand. He shook his head and couldn't hide the smile her laughter brought out.

"Trisha, did you have a question?" Jillian's humor fed through her words. The girl scrunched her eyebrows together and glanced from Jillian to

Drake and then back again. "Oh. Oh! I'm sorry, Doctor Law, I didn't know your husband was here."

Jilly's eyes widened, and her eyes darted to him. Drake moved the two steps it took to reach her before he slipped a hand around her waist. He channeled Dixon and smiled at the jailbait. "No problem. We were just going to go get an early dinner. My wife has neglected me today, and I must admit, I'm famished."

He turned his smile on Jilly. Her deer-in-the-headlights look lingered as her eyes scanned his face. He goosed her side with his hand, and she jumped. "Oh, right." She glanced back at the student. "Trisha, I'm sorry. If you'd send me an email with your question, I'll get you an answer as soon as I can."

"No problem! I'd let your husband take me," the girl gave him a brazen up and down before she finished her thought, "anywhere. Enjoy taking care of that appetite."

They watched the girl bounce out of the lecture hall, past Cliff who was still talking with a student. "Oh, my God." Jillian stepped out of his hold, much to his displeasure. He liked the way she fit against him. "She thought you were my husband?" Jilly shook her head.

"Why is that so unbelievable?" Drake followed her as she moved to the desk and started to pack up her computer.

Jillian stopped and flashed an irritated glare his way. "Right. Like you'd be married to someone like me." She shook her head and tossed her computer into her bag.

Drake put his hand on her arm, stilling her suddenly aggravated actions. "Hey, what just happened there?"

Jillian shook her head and moved away from his touch. "Nothing."

At the sound of Cliff's voice asking the students to give him a minute, they both turned. Cliff jogged up to them. "Jillian, I need to head to the lab. One of the teams we have building the artificial intelligence power unit has an issue." He turned towards Drake. "You'll be staying with us tonight?"

Drake tipped his head acknowledging the fact he would be spending the night. That worked for him. He hadn't checked in anywhere.

"Good. Depending on what's going on, I could be late. I'll see you in the morning before you leave." He extended a hand and Drake shook it. Cliff reached over and gave Jillian a kiss on the cheek. "Take him to Scrolls. The Lobster Thermidor is excellent."

He darted back to the small group, and they exited the lecture hall. Jillian placed the strap of her bag on her shoulder and motioned toward the door. "The lobster is excellent."

"That's fine with me, but don't think you've sidetracked the conversation. Why the attitude a minute ago?"

She tensed beside him as they walked down the hall toward the main exit. She shrugged and shook her head, visibly releasing her clenched muscles. "I am well aware, I'm not the type of woman you go for."

Drake opened the door for her as they walked out to the massive covered overhang. "I'm rather perplexed that you think you know what type of woman I would go for." He lifted his hands and made air quotes on the last two words.

She stopped and spun towards him. "Excuse me? I know exactly the type."

Drake threw back his head and laughed, "Prove it, Professor."

Jillian's eyebrows rose nearly to her hairline. She spun on her heel and started down the stairs.

He turned to follow as a burst of granite splintered beside him. Years of experience in warfare, being shot at, and his constant training kicked in. Drake lunged forward and tackled Jillian, rolling them both behind a parked car. He covered her with his body. Finally the sounds of shots being fired registered. "Are you okay?" He was laying on top of her and could feel her body shaking.

"What's happening?" She screamed when the bullet hit the tire on the far side of the vehicle.

"Someone is shooting at us." He pulled his handgun out of its holster at the small of his back and peeked around. Huddles of terrified students clumped themselves behind vehicles and bushes. "Stay down. Don't move. Don't make yourself a target!" His voice rang with the authority of countless missions. "Don't get up, Jilly. Don't move." She grabbed her head with her hands and clenched her eyes shut.

Drake shifted off her and pressed against the side of the car they were using as cover. He glanced at the steps and then calculated where the shooter would be based on the angle of the shots. He lifted up and peeked through the driver's side window. Several buildings across the green space could be used as a fortified shooting position. He crab-walked to the end of the car. There was no movement around him. Sirens in the distance wailed in ever-increasing volume as the campus police force and local PD swarmed the space. Drake holstered his weapon and moved to cover Jillian. There hadn't been a shot fired in over two minutes. Either the perp was waiting for them to expose themselves or they were fleeing.

Drake lifted his phone and hit speed dial. The connection to Guardian was almost instantaneous. When the operator answered, Drake hissed, "CCS, now!"

"CCS." Zane's voice came across the connection.

"Drake. Shots fired MESE Campus. Tell the campus police the shooter was on the north side of the green in one of the buildings. At least four stories up by the direction of the shots."

"Affirm. Standby."

Drake peeked over the door and watched as patrol cars slammed into reverse and backed out of the square and out of harm's way. He heard a cornucopia of cell phone alerts sounding off. The campus' emergency notification system. Unfortunately, with the times they lived in, the notification systems the schools employed were a necessity.

"Status." Jacob's voice came over the line.

"Secure. I don't see anyone down. I have a shit ton of scared kids, but from what I can tell, the shots were directed at us."

"Doctor Law?"

"Yeah." He glanced down at Jilly. Her shirt was torn, and she'd been scraped up when Drake tackled her to the ground. She was staring at him. She was afraid, but she was alive. Thank God.

"Campus police have the area cordoned off, and they are in the process of clearing the buildings. They've sent out an SMS message to all the students to shelter in place." That was Jewell's voice.

"I have a suspicion they won't find a damn thing." Drake reached down and put his hand on Jillian's shoulder. She closed her eyes and shivered. Damn it, he didn't need her going into shock.

"Sniper?" Jacob's question rang through the connection.

"I would lay odds on that, Skipper. Three shots. One when we were on the stairs. I got us to cover, and then two went into the vehicle we're sheltering behind. Nothing since. He fucked up and missed. The two bullets after we made cover were nothing but anger."

Drake knew the type well. They prided themselves on one shot, one kill. The thought that the mark had escaped would piss off a sniper. If they weren't surrounded by law enforcement right now, he had no doubt that the shooter would wait until they moved and take them out.

"No notifications of student injuries," Jewell reported.

Drake glanced at the huddles of students he could see. None of them looked worse for wear. Terrified, but in one piece. "Copy that."

He slid down the side of the car and sat down. Jillian's eyes followed him. "Come here." He motioned to her, and she scurried from where she laid on her belly over to him. Drake wrapped his arm around her shoulders and tugged her into his side. "You okay?" He held the phone to his ear as he spoke to her.

She shivered and pushed into his side. "They were shooting at me?"

"Yeah, I think so." He admitted.

"Why? They wouldn't be able to get to my invention if they kill me." Drake rubbed his hand up and down her arm, trying to give her some warmth.

"Because you don't live, the invention more than likely doesn't get presented. No invention, no problem, the world rolls along in the status quo." Jewell spoke the words Drake thought.

"Would anyone be able to reproduce your work?" Drake saw a kid start to get up. He shouted, "Get the fuck down and stay down until you get the all clear." The kid dropped like a lead weight and stared at him.

Jillian shifted so she could see the young man. "Idiot." She drew a shaky breath and shook her head. "I don't see why not. They could pick apart my work and use it as a template. The mechanics and math are solid."

"So if you weren't here to claim copyright, anyone could mass produce your product?"

"Yeah." Jillian tucked closer to him and shivered.

"Well, that is the opposite end of the spectrum," Jacob mused. "It could be someone who didn't want her invention to see the light of day or someone who wanted it for themselves. No limit on the fuckwads after that tech."

"They've cleared the three buildings to the

north. One broken window in the building directly across the quad. Still no reports of injuries to students or faculty," Jewell interjected.

"Roger that." Drake dropped his head back against the car door. "Skipper I'll need a co-pilot. Have them up here and ready to go. I won't take any chances on this. Shit has gotten real. We're not dealing with a jealous contemporary. They hired a marksman to take us out in broad daylight on a college campus."

"I'm heading to New York anyway. I'll pull Mark Jenner with me, he can meet you tomorrow morning." It sounded as if Jacob covered the phone for a moment as he spoke to someone. The connection cleared, and he continued, "Okay, he'll be with you until you don't need him anymore."

Drake knew Mark. He was a solid pilot with similar ratings. He'd be solid back-up.

Jillian answered his questions with one-word replies. He was worried about her, but until he could move, just keeping her responsive and safe was his goal. He moved to ease her position and still allow him to move if he needed to react. Thank God he'd plugged his phone in on the drive up. The full charge kept Guardian on the line while he received updates as the buildings were cleared.

"Drake, they are going to give the all clear." Three hours after they walked out of the engineering facility, Jewell relayed the news.

Once again a chorus of cell phone alerts sounded, and he watched as the students lifted cautiously from where they'd been sheltering.

Drake stood and helped Jillian to her feet as Cliff raced out of the building. "Oh, my God! I could see you from the door, but they wouldn't let me out. What happened?"

Drake motioned toward his armored SUV. "Let's get into the truck, and I'll fill you in."

"Agent Simmons, a word." Drake sent a quick look over his shoulder as the campus police chief and one other man pounded the cement in a direct line towards him. He reached in his pocket and gave the vehicle's key fob to Cliff. "Go, get inside and turn on the heat for her. Get her warm. Do not push the red button under the Plexiglas flip top."

Cliff held his daughter and looked from the keys to the vehicle. "Why, what is it?"

"An extreme duress alarm. Believe me, you don't want to push it." He glanced back at the men coming after him. There was more than enough going on without alerting every law enforcement agency in the tri-state area that a Guardian needed assistance.

Cliff's shoulders straightened, and they moved toward the vehicle as the chief stopped in front of Drake. "What the fuck is going on?"

Drake lifted an eyebrow at the chief. He got it. The man had just lived through the one thing every campus in the nation dreaded. The magic difference in this case? There had been no injuries. It didn't make it right or change the danger that the students faced today, but it was a silver lining.

"Sniper. We were exiting the building, and there was a shot that split the two of us. I pushed Doctor Law down, and we rolled behind this vehicle. There were two other shots fired. Both hit the vehicle. One sounded like it entered the engine compartment, one took out a tire." Drake turned and placed his hands on his hips. "Your emergency notification system was fast and for the most part kept those kids controlled. Your force should be commended."

"It helped that Guardian alerted us to the possible location of the shooter. That was you, wasn't it?"

"Yes, sir. Did you find any shell casings?"

"Nothing. One broken window, that was it."

"I don't have any proof, but I don't believe the shooter was after your students. There were no other shots fired to obscure his intent. Nothing to indicate an unbalanced or unstable person. This guy was a professional. When his first bullet missed its mark, he attempted another shot. In my opinion, the third shot was fired in frustration."

"So, not so professional after all?" That came from the man accompanying the chief.

Drake swung his eyes to the mouse of a man. "Wrong. He was expecting a one-bullet, one-kill scenario." Drake pointed to the building where he believed the shot came from. "The building where he or she sat in wait is at least a nine-hundred-meter shot. I can guarantee you the shooter was a professional. No pissed off student or person who'd had a mental break, or a person with an agenda would take three shots at a very specific target and then leave without anyone knowing they were involved."

The chief did a double take. "You really believe a sane person did this?"

"Yes, the person who did this was sane and dangerous."

"I'm going to need a statement. City cops will need one, too. We have the state bureau of investigation heading this way, so you'll need to stick around."

Drake glanced at the SUV. "Sir, I need to get the charges under my care to safety. Guardian will provide you with everything you need. They were on the phone with me the entire time. I'm sorry, but I'm pulling the federal trump card on this one. The sooner I get Doctor Law off this campus, the sooner the threat to the safety of your student body is eliminated."

"You mean the shooter was after Cliff's kid?"

"That is my hypothesis. Guardian can help you with any press release."

The chief's eyes closed momentarily. "Fuck me. I hadn't even thought about that. The press will be swarming."

"Yes, sir. Guardian has an entire PR division. Give them a call before you talk to anyone. They can help."

"I'll do that." The chief started to turn away but paused and glanced over his shoulder. "No offense, Agent Simmons, but I don't ever want to see you on this campus again."

"None taken, sir." Drake spun on his heel and headed to the SUV accompanied by a loud grumble from his stomach. Drake glanced down at his gut. "Shut the fuck up." He rolled his shoulders and glanced at the building from where the shots had been fired as he walked to the armored vehicle. Today needed to end. It had been one fuck ton of oh-shit with an added measure of fucked-up on the side. Since he'd opened his eyes this morning, his brother had left, and he'd posed as a human shield. Not the worst day he'd ever had, but sure as fuck, not the best either.

CHAPTER 5

Jillian placed a cool, damp washcloth against the road rash on her forearm. She was bruised, and her neck hurt from the force with which Drake had knocked her down, but considering the alternative, she'd take the aches and pains. She could hear her father and Drake talking, not the words, but the steady sound of their voices. Her hands still shook. She clenched them into fists and closed her eyes, sucking in a deep breath. Someone had tried to kill her. *To kill her.* Because she'd made an affordable, efficient energy source. If her dad hadn't called the twins? If Drake hadn't been there? A spine-chilling sensation played hell with the composure she tried to maintain. She'd be dead. Her life would be over.

That thought was the one that splintered her world. In an intimate way, as they sat on that sidewalk hidden behind the dark blue car, she'd confronted her mortality. As the campus police cleared the buildings, each minute that ticked by fueled the bitter cold reality that someone wanted her dead.

There was so much she wanted to do. So many things she wanted to experience. She had spent the majority of her life in classrooms and labs, putting off other things she'd been interested into work on making her mark in her field. She opened her eyes, tipped her head back slowly and blinked hard to stop the tears that had been falling since she locked herself in the bathroom. Would her effort to provide sustainable, clean, efficient energy be the cause of her death?

Her knees felt weak. She sat on the edge of the tub and placed her head in her hands. She shivered against the emotions that continued to assail her. Analytics. That was what she needed. Facts and absolutes, truths to weigh down the wild emotions licking at her raw nerves. Truths to silence the fears and keep them at a manageable noise level. She lifted her head and wrapped her arms around herself before she closed her eyes and made a mental list. Fact – she was alive. Today's events had been traumatic and horrifying, but she'd survived. Fact – she had Drake to take care of her. He was extremely well qualified if the events of the day were to be taken as testimony of his capabilities. He recognized what was happening and reacted. No, that wasn't right. He *acted*. He called in reinforcements, told them where the threat was coming from and worked with his organization through the entire event while keeping her grounded and sane. He was more than qualified. Fact – she had to deal with the upcoming days. There was no alternative. Fact – she needed to see this event through to the end because she wasn't going to spend the rest of her life cooped up in a lab, afraid of her shadow. She had enough money to live comfortably. She could travel. A fine sheen of apprehension fell over her like it always did. No, she didn't like to travel. She always felt alone and vulnerable. Bravery wasn't her forte.

Jillian examined her cuticles as she pondered what she really wanted to do with her life. Stupid, silly dreams flew forward from the recesses of her mind. They landed on a perch she'd forced them to abandon years ago. She wanted what her brother had found. She wanted a husband, babies, a white picket fence, and maybe a dog or a cat. She wanted an SUV with the cheesy white stick figures of a mommy, daddy, little boy, little girl, dog and cat on the back window. Hell, she'd even learn the rules to soccer. She longed for a man that would love her, for just being herself.

A silent chuckle erupted. Foolish dreams. Silly Jilly. God, Sarah Jane had tagged her correctly all those years ago. She wasn't supposed to want *domesticity*. She was a successful professional. A leading female researcher in a field inundated with men. What she was supposed to want were success, recognition, and accolades. But all of those things were hollow when you lived in solitude—no one with whom to celebrate your successes, no one to rejoice in your recognition, and no one to be proud of your accolades.

A knock at the door startled her. She jumped up and grasped at her chest. Her reflection in the mirror stared back at her.

"Jilly, you okay?" Drake's voice from behind the door reached her from behind the door.

Silly Jilly. She needed to remember that all she was to Drake was Silly Jilly. She drew a deep breath and then another. "Yeah. I'm fine. I just needed a minute."

"You know, I've been where you're at."

Jillian glanced at her feet and then at her reflection. "You've been in Cliff's bathroom?"

A chuff of laughter rolled toward her. "No, I meant I've had people shooting at me, trying to kill me."

Jillian padded over to the door and unlocked it. She opened it and leaned against the door jamb as she stared at the man leaning against the hallway wall. "You mean in the military?"

Drake gave her a sad smile. "Before and after that, actually."

"Before?" When would that have happened? Before they met at school? "You must have been just a boy."

"Yes. Uncle Bob moved Dixon and me to Louisville, Kentucky after it happened. The act never makes sense. No matter how hard you try, you can't rationalize it."

"But how do I…" She stopped and ran her hand through her hair, pushing it out of her face. "How do I walk out of this room? The people who wanted me dead are still out there. What if they come after me here? What if you or Cliff gets hurt?" She lifted a hand and wiped away a tear that escaped. "What if he succeeds next time?" She blinked hard and tried to swallow the fear. "I don't want to die." The fears she'd been trying to ignore slammed forward, smashing against her like a sledgehammer. She found herself wrapped up in his arms. Her tears fell unabated as he rocked her back and forth.

"I'm not going to let that happen. The person who shot at you today was probably hired by someone who wanted your invention to go away. What they don't know is Guardian is now on your side. I won't leave you until I know you're safe. There are city cops posted at the front and rear of the house. Guardian has assets that will take over from them tonight. They are about an hour away. They will make sure we are safe tonight and escort us to the airport in the morning. I'm not a personal security specialist, but I swear I will fuck up anyone that comes after you." He placed his hands on her shoulders and set her back, forcing her to look up at him. He smiled and winked. "I promise I will take care of you, my Silly Jilly."

That *damn* name. She slapped his shoulder without any force and groaned. "Stop calling me that."

He laughed and motioned with his head out toward the hall. "Cliff is worried. I told him you'd need some time to process what happened. He's downstairs cooking dinner."

"He's been so good to me. I didn't want him to make a big deal out of this. If he hadn't..." She wiped her cheeks again and sniffed back the remains of her breakdown.

"But he did call. You can drive yourself insane looking at what might have happened. Besides, the way he tells it, you and Matt saved his life." They walked down the hall together.

Cliff'd been amazing to her and her brother, but she could see his point. "I guess we have a symbiotic relationship. We thrived off the love he gave us, and he needed someone to love him back." She stopped and gazed up at Drake. "How have you been? Have you and Dixon started families?"

If she hadn't been watching, she'd have missed his pained look. He played it off well by shrugging and motioning toward the stairs that would lead them downstairs. She placed a hand on his arm stilling him. "You were always taking care of him. Did something happen?"

Drake shook his head. "No, our lives have been filled with wonderful people, but we haven't found that special person."

"Person?" She blinked up at him, "As in..."

A blush crept up Drake's neck. "We've discussed settling down in a relationship with one woman. You know us. I'm assuming you remember how close we are. We've watched the people we care the most about find that one special person. We want that."

"Together? You don't think you could each find someone?" It was literally the most important question she could think to ask.

He shrugged, and his blush deepened. "Maybe. I think we are both open to it, but we haven't closed the door to a single woman. Even after all the shit we went through, we are both romantics. If you tell anyone that, I'll deny it."

A glimmer of hope peeked through her anxiety and apprehension. "But you haven't found her yet?" Her muscles relaxed when he shook his head, and inwardly chided herself when she'd realized she'd done so. If she couldn't get over her hero-worship, she deserved her nickname. Jillian grasped for another subject. "So, you and Dixon live in the Midwest?"

"South Dakota. It's home. We've been adopted into a crazy family who've taken us under their wing. It's nice." He smiled and winked at her, "But,

Dixon and I have always taken care of each other and made a home wherever we landed."

"True, but it was always you who gave up what he wanted to make sure Dixon was happy." He started to shake his head, but she stopped his response. "I saw you, Drake. More times than I can count, you deferred to Dixon's desires. I was there. I saw you abandon your interests to pursue his."

Drake stared at her for a moment before his eyes softened. "You say that like it was a hardship. It wasn't. Dixon went through a lot."

"From what I remember, you both went through hell." She'd heard bits and pieces over the years, enough to know it was a miracle the twins were functioning adults.

"I'll admit our childhood wasn't easy, but through everything, we had each other, even when they…" Drake's gaze shot to the far wall before he continued. "He's my family. I'd give up anything for him."

Jillian had seen that selflessness in action. Her teenage life centered on Drake. A wallflower in every sense of the word, she had a front-row seat observing them because Cliff had been a hub in all of their lives. She added, "Or anyone." Drake's eyes cut to her, and he cocked his head in question. She chuckled. "You were so gone over Rosalinda Torres. She didn't like that you spent all your time with Dixon, or heck, even when you spent any time with me. You dropped her like a rock even though I think you liked her more than the other women you dated."

"Wow. Way-back machine activated." Drake leaned against the wall and shoved his fingers into his front pockets. "I haven't thought about Rosalinda in years. Hindsight being twenty-twenty, she was jealous and a royal diva. I was enamored with her. She was probably the first person who liked me but didn't like Dixon. I can count those people on one hand. We are a team. Where one is, the other isn't far behind, so yeah, I walked away. Dixon is part of who I am. If you can't deal with that, you don't need to be in my life." He chuckled and pushed off the wall. "What about you? Any significant other out there in California?"

Jillian glanced up at him, and a wave of doubt drizzled over her. "No. My standards are too high to keep a man around."

"Really?" They started down the stairs together.

"Yep. Nobody has ever measured up to this one guy I was head over heels in love with." She laughed at her own inside joke. She'd had been so in love with the man beside her—and she was beginning to question the "had been".

"What happened to him?" Drake asked as they stepped down.

"Oh, he joined the military and forgot about me." She glanced over her shoulder at him. "I've dated, but…" She shook her head and drew a deep breath. "Nobody's ever measured up to him." She nodded toward the kitchen. "I'm going to help Cliff with dinner." Jillian darted a fast glance at him. She'd never had the guts to actually tell Drake about her crush, but after her life-altering moment today, she wanted him to know how she felt…or used to feel. Jillian spun on her heel. Maybe.

CHAPTER 6

Drake sipped his coffee and stared out the window watching the sun come up. Two Guardian specialists were somewhere outside the house. Thanks to them, he'd been able to catch several hours sleep after patrolling the interior of the house. He made sure every window was secure, and the doors were locked. The floor above him creaked under someone's footstep. The shower in the bathroom started and drained down a pipe in the kitchen wall. The sounds of the old house surrounded him as Cliff and Jillian woke.

Drake glanced at his watch. He'd let her sleep in because he knew she hadn't slept well. The house was small and old with thin walls. Her light was on after he'd locked up the house and had still been on hours later when he'd done another security check. As he passed by her room he heard the soft sound of her computer keyboard. Thankfully, her light was out, and there were no sounds the third time he made his rounds. Just to make sure, he'd cracked open her door far enough to hear her soft, even breathing. He was the one determining take off time. He'd let her sleep. He pulled out his cell and hit speed dial.

"What's up?" Jacob answered his personal cell phone immediately.

"We are going to be late arriving at the field." Drake glanced out the window again as the shower upstairs cut off.

"Problems?" His boss's immediate concern flew across the connection.

"No. She had a bad night. I let her sleep in." Drake took a sip of his coffee.

"Roger. We are about an hour away. I'll drop Mark off, and he can do the pre-flight. Get there when you can. I'll stick around for a while, but I need to make it to Justin's before he flies to Chile."

Drake wondered if Justin was going as a Guardian asset or as a part of his ever-expanding restaurant/real estate empire, but it wasn't his place to ask. "I hear the wines down there are good."

"Really? I have no idea. As long as he stocks my cabernet, I'm good. I need him to open a small box of Tori's before he leaves. The lock is broken. It belonged to her mom, so we don't want to damage it."

"Got it. We'll be leaving here soon. Thanks for sending the assets so I could get some shut eye."

"Whatever it takes." Jacob acknowledged his thanks.

"As long as it takes." Drake hit end on his phone and picked up his coffee cup. Without turning around, he spoke, "You don't make a very good spy."

Cliff's chuckle preceded him into the room. "I was caught in an awkward position. I didn't want to interrupt a private call, so I waited."

Drake lifted his cup in acknowledgment before he finished what remained. He moved to the coffee pot and poured himself another. He needed caffeine today.

"She had a bad night?" Cliff pulled a mug out of a cupboard.

"Was up until about three." Drake moved so Cliff could fill his cup.

"She always did put up a good front. After being shuffled from foster home to foster home, both of those kids learned to hide their feelings."

"She was always shy." Drake acknowledged.

"Shy? I guess that is one way to look at it." His mentor scratched his scruff and shrugged. "Personally, I think Jillian's just quiet while she waits."

"Waits? For what?" Drake needed clarification on that point.

"Ah, that's the question, isn't it? Would you like my personal opinion?" Cliff sipped a bit of his coffee.

"If it doesn't betray her trust." Drake didn't feel comfortable talking about her without her knowing about it. He was never one to indulge in that type of conversation.

Cliff smiled and winked at him. "I'm not betraying any confidence. She knows I think she's waiting for the storybook ending." He laughed and glanced over at Drake. "Hell, she took the entire week off for the last royal wedding and absorbed every detail. My little princess is a dreamer. She's a romantic, and she's waiting for her prince to come along and sweep her off her feet." Cliff opened the refrigerator door. "I'm making omelets. Jillian likes bacon. Is that good for you?" He turned with his arms full of ingredients.

"That works for me." He moved out of Cliff's way and leaned against the far counter.

Cliff stilled and stared at the inside of the refrigerator. His voice was low, and the emotion it carried was obvious and heavy. "You're going to take care of my girl, right?"

"Cliff, I'm not going to attempt to blow smoke up your ass. There are some desperate motherfuckers out there in the world. The advantage Jillian has is that I'm a Guardian. My past is littered with people who underestimated what we are capable of doing. The people I train and work with are better than the totality of the desperation out there. I will do whatever it takes, for as long as it takes, to make sure Jillian stays safe."

Cliff stared at him for a moment before he spoke, "Good. She deserves to be happy."

"She isn't?" Drake got the sense last night as they spoke she wasn't, but he had no evidence, only his gut feeling.

Cliff lifted a whisk from the drawer and glanced at him. "Happy?" He shrugged. "She's busy. She works, but I don't think she has many friends. I know she doesn't date often but to each their own." Cliff cracked three eggs into the bowl before he glanced at Drake. "You know, she used to have a crush on either you or Dixon. I never could figure out which of the two of you it was."

Drake blinked at the revelation. "On one of us?" He remembered her always being around, but a crush? Hell, he never saw Jilly act like a love-sick teenager, and between him and Dixon…oh, well that explained it. She must have had a crush on Dixon. That was why *he* never witnessed anything.

"Oh yeah, and it was bad. When she was a senior in high school, especially. I know she carried that torch well into college, hell, probably until you two graduated and left." Cliff chuckled and poured a dollop of cream into the bowl before he started whisking the eggs. "She would never tell us which one of you two she was crushing over, but her brother would tease her about it. Poor Jillian, with her braces, thick glasses and the fact she was all elbows and knees? Hell, she was mortified when we caught on and never would reveal which one of you hung the moon and the stars."

Drake set his coffee down, suddenly awake and very interested in the conversation. "I had no idea."

Cliff laughed as he laid strips of bacon into a frying pan. "No doubt. Back then she would have died of embarrassment if she'd thought either of you knew. Today, Jillian is confident in her science and in her profession. In anything else, she's still that shy, ugly duckling." Cliff tapped his head. "At least in her own mind. She doesn't see the beautiful woman she's become."

Drake watched Cliff work as he thought back to the words she'd whispered as she'd moved past him yesterday in the lecture hall. *Silly Jilly was a teenager. In case you hadn't noticed, I'm all grown up.* Oh hell yeah, he noticed. The question was, what did he do with that information? If she'd had a crush on Dixon, would expressing his interest in her be wrong? Yes. He'd never infringe on his brother's territory. Dixon deserved to be happy, and if Jillian had the potential to make his brother happy, there was no way he'd fuck that up. *Hell, did he even need to worry about it though?* The answer to that was blatantly obvious. No, he didn't. He was on a mission. His actions had already been dictated by Guardian. He'd fly her to San Jose and then take her back to the ranch to safeguard her invention and keep her out of harm's way.

"Good morning." Jillian smiled and spoke as she entered the kitchen. He lifted his cup in response. A swept back ponytail confined her hair. She wore a pair of stylish, dark-brown framed glasses that bore no resemblance to the ones she'd continually pushed up her nose as a teenager. Dense lenses no longer hid glorious brown eyes. She wore a pair of skin-tight dark jeans that hugged her thighs and ass while perfectly framing her taut body. The clingy long sleeve shirt did nothing to cover her curves. The press of her breasts against the thin material outlined their fullness and accentuated her gorgeous body. His eyes followed her as she bent over searching for something in the refrigerator. *Shit.* He pulled his attention away from her and straightened, glancing at Cliff to make sure the man hadn't caught him ogling his daughter's assets.

"Good morning. Did you sleep well?" Drake asked before he took a long pull of his coffee.

Jillian flipped a cross look at him. "No, hence the glasses. I couldn't stand the thought of putting in my contacts." She grimaced and headed towards the coffee pot. "Morning, Dad."

Cliff winked at her. "Morning, princess. Ready for a new adventure?"

Drake watched as she tensed and poured her coffee.

"Sure." Her posture contradicted the confidence in her tone. Her shoulders rose as she drew a deep breath before she turned to meet Drake's gaze. "When do we leave?"

"If you're packed and ready, we can leave after breakfast. I've checked the aviation weather sites; the weather is clear for the most part from here to San Jose. Afternoon thundershowers are always a concern, but we have a beautiful day."

Jillian leaned against the counter. "How long have you been a pilot?"

Her lips pursed as she blew on her coffee. Her bottom lip was fuller than the top, but the top formed a perfect cupid's bow—an altogether enticing pair of lips. She took a sip, breaking his gaze. *Shit.* What had she asked? Pilot. Right.

"You don't remember?" Her brow furrowed, and she shook her head.

"Dixon and I started taking lessons in our junior year at Louisville. Our uncle's boss paid for them. After we got our license, we flew her to meetings and on short trips in her Cessna. That was so much fun we decided to take lessons to pilot helicopters. When we joined the military, we continued to get qualified in different aircraft. Hell, we were stationed stateside for the first three years of our hitch. Basically a nine-to-five gig. We flew out of a small airfield across town from the base and piled up certifications." Drake shook his head. Gabriel had crossed their path three months after they hit their first duty assignment and life had never been the same. He funded their flights, certifications and extracurricular activities. The man waited until they finished their hitch, then introduced them to Jacob.

Jillian froze with her coffee cup halfway to the counter. "Please tell me we aren't flying to California in a Cessna or a helicopter."

He just smiled at her. Wait until she met Gracie.

After breakfast, Drake loaded their bags into the truck. He spoke with each of the Guardian operatives who had watched over them last night. There was nothing to report, no suspicious activity or anything concerning during the night. He thanked them both and headed back inside knowing they would remain on post until they departed, and one would follow them to the airfield. Jillian was in the kitchen with her father. He could hear their voices as he entered the house. He stopped just inside the door, and Cliff's words drifted to him.

"You call as soon as you get in."

Jillian answered, but Drake couldn't hear what

she said. He leaned against the door jamb. The Jilly he remembered had been quiet, studious and happy to be included in any of the numerous projects he and Dixon had worked on. Hindsight being twenty-twenty he could now see she'd been eager to be with them. Hopefully, Dixon would take time off after his assignment in that cesspool, so Drake could re-introduce them. She was smart and beautiful, just the type of woman his brother needed.

"You need to tell him."

Drake's ears perked up at Cliff's comment.

"Why? What good would it possibly do? Besides, I still think he sees me as a nerdy teenager."

Drake shifted his weight. He should probably go back outside, but her words held him super-glued to the spot. Was she talking about him? It sure sounded like it.

"Anyone with eyes knows you're not that girl anymore."

Drake agreed with that statement. One hundred and fifty percent.

"You're right, I'm not that person, and I no longer have a schoolgirl crush on a boy who never even knew I was alive."

Drake shook his head. He'd known she was alive back then. Hell, he'd gone out of his way to include her when she was around. Had he any interest in her other than being nice and involving Cliff's kid? No. But at that point, he and Dixon were just starting to live and experience the world without the confines of their past binding them. They were young, and they not only played the field, they dominated it. One thing neither he or Dixon would ever do was play games with their mentor's daughter. Even if she'd been a little sex kitten back then, neither one of them would have made a move on Cliff's kid. Through all the shit their parents had put them through, they'd come out with a healthy sense of manners and propriety. The darkest type of evil, like their parents, did one of two things to a person. It showed you the evil you'd become if you allowed it to consume you, or it showed you what you needed to fight against to ensure evil did not win.

Drake reached back and opened the screen door soundlessly before he shut it loudly and started down the hall, letting the heels of his cowboy boots hit the old pinewood floors harder than necessary. He stopped in the doorway. "Are you ready?"

Jillian nodded and leaned into her dad for a hug. "I'll call."

"You better." Cliff hugged her before releasing her. He reached his hand to Drake. "Take care of her and yourself."

Drake clasped his hand and pulled him in. "I'll look after her."

CHAPTER 7

"Wow, that is so not a Cessna." Jillian gawked at the sleek, black jet. It had a golden symbol on the tail along with numbers and letters. It was shiny, beautiful and ... big.

Drake pulled to a stop and put the car into park. He smiled out the windshield as he gazed at the aircraft. "Jillian, meet Gracie."

"Excuse me?"

"Dixon named this bird. She's been the means of grace for many people. We've flown our teams and personnel to and from dangerous situations in that plane. She's carried our family and friends, and she's sheltered a few lost and hurting souls. She's our favorite."

Jillian's attention was no longer on the aircraft. Drake's words as he looked at "Gracie" carried so much emotion her eyes had been drawn to him. He glanced at her and shrugged. "Ready?" Color rose from his neck to his cheeks. He'd been embarrassed by his outward display of emotion.

The boy she idolized was still under the man that stood before her. "You've become an amazing person, Drake Simmons."

He shook his head and moved to open his door. "I'm nothing special."

She laid her hand on his forearm. It was a gesture she couldn't seem to stop, no matter how many times she forced herself to remove her hand. She felt warmth rushing to her cheeks, too. "No, that's not true. We've both had horrible childhoods, and we've both overcome them. I know genuine goodness when I see it. You *are* a good man. I can tell by the way you talk about your brother, your new family, and even Gracie, here. You *care*. That makes you amazing in my book, so please, don't shrug it off. Accept the compliment and let me admire what I see in you."

He stared at her for a moment. "Thank you."

She winked at him. "See, it wasn't that hard was it?"

He laughed and stepped out of the vehicle. "More so than I'd like to admit."

A man exited the aircraft and waved before trotting down the entry steps. Drake lifted a hand in acknowledgment and pulled their bags out of the vehicle. Jillian watched the other man approach. He was bulky, mid-thirties and bald. Tattoos covered his arms and peeked out of the collar of his shirt. The total effect was exceptionally sexy. He saw her and smiled wide. It was a fantastic smile she had no choice but to return. He stopped in front of her and extended his hand. "Mark Jenner."

"Jillian Law. It's nice to meet you."

Mark nodded towards Drake. "I'm here to make sure he doesn't screw up."

"Like that would ever happen." Drake shut the door and locked the vehicle before he shook Mark's hand. "Where's the ground crew?"

"I sent them off about an hour ago to grab some lunch. Alpha said he will send someone to get this truck, just send the keys to the office when you get back to South Dakota."

"Will do."

Drake lifted their luggage as if it were weightless. They walked toward the aircraft as the men spoke, with Drake still toting the bags. She didn't know how he did it so effortlessly because hers was heavy. Most of the discussion pertained to the aircraft and something about a flight plan. Instead of trying to comprehend the content of the conversation, she absorbed Drake in his environment. He oozed confidence. He and Mark joked around, but it was clear Drake was in charge.

After they finished the walk around, Drake placed the suitcases in the luggage hold before he reached out and took her hand. The simple touch shocked her into a stupor. He continued to talk with the other pilot, oblivious to her current brainlessness.

He tugged on her hand, and she followed him as they walked around the aircraft again. His thumb stroked the back of her hand as he spoke and laughed with Mark. They finally made it full circle and Drake released her hand at the stairs to the cabin. She missed the contact immediately, but his hand landed on the small of her back encouraging her up the stairs. She grabbed the handrail and used it to steady her steps into the aircraft.

The opulence of the cabin stopped her short. Wow, she wasn't in Kansas anymore, Toto. Huge leather chairs formed a conversation pit, and a plush dark brown leather couch lined one side of the cabin. The chairs had end tables made of wood and gold accents, and the carpet on the floor was so thick her foot sunk into the pile. Stunning in an ultra-rich, you-must-be-dreaming way. She jumped at Drake's chuckle.

"Not bad, huh?"

Jillian spun on her heel. "Not bad? Is this real?"

Both Drake and Mark laughed at her. "Yes, it's real." Drake pointed. "That will be your seat when we take off. After we get to cruising altitude, you can come up into the cockpit and visit with us. There is a jump seat up there. It isn't the most comfortable in the world, but at least you won't have to be alone." He pointed down the hall as Mark headed toward the cockpit. "There's a bedroom back there along with a full bathroom. I know you didn't sleep well last night. If you'd like to lay down, feel free to use it. Otherwise, there is a full galley through here." He put his hand on her back and moved her forward. A shiver ran through her at his touch. Damn, how was she supposed to concentrate when he did that?

"The refrigerator is stocked, and the microwave works just like a normal one would. The only caution I'll give is to make sure you secure all the doors with these little hooks when you open them or close them. Drake showed her the small latches. "Coffee pot here. Hot water dispenser for tea here. All the makings are in this cabinet." He moved through the galley and pointed out things she may need. Her head nodded north and south, but her mind focused on his light touches and soft tone.

"Drake, the ground crew is ready."

She jumped at Mark's voice over the plane's intercom.

"I'm going to close up the aircraft. You get yourself strapped in. I'll let you know when you can move around. Okay?"

Jillian nodded and made her way to the huge leather chair where she strapped in as Drake closed the main cabin door. He winked at her as he headed to the cockpit. Jillian watched him settle into the left side seat and put on his headphones. Something Mark said made him laugh. The sight of the man in his element, and happy, stole a piece of her heart. All the admiration she had for him as a teenager came rolling back in a wave the size of a tsunami. She could feel it swelling but the emotions she once felt for the man were nothing compared to the place she now found herself. She could very easily lose herself in Drake Simmons. If he treated her with the same disregard now as he had then…the heartache she'd suffered as a young woman would be nothing compared to what she'd suffer now.

~

They hadn't been airborne twenty seconds before his co-pilot started in on him. "That is one hella beautiful woman you got there. When did you latch on to her?"

Drake smiled at Mark's words. He made sure the coordinates were entered into the plane's navigation system and engaged the autopilot function as he replied, "I haven't latched on to her."

"No?" Mark's hand stalled as it reached for a switch above his head.

"No." Drake reached over and completed the move for his co-pilot.

"Then you wouldn't mind if I got to know her better?" The shit eating grin Mark gave him indicated he knew exactly how much it would bother Drake if he started hitting on Jillian.

"What do you think, asshole?" There was no malice in Drake's reply, just two men tossing harmless barbs at each other.

"Wow, no need to get defensive, cowboy. You said you hadn't latched on to her, so that makes her available, right?"

Mark's pearly whites made a brilliant appearance in a smile so innocent Drake laughed. "She's an old friend. I've known her since she was…hell, sixteen or seventeen, maybe? She was in high school when we first met her dad. We lost track of each other for about ten or twelve years."

Mark's brow furrowed. "Dude, how the fuck do you lose track of something like her?"

"Easy. You join the military, get recruited to Guardian, fight alongside your team through the devil's armpit of pure evil, get shot at, blown up, and try like hell to find ground zero after they patch you back together."

Mark blinked and then nodded. "There is that." He glanced back toward the cabin. "What's her story?"

"She's in need of a PSO. I'm available, so I took the assignment."

"Since when do you work as a PSO? I mean, I get that you were on one of the original teams, but PSO?"

"The original Alpha Team, yeah," Drake confirmed.

"Dude, we need to sit down and have a case of beers. I'd love to hear some of your war stories."

"Yeah, someday." Drake would never take the man up on his offer. What he and his brothers in arms went through was classified and in no way eligible for a drunken episode of *Spill Your Guts*.

"So how do you rate PSO duties?"

Drake answered, "I've been training Personal Security Officers for...damn, almost four years now. It started out as physical training. Then we went down a trainer, and I stepped in. The classes are intense and focused. I learned as the class learned and then I started developing logical, follow-on classes. When we finally got a new instructor, I kept my fingers in the pot, so to speak." Meaning he approved all the training plans, taught four classes on explosive and incendiary devices and, in conjunction with Dixon, oversaw all physical training at the complex.

"So she's got a stalker or something?" Mark glanced back into the cabin. "I could see how someone could be obsessive about her."

"She had some threats because of some work she's doing. It will be a quick out and back. We need to retrieve some equipment in San Jose. We'll get what she needs Monday morning and then we'll head to the complex in South Dakota."

"A weekend in San Jose? I could do worse." Mark reached over and unbuckled his seatbelt. "Seriously, you got no claim on her? You mind if I see if she's interested?"

His jaw tightened at the question. No, he didn't want Mark hitting on Jilly. Mark was a well-known carouser. He had an entire bed frame notched with his conquests—surprising the thing still held together. But Drake had zero right to make any decisions for Jillian, other than ones to ensure her safety. He shrugged and turned away, "Take your best shot, man. She's her own person."

"Right. Thanks for the clearance. I'm going to rustle up some lunch for us because I'm starved. I'll send her up here until I get done. You want anything?"

"Dude, I'm not turning down food."

Mark winked at him and extracted himself from the co-pilot's seat. Drake could hear their voices, although the words escaped him. Jillian's laughter, however, did not. It made him smile. When Jilly laughed, it came from deep inside her, and nobody could doubt the woman's joy.

"Mark said it was okay to come up?"

Drake turned and saw Jillian braced against the small door. "Absolutely. You can sit there," Drake nodded to a fold-down jump seat, "…or in Mark's seat. Just be careful not to touch anything as you climb in."

Her eyes rounded and she pointed to the vacant co-pilot position. "Really? I can sit up there?"

"For a while, sure."

"Wow." She moved cautiously into the cockpit and bent down, nimbly sitting in the seat, being careful not to come close to the instruments. "Best view, ever."

"Not bad is it?"

"Not bad? Seriously, you could charge ten times the price of first class for a thrill like this."

"I think the FAA would have a problem with that."

"Probably, but wow." Jillian leaned forward and then to the side. "I can see forever."

"I don't think forever is a distance," he deadpanned as he watched her.

"Hey, don't be a wise ass, and aren't you supposed to be flying this?"

"Autopilot. Forever isn't a distance. I wasn't being a wise ass." He lifted a finger with each point in challenge.

"Really? Last time I checked forever is a continuum. It could be considered a measure of distance. If you weren't being a wiseass, you were being a smart ass or just an ass. I'm not sure which right now."

"Probably just an ass, Dixon says it's my default setting. And while forever is an expression of a continuum, it is not a measurement of distance; it is a measure of time."

"A pragmatic and uninventive use of a new concept. Open your mind to the unlimited possibilities!" Jillian narrowed her eyes at him before a small smile flitted across her expression. "Infinity."

Drake laughed, he knew where this conversation was going. "Infinity plus one."

"Uggg...no." She held up a finger and then pointed it directly at him. "There are multiple infinites defined individually, and those shades of the reality are subject to distinctive operations and disparate laws. Why can't there be the same functions for forever as there are for infinity?"

Okay, so maybe he actually had no clue where the conversation was heading. He knew Jillian was intelligent but damn... He followed her concept of forever. The possibilities were mind boggling. He shook his head. "Is *that* the kind of thinking that led to your latest invention?"

"What do you mean?" Her question held a tinge of…hell, defensiveness, maybe?

"I didn't mean to insult you, Jill. I'm immensely impressed with your mind. You've got a way of looking at things that are new to me and uniquely refreshing. No wonder you've been able to make advancements on old technology." She nodded and looked out the cockpit window hiding most of her face from him. "I honestly didn't mean to hurt your feelings."

She glanced back at him, and it was possible her eyes held a bit of mist. "You didn't. I'm used to people scoffing and putting my thoughts down as hair-brained and impossible. But it is the what-ifs that interest me. What if you didn't confine yourself to thinking about processes the same way as your predecessors. What if you take the risk? If you fail, you fail…" Jillian trailed off at that point and stared out the window, lost in thought.

"But what if you don't?" Drake finished her line of reasoning.

She swung her gaze at him. It lingered before she responded, "Right. I don't want to be the one afraid to take the risk. Not anymore." She fell back into that far away gaze and stared out the window again. In that minute, he saw the insecure seventeen-year-old with braces, and glasses sitting quietly hoping to be included.

"I'm glad. So tell me about you." Drake reached down and unlocked his chair, swiveling it a few degrees so they could talk more easily.

"About me?" She chuckled humorlessly. "I'm boring. I got my undergraduate degree, went on to my masters and then my doctorate."

"Boyfriends? Relationships?" So much for being subtle. Drake felt his neck get hot. He'd blame it on the sun coming through the cockpit windshield.

"A few. None that stuck around."

"Why?"

"Ah, that's the twenty-thousand-dollar question." She thought about it for a minute and cocked her head back and forth before she answered. "I don't think any of them were willing to become the men I wanted them to be. I have a couple of mandatory requirements. First, they have to be gentlemen, which is harder to find now then you'd think, and second, they have to be intelligent."

"So, you can discuss your thoughts with them?"

Her head swung toward him, and she was clearly surprised. "Exactly, I mean they don't have to have a doctorate, but would it hurt to be interested in my life's work? I know it can be boring and repetitive, but inching closer and closer to that breakthrough is exhilarating!"

"You never had a boyfriend that was a gentleman and intelligent?" Drake was feeling sorry for mankind on one hand and lucky as shit on the other.

"Oh, I didn't say that. I said I had a high standard. I lived with a physics professor for a year."

Drake tried like hell to keep his expression passive. "Did you love him?"

"Love? No. It was comfortable. We understood each other's work and occasionally bounced ideas off each other."

"What happened to end the relationship?" He wasn't sure he really wanted to know, but any data she'd give up about her past would only benefit his future decisions, because having a future with Jilly in it, even as just friends, was going to happen.

She gave a soft huff and suddenly found her fingernails interesting. "He found another woman."

"While he was living with you?"

"Technically, I was living with him, but, yes. It was classic. I walked in on them together. He had her bent over the couch." She swallowed hard and then shook her head. "That was enlightening. He claimed he didn't have a strong libido. We had sex on rare occasions. Guess he saved it up for her."

"What is his name?" God, he prayed that came out non-threatening because right now he wanted to reach down that bastard's throat and pull out his heart.

"Who? Clay?" She shot a glance at him. He must not have done a great job at concealing his anger because her eyebrows shot heavenward.

"Clay what?"

"Oh…no. No, you don't get to be offended for me. Believe me, I learned my lesson. Since we parted ways, I only hook up when I know there will be no strings attached. It is easier to keep yourself safe that way."

"But that isn't living." *Whoa*. Drake snapped his mouth shut. Shit, maybe he needed to listen to himself because he'd been doing the same thing as Jillian. Scratching an itch and keeping away from any form of commitment was the go-to game plan for Dixon and him. Hell, they even shared women so they wouldn't form attachments. They'd tried dating separately, but that always ended before it started—no doubt because of the baggage each of them carried.

She shrugged. "It works for me. For now. Eventually, I want the white picket fence, the big porch with a swing where I can rock my kids. I want pets, and a home and a husband that wants the same thing."

Drake considered her desires before he asked the obvious question. "What about work?"

She blinked at him as if trying to understand his question before she asked, "What about it?"

"Do you plan on working when you find this white picket fence scenario?" He figured if she was talking, he'd continue to rake in any information he could obtain.

"Duh?" She blinked at him as if he'd grown a second head.

Huh, well, all right then. He glanced out the windshield to hide his embarrassment. "That's a lot to put on your plate."

"See, that's just it. I don't think it is, because I want a man who will stand beside me. A marriage is a partnership. It isn't *me* taking care of *him*. I don't want to be the only one cooking dinner and cleaning the house, especially if I'm working. How is that fair? I want a husband who wants a family as much as I do and is willing to do more than go out and work his eight hours. I don't want one who comes home and expects me to cook, clean and wait on him all while doing my job, plus taking care of the kids and the house. That dogma is so nineteen fifties. I get that it works for some, but it would never work for me."

"I can see that. Most of the families I know at the complex are not typical." Ember was a doctor and Joseph, well he wasn't really positive what Joseph did on a daily basis, but the man lived for his family. Chief and Tatyana…well that relationship was as atypical as they came. Between the two of them, he got maybe ten sentences a month, but they worked damn well together. Anyone could see that.

"What do you want in a wife?" Her question catapulted him out of his thoughts.

"Wife?"

She laughed at him. "Yes, wife. Don't look so afraid. There is no law saying you have to have a wife, but if you did, what would you look for in her? Or maybe a him?"

Drake felt his neck get hot again. What was it about this woman making him blush? He couldn't remember the last time he'd let someone embarrass him. He stalled and checked gauges and readings that didn't need to be monitored.

"Well?"

Drake shot her a glance, mentally grabbed his balls, and answered. "I don't know. There are a lot of things that would have to fall into line before I'd ever think of getting that serious with anyone."

"Understandable. But if those things fell into line, what would you look for?" She turned in her seat and carefully lifted her leg, making sure not to touch any equipment.

"Well, the obvious of course, someone who loved me."

"Of course. Go on."

"They'd have to be okay with living with me at the complex. That is non-negotiable."

"Yeah? Tell me about that place."

"The complex?"

"Yes, you haven't said much about it."

"There really isn't a lot I can say without trespassing boundaries that shouldn't be crossed."

"Just how big is this complex?"

"Well, it has definitely grown since its initial concept. Currently, we have thirty-five full-time employees. That includes doctors, pharmacists, medical technicians, PT's, educators, managers, and various others that lurk in the shadows." He grinned at his own inside joke.

"All of this, and it's in South Dakota?"

"Yes. On a ranch. The family I told you about, the one that adopted Dix and me, the Marshalls?" Jillian nodded, encouraging him to continue. "They have a massive ranch. The complex is located over the hill from their ranch house, and they recently completed another long-term lease for an additional one hundred acres. Guardian has some interesting plans for the land."

"So this complex is thriving?"

"It is."

"In the middle of nowhere?"

"Well, it is remote, but there is a small town about a half hour drive from the complex. Hollister is about midway between Newell and Buffalo. Hell, it's actually built around the junction of the highway. Go north, and you're in Buffalo. Go east, and you'll hit Newell. Neither of those communities are large, but they are hubs for the ranchers in the area. Anyway, Hollister is where most of the people who work at the complex live. The influx of income helps the community, and they, in turn, keep nosy people out of our business. Not that anyone usually comes looking for us, but when questions are raised, that town closes ranks. Some of the best people in the world live up there.

They work hard because they don't know any other way. Honest people. Salt of the earth."

He glanced at her and did a double take at her expression. It was soft and dreamy. "You love it in South Dakota. I can tell by the way you talk."

"I won't deny it. It's home for both Dixon and me."

"Where is Dixon's assignment?"

Drake let out a harsh laugh. "New York City."

"I take it you aren't happy about that?"

"I'm not." Drake rolled his shoulders.

"Lunch is ready." Mark's voice preceded him as he entered the cockpit. Jillian carefully extracted herself from the seat and turned sideways to slide by Mark. Drake glared at the man. He could have moved so there wouldn't be any contact. Mark winked at him and headed back to the galley kitchen after Jillian. The asshole.

CHAPTER 8

Mark's flirting was fun, for about the first hour. Jillian finally sought refuge in the bedroom, feigning a headache. Although Mark had a wicked sense of humor, he wasn't the man she wanted, and that was a shame because he was very attractive and obviously interested. Had she misinterpreted Drake's interest this morning? Perhaps the hand holding and small, gentle gestures were remnants of the friendship they once shared.

She sat down on the bed and flopped back against the stack of artfully arranged pillows. Her life had toppled onto its head in the last twenty-four hours. Someone had tried to kill her. For what? Technology? No matter how she tried, she didn't understand how killing her would benefit anyone. Did she plan on patenting the invention? Yes. Would it be a game changer for the energy industry? Absolutely. Low cost, high-efficiency energy that could power third-world countries and revolutionize first-world tech was an ultimate game changer. Would the oil companies and countries that held biofuel monopolies be willing to kill to prevent distribution of tech that would benefit the whole of civilization? Jillian shook her head. In concept, perhaps, but people really weren't that evil. Were they? She didn't believe in such things as paid assassins, at least not in America…not since President Kennedy. His death had been debated and dissected with everyone pointing fingers at random conspiracy theories both internal and external. The arguments for any assassination claims after that event had always been debunked, at least as far as she knew. That drama was reserved for Hollywood.

She rolled onto her side and plumped a throw pillow to support her head. She couldn't find a common thread for all the events of the last week. Well, except that they'd happened to her. A soft knock at the door produced a major eye roll. Mark obviously didn't take hints very well. Jillian moved off the bed and opened the door.

Drake held out a small packet and a tiny bottle of water. Jillian opened the door farther and let him in. "Mark said you had a headache. I brought you some pain relievers."

She took the packet from him and eyed it. "Can I make a confession?"

Drake's eyebrows drew together. "Sure."

"I don't have a headache. I'm suffering from overexposure."

"I don't understand."

"Mark is fine in small doses, but..." Jillian handed the packet back to him.

"Oh, no fucking way. I'll kill the jerk."

She grabbed his arm as he spun. "No, hey, it wasn't like that. He was a gentleman. I guess I'm more tired than I thought." *That sounded plausible, right?*

The tension drained from Drake's body. "Are you sure?"

"Positive. I just needed a few minutes to be quiet and process...everything."

Drake nodded and glanced back toward the front of the plane. "I'll head back up then."

"That's not necessary. Can you be back here for a few minutes?"

"The aircraft is on autopilot, and Mark is capable of flying the plane if something goes south. Why?"

Jillian's mind blanked at the question. *Why? Because I like being near you? Because I want to learn more about you. Because I'm stupid and still reeling from my teenage crush and hell...* Drake shifted on his feet, and she blurted, "I wanted to ask what was going to happen when we get to San Jose."

"We'll go to your place and hang out until Monday morning. Keep a low profile." Drake dropped into a small chair permanently fixed in the corner of the bedroom. "You're okay with me staying in your apartment?"

"Yeah, no problem. I have a sectional that is killer comfortable. I'd give you my bed, but it's a twin. Somehow, I think your legs would hang over the end."

"A twin bed? I thought only kids had twin beds." Drake extended his long leg and propped it up on the edge of the bed. "And, as you pointed out, you're not a kid anymore."

Jillian groaned inwardly at her brash comment yesterday. *Hell, was it less than twenty-four hours ago that this man had walked back into her life?* "I did say that, didn't I?"

"You did. And I must say, I agree."

"Yeah, well being grown up isn't all it's cracked up to be, you know?" She laughed and shook her head. "Man, I couldn't wait to get rid of those braces and glasses, to grow into my body and stop being a gangly, frizzy-haired teenager with zits."

"I liked her. She was a good kid."

Kid. Right. Jillian took that hint. At least she knew he never saw her as anything but a kid. Well, congratulations, old girl, you're the only one harboring past feelings. Good to know. She sat down on the bed and flopped back on the soft duvet cover.

"Seriously, why do you have a twin bed?"

"I have a twin bed because it doesn't feel as lonely to sleep in it as the king-sized mattress I used to own. I guess that's pretty lame, isn't it?"

"No. I don't think so. You adjusted to help yourself feel more comfortable."

She lifted up onto her elbows and examined him for a moment. He stared back at her, his expression unreadable. "Have you ever been lonely, Drake?" She sat up. "I mean, I know you have Dixon, but is that enough for you? Am I stupid for wanting the dream? Is it because of my past that I want a family so badly?" She shook her head and then laughed, holding up a hand before he could respond. "Forget I asked. I must be exhausted. I don't make sense, not even to myself. You must think I'm a blithering idiot. Hell, *I* think I'm a blithering idiot."

Drake pulled his boot off the bed, stood up, and moved to the door. "Get some rest, Jilly."

"Jillian." The correction was a reflex.

"Right, sorry." He rubbed the back of his neck before he spoke, "I do know what it feels like to be lonely. My brother is a big part of who I am, but is that connection enough?" He reached for the door handle and paused to glance over at her. "Probably not. I don't know if everyone gets a happily-ever-after, Jillian. I've seen some of my closest friends find it, but is that going to happen for me? For you? I can't answer that question. I don't think anyone can. Get some rest."

The door closed with a quiet click. Jillian flopped back down on the bed and stared at the curved ceiling. She closed her eyes and drew in a breath. Her "happily-ever-afters" centered on a specific Prince Charming. Well, hell, she'd jumped ahead about a hundred steps, hadn't she? The man had done nothing but hold her hand today, and she was mentally scribbling hearts and arrows and dreaming like a schoolgirl. God, she *was* pathetic. Jillian grabbed another pillow and shoved it over her head. Maybe she did need a nap.

~

Drake stopped by the galley, warmed and ate the plate of food Mark had put in the small refrigerator for him. Jillian's words echoed in his head. Being alone and being lonely were two different things. Since they'd been reunited, he and Dixon hadn't been separated much. When duty or the military forced the issue, they did what they needed to do, but always came back together. Yet at times, even when Dixon was right next to him, Drake was lonely. Not alone, but lonely. He and Dixon filled that void with words, banter and bullshit. It was all a way to make sure people didn't look too close, see through the smoke to the dark hollow places that haunted both of them. It never failed. People thought they were funny, or obnoxious, or intelligent, but nobody saw them as damaged, lonely, and hurting. They made damn sure of it.

Jillian was a beautiful, intelligent woman, and she had a dream for her future. Drake couldn't see himself as part of what she wanted. He had obligations to Dixon. Maybe someday Dix would find a woman, then Drake would be able to consider his future, but until that point, he'd manage. It had always been his responsibility to take care of his younger brother. Even if Dix was only twenty-six minutes younger. It was who and what they were. Two parts of a whole that had been broken and shattered almost beyond recognition. He'd slapped glue on himself and carefully pieced Dixon back together. Neither of them were the kids they had once been, but age and life hadn't dulled the need to ensure Dixon was safe, both mentally and physically. He'd give his last breath to his brother without a second thought. He wasn't sure he'd ever find a woman who'd stand on an equal level with his brother. He wasn't relationship material. Not now at least.

Finished with his meal, he stacked the dirty dishes in the small cupboard that would be serviced when they landed and made sure all the latches were secure before he grabbed a bottle of water and headed back to the cockpit.

Drake and Mark shared a comfortable silence.

Mark was reading something on his tablet and Drake didn't feel much like talking. The hours and miles slipped by, and conversation was sparse, but not strained. Drake got up to stretch and went back to check on Jillian. She was sprawled out across the bed, asleep. He watched her for a few minutes before he silently closed the door, grabbed two more waters and went back to the cockpit. He handed one to Mark as he slid back into his seat and strapped in.

"How's our girl doing?" Mark asked when Drake folded into the pilot's seat.

"She's out. She didn't sleep well last night."

"You know that how?"

Drake opened his water bottle and took a drink before he replied. "I spent the night with her."

"Dude, did you or did you not tell me there was nothing between the two of you?"

"I did."

Mark raised an eyebrow at him.

"I was up patrolling the house because someone tried to kill her yesterday."

"Okay, that explains your actions, but not hers."

"What do you mean?"

"She's into you."

"You're mistaken." Drake couldn't afford to let a

flight of fancy pull his attention away from his primary task.

"Maybe you should tell her? I've been over here nursing my wounded pride. I mean, dude, I used all of my best lines on that woman. Nothing worked. If she isn't into you, there is someone else, because I'm a lady-killer, and let me tell you, there was nothing there. I struck out swinging, though."

Drake chuckled. "Struck out, huh?"

"Shut up. You were all touchy-feely with her this morning. What did you do, set me up to watch me go down in flames?" Mark cocked his head at Drake. "You did, didn't you? Man, what did I do to you to deserve that? I thought we were friends."

Drake couldn't contain his laughter and raised a hand, one finger extended, asking for a moment until he got himself together. "Oh, shit, dude! No, I didn't set you up. If you struck out, it was because Jilly wasn't interested, no other reason."

"How could she not be interested? Look at me!" Mark curled his arm, bulged his bicep, and kissed it.

"Narcissistic much?" Drake barely got the words out and had to hold his stomach he was laughing so hard.

"Nah, man, this isn't narcissism, this is a well-developed sense of self-esteem. I'm a teddy bear with muscles and tattoos. Women love me."

"Most women." Drake corrected. Mark flipped him the bird for his efforts.

The plane's dedicated communications system lit up, and Mark's smile dropped immediately. Both men snapped their headphones on.

"GDN101, this is Guardian Control."

Drake flipped the switch and centered his mouthpiece so his words wouldn't be muffled. "Guardian Control, this is GDN101."

"Standby for Alpha."

Drake sent Mark a sharp look and received one in return. "GDN101, the FAA has issued an Airworthiness Directive, grounding all G6's effective immediately. There have been two crashes in the last twenty-four hours, and although there is no known connection to the airframe, the FAA is mandating a safety stand down."

"Mechanical issues suspected?"

"Negative, not at this time. Pilot error suspected in both instances, however, two in twenty-four hours is enough for the FAA to act."

"Roger that. We are thirty minutes from our initial approach into San Jose." Drake knew there was nothing wrong with the aircraft. The

G6 was the sturdiest plane he'd ever flown, and it had a top-rated safety and maintenance record. The aircraft was damn near infallible. But two crashes in twenty-four hours was concerning.

"Affirmative. You'll need to wait out the safety stand down or drive to your original destination. When you get the lay of the land let me know."

"Roger that, Skipper. Do we have any further information on the case?"

"Jewell is running down rabbit holes and eliminating scenarios, but we are still at the starting point. Nothing makes sense about the shooting yesterday. Why take out the person who has the tech? I could understand kidnapping or blackmail in this situation, but sending a hired killer? Everyone here is scratching their heads, and that puts me on edge. Be careful out there. Don't take any unnecessary chances."

"Roger that, Skipper. I'll call as soon as we get settled in San Jose."

"Affirm. Archangel has a PSO heading your way to watch your six at night. He has your cell number and will contact you when he arrives."

That was a godsend. He needed to sleep tonight. Hopefully, Jillian's apartment wouldn't be a logistical nightmare to secure. "Affirmative. Thanks, Skipper."

"Be smart." Jacob cautioned.

"Never going to happen." Drake retorted. The laughter of his friend and boss rang loud in the cabin before the radio went silent.

Drake pulled the headset off and scanned the controls in front of him, looking for any indication of a problem.

After long minutes spent checking every gauge and going over the controls with a fine tooth comb, Mark broke the silence. "There is nothing wrong here, man. This bird is solid." He nodded to the door behind them. "You want to go wake her up for landing or should I?"

"I'll do it. Be right back." He unstrapped and started to get out of his seat, not expecting to see Jillian walking toward the cockpit.

"Hey, you." Drake mentally rolled his eyes at himself. *Brilliant conversationalist, aren't you?*

She blinked and wrapped her arms around her stomach. "Hey. Are we almost there?" The sleepy rumpled look was very attractive on Jillian.

Drake dropped back down into his seat. "On our initial descent. I was just coming to wake you up and get you strapped in for landing."

A low, sexy laugh flitted around the cockpit. "Oh. Wow, that sounds way kinkier than I think you meant it to sound." She winked at him and pivoted on her heel.

Drake blanked out. He had no response for that comment. None. Mark chuckled and waited for Drake to strap back in. The second his headset was back on Mark quipped, "I'm telling you, that woman is into you."

Drake ignored his co-pilot's comment, although he found himself considering the possibilities. Possibilities that before yesterday, he wouldn't have believed existed.

CHAPTER 9

Jillian waited for Drake as he pulled their bags from the aircraft. Did she appreciate the view of the bulging muscles under the tight shirt as he flexed to retrieve the luggage? Oh, dear, yes. Yes, she did... and that type of thinking needed to stop. He walked toward her with the bags. "Guardian has a car waiting for us out front."

Jillian fell into step with him. She turned and looked over her shoulder. "What about Mark?"

Drake stopped, causing her to bump into him. "What about him?"

She held a hand against his chest and stepped back, putting distance between them but not before she was able to breathe in the addictive cologne the man wore. The dark spice filled her sense and wrapped around her. Intoxicating, distracting and addictive, the adjectives didn't come close to describing the need that thrummed just under her skin. She drew a shuddering breath and tried to form a coherent response to Drake's question. "Oh, ahh…does he need a place to stay? It would be really tight, but he could come with us."

"He's good. He has to babysit Gracie. The FAA grounded all G6's pending a safety review."

"Say what?" She glanced back at the gleaming aircraft. "That plane wasn't safe?"

Drake chuckled as he pushed open the door and awkwardly held it for her while juggling the luggage. She skipped through the door and glanced around the private airstrip's small terminal building. "She's perfectly safe. There were two accidents in the last twenty-four hours, and both involved that airframe. While pilot error is suspected as a cause for both incidents, the FAA has to exert its due diligence. The stand down is a normal procedure in these types of events."

Drake made it through the building by the time he was done talking. He stopped and looked out the front door. A large SUV was parked at the curb. She watched as his eyes roamed the exterior of the building.

"What are you looking for?" she whispered.

"Just checking for anything that seems off." The driver's side door of the SUV opened, and a man trotted around the vehicle toward them.

Drake dropped the luggage that was in his right hand, grabbed her arm, and tugged her unceremoniously behind him.

"Mr. Simmons?" The man extended his hand. "I'm your ride to San Jose." Drake didn't move or respond, and Jillian peeked around Drake's arm. Puzzlement flitted across the man's face. "Oh, I'm supposed to say Cobalt." Drake relaxed and reached for the man's hand. "Next time, lead off with that."

Jillian kept her mouth shut and watched. The driver apologized several times while loading the baggage and then again after they got into the vehicle.

"So, do you work for Guardian, too?" Jillian asked the driver, more to be polite than anything else. Drake put his hand on her thigh and squeezed it. A small shake of his head silenced her. The silent trip to her apartment took less than a half hour. With luggage in hand and the driver dispatched, Jillian led Drake to her apartment. The front door had been damaged, but she had expected that. The police told her the apartment manager was able to secure the door with her deadbolt, but they didn't tell her about the gap in the door at the bottom. A cat or a small dog could easily fit through the opening.

Drake placed the luggage by the front door, bent over and stood up, holding a wicked looking handgun. "Where did you get that?"

Drake chuckled. "A concealed holster." He extended his hand for her keys. "The same place I retrieved it from yesterday during the shooting on campus."

Jillian blinked and handed him the keys. Somehow she hadn't noticed the gun. *Why hadn't she noticed it yesterday?*

Drake opened the door and pulled her inside. He shut it, leaving the luggage outside. His finger over his lips, he gestured for her to be silent. She nodded. He pointed at the spot where she stood. Not a problem. She wouldn't move an inch. He spun and walked away, and that's when she got the first glimpse of her apartment. The paintings on the wall had been destroyed. The canvas drooped in shreds from the frames that were askew from the hangers. Filthy words, spray painted on her walls in four feet high letters, screamed at her in red and gold hues of hatred. The sectional she adored had been destroyed. Stuffing from its wonderfully soft cushions lay in white mounds on the carpet beside the other shattered remains of her life. Small figurines of angels she'd collected throughout college were thrown from the curio cabinet that once held them against the wall across the room. They lay in shattered pieces. Ruined. She stepped toward the rubble. Why? Why would anyone do this?

"The rest of the house is trashed, too. They must have been alerted to the cops coming before they made it to your closet. Your clothes look relatively untouched. Go get whatever you'll need for an extended stay away. I'd prefer if you traveled light. No need for fancy clothes. The ranch is a blue jeans type affair." Jillian nodded and moved to step past him. His hand reached out and stilled her. She glanced up at him. "I'm sorry someone did this to your home. It looks like kids. They destroyed shit they couldn't steal. It looks like your electronics were what they were after." He motioned toward the empty entertainment center.

She nodded and headed into the bedroom. The

first three drawers of her dresser were pulled out, and the contents were scattered over the floor. Jillian walked over the clothes to get to the closet. There was a box where she kept photos of her parents. She'd scanned them into her computer and loaded them on the cloud so they'd always be there, but... She dropped to her knees and moved a stack of clothes away from the box. She opened the lid and smiled. The small envelope of photos was still inside along with her college class ring, the tassels off her graduation caps, and pictures of her, Matt, and Cliff on the day they went to live with Cliff.

Jillian stared at the small box in her hands. They trembled no matter how hard she clenched the pressed cardboard. She lifted her eyes and took in the devastation beyond the door of the closet. From floor level where she knelt, the senselessness seemed even more devastating.

The sound of Drake's boots as he walked down the hallway toward her room punctuated the stillness of the apartment. He entered the room and zeroed in on her. Careful to step around the clothes strewn across the floor, he made his way to her and knelt. His large hand reached out and picked the top photograph out of the box. It was of her and Matt. He smiled at the image. "Are you okay?"

She shook her head. "No, not really."

"I've booked a hotel room. We'll stay there until Monday. We should probably go." He glanced around. "Can I help you pack? Is there something you want me to try to find?"

"No, everything they destroyed can be replaced. Everything except these mementos. I'm lucky they didn't find them." Jillian gave a despondent glace around the room. "I know, rationally, this was a random act, but inside?" She tapped her fingers over her heart. "Here, it feels like I have been picked up and dropped into a world that doesn't make the slightest sense."

"I know, sweetheart." Drake's hand under her chin brought her eyes back to him. His thumb swept moisture off her cheek.

She leaned into his touch. His strength and his presence intimated a connection she knew wasn't really there, but right now, she wanted to believe he cared for more than the person she used to be. Moving away from him, she closed her eyes and shook her head. The use of the word sweetheart was nothing new. He'd called her that when she was a teenager. It was one of the things that fueled her teenage addiction; but now, just as then, it was just a term of endearment meant to reassure her. She pushed to her feet, and he stood with her, taking her arm to help her gain her balance. She gave him a sad smile. "Thank you, again."

"For what?" Sincere confusion flashed across his expression.

"For being where I needed you to be. For being who I needed you to be." She forced a small laugh, one she didn't feel and wasn't sure she'd properly managed. "I seem to be in need of a hero lately."

He pulled her into his arms, the little cardboard box between them. "I'm honored to be your hero, Jill. I wish you didn't have to experience any of this. We will get through this, and then you can resume your life."

Jill drew a deep breath and inhaled his scent before she nodded and stepped back. Resume a life devoid of the man who, once again, left footprints so large no one else would ever be able to fill them.

It took thirty minutes to sort through the destroyed clothes. Her jeans hung in the closet, so she had a portion of her wardrobe covered. Casual tops were going to be an issue. Most of them had been dumped out of the dresser and spray painted. Her business apparel provided long-sleeved shirts and several other choices, but all were inappropriate for a ranch. Jillian drew a long deep breath and released it before repeating the process. She wasn't going to cave to the stress pushing her down. She put the clothes she could salvage into her suitcase and headed back to the closet for her intimates. She kept her underwear in a silk-lined basket in her closet. The lingerie was expensive, flimsy and a complete indulgence. She grabbed two pairs of boots and a pair of sturdy walking shoes along with the basket and headed back into the bedroom. Fingers hooked in his front pockets, Drake leaned against the door jamb. She gave him a quick smile and packed the clothes she had stacked on the bed before she cast one last glance around the room. Her jewelry box had been smashed, and there was no sign of any of the items she'd left. A watch, several rings that didn't mean anything to her and a drawer full of earrings, most of which were purchased at department stores, were missing. They'd get little to nothing from pawning those items.

"Are you ready?"

Jillian jumped at Drake's question. She'd been so lost in her thoughts she'd forgotten he was waiting. "Yes, I think so." Her glance bolted from the devastation to him. "No, wait, I'm not." Jillian headed out the door and brushed past Drake who moved out of her way.

"Where are you going?"

"You'll see!" Jillian hopped over her broken glass figurines and into the kitchen. Bingo! The cabinet on top of the refrigerator was undisturbed. She looked around for her little step stool, but couldn't find it in the rubble of what was once her kitchen. She stood on her tiptoes and stretched for the handle. Drake's arm appeared, and she felt him place his hand on her hip, steadying himself as he leaned over her.

"What's up here?" He opened the door, and Jillian applauded at the sight of two red and black boxes with a gold embossed label. "Are you shitting me?"

Drake's question brought a bubble of laughter out of her. "All they took didn't equal the cost of those two bottles."

"Is this the real thing?" Drake carefully handed her one box and then reached back up for the other.

"Oh, yeah. Two bottles of Louis the XIII Magnum. Eight thousand dollars a pop. The best cognac in the world." Jillian opened the front panel of the red leather box and ran her finger over the blown glass details and fleur-de-lis bottle stopper. "I bought these when I sold my first patent for mega bucks. I was going to give one to Clay so we could toast my success. That was the day I came home and found him." She closed the lid and smiled up at Drake. "I want to drink one of these tonight."

"What, the whole bottle? Eight thousand dollars worth of alcohol in one night?"

"Yep." Jillian stacked the boxes. "Get the suitcases. We can take my car to whatever hotel you've booked for us." She led him out of the apartment and to the covered parking provided for her unit. As soon as she indicated her vehicle, he came to an abrupt halt.

∼

"That is not a car." Drake lowered their luggage to the sidewalk and stared at the tiny car. "I have duffle bags bigger than this." He'd seen cars like this on the highway and wanted to ask the people driving them what part of their brain they'd lost. It was the size of a roller skate. A child's roller skate!

Jillian laughed and opened the trunk…well, the back end, not the trunk, because the small little partition between the rear bumper and the front seat was anything but a trunk. A glove box maybe. "You can't even fit the alcohol in here. Nope, not getting in this thing."

Seriously, a golf cart would have more room than the little black SMART car that sat in her parking spot. Even if he could get over the pink stripes on the damn thing, there was no way they would get the luggage and his long ass legs into that vehicle at the same time. Hell, the top of the roof hit him at his belt buckle.

"Stop being a baby. Put this suitcase in length-wise and then put the duffle on top."

Drake did as she asked and then watched as she slid the two bottles of alcohol safely next to them. He whistled, "Well, I'll be damned."

She shut the hatch and shrugged. "I was surprised, too." She nodded to the passenger side and went to the driver's side door.

Drake eyed the space and shook his head. "I'm not going to fit."

"Sure you will. There's more room than you expect." She slid into the seat.

Drake rubbed his jaw and opened the door. The

cell in his pocket vibrated. He stepped back and eyed the tiny car as he answered his phone. "Go."

"Status?" Drake recognized Jacob's voice immediately.

"Secure. We have to relocate. Her apartment wasn't just broken into, it was vandalized. It isn't livable."

"Do you need us to send in contractors to get it back up to speed?"

"I'll let you know about the interior. I'm not sure what she wants to do with it right now. At a minimum, the front door needs to be replaced."

"Roger that. I'll get the info from Jewell and send it down to operations. We'll try to get it secured tonight."

"Thank you." Drake put his foot inside the vehicle and tried to sit down. His knee met his ear. Literally. He sat down, leaned over damn near into Jillian's lap, and pulled his right leg in after him. He grunted when his size thirteen snagged on the door. He grabbed his knee and pulled it towards his chin. His boot disconnected from the frame and he whacked his chin with his knee. He grunted. Fuck him, that was going to leave a bruise.

"What the ever loving fuck are you doing? And

if you are doing what I think you're doing why the hell did you answer the phone?"

"Fuck!" Drake tried to shift positions, brought his elbow down and hit his funny bone. "Son of a bitch." He wasn't in a position to look, but whiny sounds of mirth being ruthlessly strangled came from the driver's seat.

"Where are you?" Jacob growled.

"I'm trying to get into her car."

"Dr. Law's car?"

"Yeah." His shoulders packed the inches that separated him from Jillian as he tried to contort himself into the vehicle. He craned his neck around to peer at her. She held her hands clamped over her mouth in a futile effort to dampen her howls as her eyes bled tears of laughter and her right shoulder jerked spasmodically against his side. Great.

"What the fuck kind of car is it?"

Drake reached over with his left hand and tried the grab the passenger door. He wasn't bendy enough. His knees pressed hard against the dash; which rammed his hips against the seat back, jack-knifing him tightly between the seat cushion and the roof—all accompanied by howls of savagely muted mirth. Fuck if he could figure out how to close the door. "Ahh…it's like one of those SMART cars."

"You've got to be kidding me." Jacob started laughing. Drake removed the phone from his ear, extended his arm out as straight as he could, angled the phone to get the knees to ear position he was in and snapped a picture. He thumbed the commands on the phone and sent the selfie to Jacob's email.

"Check your email, and by the way, I'm renting an SUV for the drive to the ranch. You're reimbursing me. I'm also making you pay for at least four chiropractor visits."

Drake heard Jacob click his computer keyboard and then pulled the phone away as Jacob's guffaws damn near split his eardrum. Drake couldn't help laughing at the absurdity of his knees planted against his ears, and Jillian's keening whines of hilarity added to the seriously stupid situation. "Hey, Jacob?"

"Y…yeah?" Jacob managed between fits of laughter.

"The car…it's black, with pink stripes." Drake threw his head back from the phone as Jacob's wild shrieks of laughter ripped through the connection. Jillian had abandoned any attempt to hide her reactions and was hiccupping and sobbing with laughter. Good, at least he'd made her day lighter. He disconnected the call and managed to shut the door. He glanced at Jillian. "Woman, I hope you have a can opener."

CHAPTER 10

*E*xiting the vehicle wasn't as tricky as the pretzel imitation he'd done to fit into it. Once Jillian was out of the vehicle, he opened his door, tipped over her seat, pulled his knees up and got his big-ass feet clear of the door jamb. Once both legs were out, he grabbed the top of the vehicle and tugged himself to the edge of his seat. From there, it was a matter of standing up and grabbing the roof of the car to allow his legs to regain feeling. He'd survived. Barely. He straightened slowly, placed his hands at the small of his back, and arched backwards.

He moved to the back of the vehicle and took out the luggage as she locked up her car, her eyes still leaking and her lower lip held between her teeth in a ferocious attempt to quiet her laughter. He didn't understand the efficacy of a lock when two men could lift the vehicle into the back of a pickup. What she really needed was a cable and a padlock like people used on their bikes. He grinned at the mental image of the car chained to the cement parking stop.

"If I weren't depending on you to possibly save my life, I'd have videoed that last thirty minutes. Slam dunk to go viral on YouTube and…oh my… blackmail gold." She cleared her throat and fought for a straight face while he shot her a look of disgust and proceeded to ignore her. As soon as she turned away, for a moment, he succumbed to a broad grin and silent laughter, but when she turned back again, his face was a blank.

Their room was a double king. It was obviously the best Jewell could come up with on such short notice. The PSO that was shadowing them had arrived. He told the man to get some shut-eye and where they would be for the evening, then made arrangements for the man to check in at eleven that night so Drake could get some much needed sleep.

Jillian flopped down on the bed and bounced

right back up. "Food. We need food if we are going to drink tonight."

"Not we, sweetheart. One of us is working tonight to make sure the one who is drinking remains safe." Drake watched her expression as she realized what he was saying. She drew a breath, straightened her shoulders and gave him a nod.

"Got it. Then I need food to soak up the vast amounts of alcohol I intend on consuming, and you need to get something non-leaded to drink." She whipped her ponytail over her shoulder, grabbed her small bag and went into the bathroom.

Drake ambled over to the small desk and pulled out the take-out menus from the folder provided by the hotel. He glanced at the closed door and called to her, "Italian, Mexican, Chinese or Thai?"

"I don't care!" Her shout preceded the sound of the shower. Drake stared at the door trying to block out the image of her naked—the only thing separating them a flimsy door. He dropped the menus and hit up his phone. What he wanted wasn't food. No matter what he ordered, one of his appetites would remain unsatisfied.

Jillian blinked back the feelings of rejection. She was a job. Somehow in the course of the last twenty-four hours, she'd forgotten that. She would be paying Guardian, which meant she would be paying Drake. She was his job. Why did she have a problem internalizing what she was to this man? She was Silly Jilly, and she was a job. She stepped into the warm jets of the shower and dropped her head under the stream, blocking the world out. She took her time washing her hair and luxuriated in the never ending flow of hot water.

She changed into the yoga pants and oversized t-shirt she'd packed as pajamas before combing out and braiding her hair. The room was dark except for a dim light in the far corner. Drake sat looking out at the setting sun. A plethora of takeout containers sat beside him. A small plastic cup sat beside the Louis the XIII bottle. Jillian padded over and sat down on a matching chair on the other side of the table.

"I wasn't sure if you'd changed your mind." He nodded toward the elegant round bottle.

Jillian shook her head. "Nope. Open it, would you?"

Drake reached over and picked up the bottle. He made quick work of the seals and pulled the cut crystal fleur-de-lis stopper out. "It is a shame we don't have a crystal snifter for this." He poured about a half inch of the brown liquor into her cup, replaced the stopper and smiled at her. "I have a friend who likes expensive cognac. He gets a bottle once every four months from our employer. I've watched him while he babies cognac. You're supposed to cup it in the palm of your hand to warm it and swirl it around to get the bouquet or the nose of the liquor."

Jillian picked up the plastic cup and gazed into its depths. "Yeah, that would be lost on me. I like martinis." She put the cup to her lips and slung her head back, downing the liquid in one gulp. The fire made her nose burn. She gasped at the burn and put the cup back down. "Hit me, baby, one more time."

Drake laughed and picked up the bottle. "You did not just quote a Britney song to me did you?"

Jillian laughed, and as he poured she asked, "You did not just recognize a Britney lyric, did you?"

"Ah…one point for Doctor Law." Drake put the bottle down and opened the containers on the table. "I ordered several different things, wasn't sure what you liked." She glanced down at beef, chicken and fish tacos, with smaller containers of rice, beans, chips, and salsa. Jillian grabbed a chicken taco and a small handful of chips with salsa. She watched as he took his food and they both settled into the chairs again.

"Maybe you should put that bottle over here by me." She was going to get drunk tonight. She deserved it. Hell, she earned the right.

"Maybe you shouldn't get too tipsy." He poured a small amount into the bottom of her cup. She tossed it back and held it out to him again, daring him to turn her down.

"Seriously, I'm only thinking of your safety here."

Drake poured a good amount into her cup, and she set it down while she demolished her chips. "I am absolutely positive you can, and will, protect me whether I be fully functioning or blotto drunk."

"Blotto? Is that a technical term?" Drake spooned some rice onto his plate.

"Yepper. Defined as shitfaced, snockered, and drunk as a skunk." She drank half the cognac in her cup and felt the warm buzz of alcohol running just underneath her skin. It smudged out the sharper edges of the day and allowed her to examine the events from the time of the shooting until now with a little distance. Lord knew she needed distance. "We're driving to South Dakota?" Jillian put her empty plate on the table and picked up her drink. Outside, the lights of the city were starting to twinkle in the dusky night sky.

"I think that is probably the wisest decision. Nobody knows you're with me. I'll rent the vehicle, and we'll head east. We don't have to hurry. We can enjoy ourselves even, play tourist. Maybe stop at Yellowstone and see the sights."

Yellowstone. Bears and trees, and well, she thought of picnic baskets and a cartoon bear with a hat and tie. She shook her head to clear her thoughts and turned in the chair, surprised at his suggestion. "You'd be willing to do that?"

"Sure, why not? I mean, look at it logically. There is no way anyone knows Guardian has you in protective custody, and even if they figured that out, the chances of them deducing I am the Guardian protecting you are next to zero. Right now, Mark is moving your car back to your apartment."

"How?" She glanced at the desk where she'd left her keys.

"With your keys. Don't worry, he's shorter than

I am. He won't break your car, and he'll secure it when he parks it at your apartment."

Jillian downed her liquor and deliberately stretched her cup out to Drake again. He sighed and poured a smidge into the bottom of the cup. She waited until he set the bottle down and picked it up, filling her cup a quarter of the way to the top before she put the stopper back in the decanter. She leaned against the back of the chair and swirled her $8,000 cognac in her $0.05 plastic cup. "Explain your rationale."

"First, back east, someone was trying to get to you. They will obviously keep looking for you. If they don't find you there, where do you think they will check next?"

"Here." That was a simple deduction, granted, one she hadn't thought of earlier, but hey, to her credit, she wasn't used to being shot at. "Does anyone get used to the idea that someone's trying to kill them?"

Drake leaned forward and looked out the window, his elbows on his knees. "It has been my experience that you become hyperaware. Everyone and everything becomes a threat. You hedge your moves in anticipation of a possible situation."

"That doesn't sound like fun. I want to have

fun, don't you?" She nodded her head in a agreement with herself. "I like the idea of driving to South Dakota while playing touristsess…" Jillian scowled. "Sightseers."

Drake chuckled at her and reached for the decanter, placing it between his feet.

Whatever, she had a good portion still in her cup.

"I'm glad you like the idea. It is the simplest way to keep you safe."

Jillian squinted her eyes at him and tried to play that logic through, but for some reason her thought process was hazy. "How so?"

He shrugged, "The likelihood of someone following our flight path back to San Jose is slim. If they do show up here, they will be looking for you. Your apartment and work are where they will focus their attention. The city is too damn big to find you, especially if you don't leave an electronic trail."

"Credit cards, emails and such like that," Jillian added just to let him know she was not yet blotto.

"Right. Cell phone, too. I took the liberty of taking your battery out of yours, by the way."

"Wait, what if Dad calls?"

He winked at her. "I had Guardian call him and

give him an emergency number to use if he needed to get in touch with you. Other than that, you can call and check in when we get back to the ranch."

She lifted her legs into the chair with her, bracing her heels on the edge of the seat, and hugged them with one arm. "Okay, but I don't understand why we don't drive straight to your place. Why the touriss, touresssess...sightseeing thing?" She rested her cheek on her knee when she turned to regard him. But for the light thrown from the small lamp behind her, the room was completely dark.

Drake turned to her and stared at her for several long seconds. "I'm being selfish, Jilly. I want to spend time with you. I want to get to know you."

It was dark, and she was well on her way to being drunk, but she saw the desire in his eyes and that revelation sent a chill of anticipation through her. She set her five-cent cup down and gave him her full attention. "Why?"

He chuckled. "Because a wise man told me to start paying attention to what was in front of me."

Jillian squinted at him and scrunched her nose. "Dad. Dad told you I had a crush on you." Mortified, she dropped her head onto her knees. "Ohhh, gaaawd…how could he do that?"

"No, he didn't tell me you had a crush on me. He did mention you might have carried a torch for either Dixon or me when you were younger." Drake let out an embarrassed chuckle and shrugged. "He may have told me I might want to start paying attention to what is in front of me."

Jillian lifted her head and propped it up on her hand. "I like Dixon," she shrugged, "but I didn't have a crush on him." A yawn escaped, and she covered her mouth. "Sorry."

"I'm not sure what you're sorry about." Drake's words carried a warmth she had to be imagining.

Drake had a bemused smile on his face. He was so handsome. Did he know that? "Do you know that?"

"Do I know what?" He chuckled.

"That you are handsome? And sexy. Sooo fucking sexy. Sex on a stick. A woman's wet dream. Yummy even." She wrinkled her nose and gave him her take on a sultry growl.

He laughed and rubbed his face.

Whoops, did she say that in her big girl voice?

Finally, he turned his gaze to her. "I think you're drunk."

"I'm not as think as you drunk I am, and I don't care if you know that." She stalled for a moment and shook her head with a frown. "Came out wrong. Don't care if you know I want you, 'cause I do." She blinked at him to put him back in focus. "Do you want me?" The warm fuzzy feeling became cotton batting around her. Yep, she was now blotto.

"Yes, Jilly, I want you."

"Name s'not Jilly." She wagged a finger at him.

He stood, and her eyes followed him up…way up. He was so tall. She bent backward and almost overbalanced in the chair but straightened at the last moment. He bent down and swooped her up. She may have squealed a little bit.

"Yes, you did squeal. Just a little bit."

Jillian wrapped her arms around his neck, bit her lower lip, and snorted. "Whoopsie… did I say that?" He was so close. His sexy mouth was right in front of her. "Brace yourself, Mr. Simmons. I'm going to kiss you." Jillian leaned in and pressed her lips against his. Even through the haze of alcohol, she felt an unmistakable jolt of desire split every atom in her body, scramble it into a frenzy and then zap her with lust. She moaned as his tongue licked her lips. She opened for him and reveled in the kiss. "Oh…god…I just knew it'd be epic."

He smiled against her mouth and lowered her onto the bed before reaching behind his neck to unlace her fingers. "When we make love, Jilly, you won't be drunk. I want you to remember everything we did together." He kissed her nose and pulled the comforter over her. "Go to sleep, sweetheart."

"Drake, don't leave me." She watched him turn his chair and sit down beside her.

"I won't leave you. I promise."

Jillian curled into the pillow and hummed contentedly. "If this isn't real, I'm going to be so fucking disappointed in the morning."

CHAPTER 11

*D*rake waited until he knew she was asleep before he cleaned up the dinner containers and poured her very expensive alcohol back into the fancy decanter. He lifted the bottle and chuckled. She hadn't really had that much, but it was enough to do the trick. She was a funny drunk, trying to be logical and follow his justification for the lengthy detour. What he didn't tell her was the longer she was completely off the grid, the longer Guardian had to figure out who was after her and why. Tomorrow, when she was sober, they'd discuss taking her invention with them. They could leave it in the safety deposit box and slip away or wait until Monday morning and take it with them. Either way, the likelihood of anyone knowing where she was would be slight at best.

His phone vibrated in his pocket. He glanced at his watch and frowned. It wasn't time for the PSO to check in for the night. He palmed it and blinked at the screen before he smiled. Jade rarely reached out, but when she did, it was always a surprise. Her text read:

>*I don't like rules. D checked in. He's okay.*

God, he loved that rule-breaking woman. Jade was a twin, granted not an identical twin, but she got Dixon and Drake. The fact that she bucked Archangel's and Guardian's protocols to let him know Dixon had made contact and he was all right said a lot about the woman. She was a rebel and was using her position to cherry pick information for him. Damn, she had balls the size of Texas.

Drake grabbed the remote and turned on the television, keeping the sound down low. He stretched out next to Jillian in the king bed and drew a deep breath. He'd started something tonight. Something that could blow up in his face. Jill was the first woman in ages who interested him. He liked her, loved the way her brain worked, and the sexual attraction he felt? Fuck, the entire situation was a volatile cocktail. One wrong move and he'd lose everything. His mind drifted to Dixon as he flipped through the channels. Dixon would need him after this mission. Jillian would have to be okay with that dynamic. It was nonnegotiable.

His phone vibrated again. He answered it, heading into the bathroom so he could talk without waking Jillian. "Go."

"That any way to answer a phone, son?"

Drake smiled and shook his head. "No sir, but it was the way I was taught by Guardian."

Frank Marshall grunted at the other end. "Checking in on you." Frank knew how much dropping Dixon off in the middle of a fucking mess would cost Drake. He knew it without Drake saying a fucking word. "You were pretty riled at him when y'all left. Did you make your peace before he went his way?"

"I don't know. I tried, but I don't understand why he needs to do this." Drake shook his head as he spoke. "That bastard almost destroyed him."

Frank grunted before he growled, "So, of all the people in the world that you know, physically know, who is the smartest?"

"Dixon," Drake replied without thought. Then

he smiled as he thought of Jillian. It was nip and tuck.

"When you are in a firefight, who is the one person you want at your six?" Again, Frank asked in that direct, no-shit way he possessed.

"Dixon." The answer was immediate and finite.

"So why do you think he isn't capable of doing what Jason's asked of him?" He could hear Frank unwrap a piece of candy. He was addicted to that taffy.

Drake considered the question before he answered it. "He's more than capable of doing the mission, Frank, but that man scarred him. Hurt him in ways you can't imagine. I'm not afraid Dixon can't do what he needs to do. I'm afraid of what will happen to him when he does."

Frank cleared his throat before he spoke. "He will do what he needs to do to protect himself. Trust your brother, Drake. You two survived in this world this long by doing that. Keep doing that."

"Yes, sir." That was an automatic response, too. Frank Marshall was many things to many people. But to Dixon and Drake, he was the positive father figure they'd never had.

Frank sighed. "Listen, you and Dixon are my

boys. Don't care about no damn genetics. If you need to talk, about anything, I'll be here."

"I know that. You know how much Dixon and I care about you and Miss Amanda, right?" Drake wanted him to know, needed him to know it.

"I do. When you coming back?"

With Frank this conversation was easy. He knew the nature of the job, and although he didn't know the specifics, he knew if Drake wasn't back it was because Guardian had him busy.

"Could be up to two, maybe three weeks. Need to keep someone off the grid and away from people."

"Then bring 'em here." The growled voice added the "dumbshit" even though his words didn't.

"Ah…well…" Drake rubbed the back of his neck. "I'm being selfish on this one, sir. Going to take some time to get to know her better."

There was silence for a long moment. Frank snorted and then said, "Well, it's about damn time. Bring her home when it's right for you. Can't wait to meet the filly who chased you down."

"Don't know if it's just wishful thinking or if it's actually something, but I want to find out."

"Good. You call me every now and again so I

can stop Amanda from worrying. Can't have both of my boys out of communication."

"I know Dixon checked in today." Drake didn't want Frank and Amanda to worry, so he'd share his ill-gotten update.

"I can lay odds on which one of the kids broke protocol and told you."

"I have no idea what you're talking about, sir."

"You're a horrible liar. Take care of yourself and your filly."

"Yes, sir." Drake laughed as the phone disconnected. He had another hour to wait until his back up arrived. He checked on Jillian, who hadn't moved since she'd fallen asleep. The remote in his hand again, he started flipping through the channels. Even with Dixon gone and the stress of that operation bearing down on him, Drake felt light. Lighter than he'd ever felt, and it was all down to the woman sleeping beside him. Now he just needed to ensure he didn't fuck it all up.

CHAPTER 12

Jillian dropped her head under the shower. All things considered, her hangover wasn't as bad as it could have been if Drake had let her slam the cognac the way she wanted. He left a note for her telling her not to leave the room; there was a person from Guardian watching the hotel; she was safe; and he'd be back with breakfast. Her stomach rolled at that thought.

She needed to talk to him, to make sure what she remembered of the events of last night were actual memories, and not dreams her overwrought imagination had manufactured. She was ninety-nine percent positive the kiss had been real. Then there was the admission he wanted to spend time with her and get to know her. She remembered the words, the way his eyes looked and the desire she felt when they kissed. *God, when they kissed.* Jillian shivered under the hot water. A visceral reaction to his long-awaited touch.

"Jilly, I'm back. I have coffee."

She'd left the bathroom door open a crack so the steam wouldn't fog the mirror and it was evident by the volume of Drake's voice he was standing in the bathroom. She gathered the shower curtain in front of her body and peeked out. *Oh damn.* A tight black t-shirt, black jeans, a tooled leather belt with silver, platter-sized belt buckle and boots. *Gah.* Her sexy cowboy. Who'd have thought she'd find "home on the range" so appealing. No, she wouldn't change the way he dressed for the world. Her eyes drifted back up his tight, ripped body, to a knowing smirk. The hunger in his eyes cleared any doubt the events of last night were as she remembered. They'd really happened. She let the shower curtain fall a little, and Drake's eyes chased the expanse of her exposed skin.

"We need to talk when you get done." Drake leaned against the vanity, not three feet away from her.

"Talk?" Jillian pulled her bottom lip into her mouth and cocked her head. "I don't want to talk right now."

She dropped the shower curtain as she turned and presented the expanse of her backside to him. A low rumbling growl brought her head around. The black t-shirt landed on the floor, and his boots flew off, ending up somewhere on the floor. Jillian placed a hand on the back wall of the shower, steadying herself. Drake's eyes met hers as he unbuckled the belt and unzipped his jeans. She lifted an eyebrow in a silent dare. The corner of his mouth ticked up. He slid the zipper down, exposing skin instead of underwear. "Naughty boy." Jillian turned to face him exposing herself completely to his view.

"Fucking hell, you're beautiful." Drake pushed down his jeans.

She swallowed hard, pushing back her nerves, which made an unscheduled and unwanted appearance when she took in the size of Drake's cock. He was erect and larger than any man she'd ever been with. Her eyes lingered on his member as he reached down and stroked it. She ran her eyes up his body, stopping when she met his stare. "Ummm…wow." Laughter burst from Drake, and she chuckled as well. "Eloquent as always, Dr. Law." Drake stepped into the shower and pulled the curtain closed behind him. He reached for her, wrapped his arms around her waist, and pulled her into him. She tilted her head up. He smiled slowly and bent down to kiss her. Jillian shivered as his lips ghosted over hers. "Breathe."

A whoosh of air expelled from her lungs. She hadn't even realized she was holding her breath.

He kissed her again before he murmured. "I've got you. Just relax."

Drake seduced her with long, languid, sensual kisses, punctuated by the wandering of his calloused hands against her hypersensitive skin. Her hands slid down his arms, learning the bulk and movement of his muscles, the feel of the ridges and valleys that defined his masculine beauty. She chased his lips as they luxuriated in each other.

He maneuvered her against the wall and lowered to his knees. She dropped her hands to his shoulders. He leaned forward and kissed her stomach while his hands framed her hips. With excruciating slowness, he made his way lower until he lifted one of her legs and placed it over his shoulder. She gripped the hair at the back of his neck with one hand and braced against his shoulder with the other. He interspersed kisses of her inner thigh with small, tantalizing bites he would then lick and soothe. The tease was excruciating. Her greed consumed her, and she used the hand at the back of his neck to let him know where she wanted him. A low rumble of laughter rose through the steam.

"Oh, my God!" she gasped, and her head hit the wall of the shower when his lips finally met her sex. "Drake!" She was at a loss as to what to do. She wanted more, needed it, but she didn't want to climax because she didn't want this moment to end. His tongue swirled around her clit, driving her insane as his hands cupped her breasts and teased her sensitive nipples. When he pinched them, she lost her mind. The combination of sensations pulled wanton sounds from her she couldn't deny or stop. She used both hands to grip his shoulders and thrust against his mouth, lust-filled and driven. She clenched her eyes shut, focusing on nothing but reaching the peak of the mountain he was pushing her up. He added his fingers to his efforts, and she shattered. Reds and whites burst against the black of her tightly closed eyes. The second the wave of her orgasm released, and she melted into a somnolent state, aware

Drake had risen and now held her, but unaware of how that happened. She slid her hands up his arms and linked them behind his neck before she opened her eyes. The dark passion she found in his eyes made her heart pound. He wanted her. She could see his need. She could see his desire. "I'm on the pill." Drake reached down and cupped her ass, lifting her as if she weighed nothing. He pinned her back against the wall. She scrambled to lock her arms around his neck, realizing what he wanted. "You can't hold me up that long!"

Laughter filled the shower. "I could hold you like this all day. You weigh next to nothing." He kissed the junction between her shoulder and neck. She tipped her head to give him access. The tip of his cock met her sex, and she moaned against the lips that sealed hers. He loosened his grip, and she felt him enter her. She tightened her grip on him, his size taking her breath away. "Relax, sweetheart. I won't hurt you. I promise."

Jillian nodded and dropped her head against his shoulder. Her arms and legs wrapped around him. He controlled everything and freed her to just…feel. Feel his body as he worked his way into her. Feel as he held her bottom, lifted her and pushed in. Feel her insides ripple and clench around him as he slowly started to stroke in and out. Feel as he trembled and tightened his grip. Feel as her body shattered again and he lost control; his sure, measured strokes morphing into a chase for his own release. Jillian trembled in his arms as she felt everything, including emotions that were far too early to acknowledge.

Drake carefully lowered her, severing their connection, but not their hold on each other. She leaned against his chest and hummed when his hands roamed over her back. "That was…amazing."

He dropped a kiss to the top of her head. "You are amazing." She lifted her head so she could see him. His blue eyes held hers. The intensity of his gaze held emotions that she pretended not to see or acknowledge. It was too soon. She had to be projecting her feelings into his actions.

She reached up and cupped his cheek with her hand. "I want to get to know you, too, Drake. I want to know the man you are now."

A devastatingly handsome smile split his face. "So you do remember last night?"

She crossed her eyes at him. "I do, I may have had a bit too much—"

"A bit?" He teased before he dropped a kiss on

her, silencing her objection before it began. The way the man kissed consumed her, fogged her brain. She loved the way he took possession of her very being with each kiss. Drake was all consuming. Her teenage anticipation was nothing compared to reality.

He pulled away, slowly, dropping kisses against her cheeks, her nose, and her eyelids before he reached behind him and turned off the water. He helped her out and wrapped a towel around his waist before carefully and meticulously drying her from head to toe.

"What did you want to talk about?" Jillian asked as he wrapped a towel around her.

"I need to find out what you want to do about your invention." Drake took her hand and led her back into the hotel room. There were two cups of what she assumed was coffee and a white bag on the table. Drake popped the top of the cardboard cup. Steam still wafted off the drink. He passed it to her when she sat down.

"What do you mean? I thought we were going to get it and take it back with us."

"We can do that, or we can leave town now and keep your invention in the safety deposit box." He took a sip of his coffee before he opened the bag. "Blueberry, banana or chocolate?"

"Too hard to choose. Can we share?"

He smiled and winked at her, pulling six muffins out, one at a time. "You eat what you can."

She grabbed a plastic knife from the bag and sliced three muffins into quarters. Picking up a small portion of the banana, she leaned back in her chair and considered her options as far as Delbert, as she was now thinking of her invention, was concerned.

"Would it be a bad thing if I wanted Delbert to come with us?" She ate a bite of the muffin as she waited for him to respond.

Drake swallowed the food he had in his mouth and took a sip of coffee. "No. Bank safety deposit boxes are not secured in the same way by all banks. Some place the boxes in vaults, others have secured rooms. There have been several instances where thieves have broken into safe deposit storage rooms through unreinforced ceilings."

Jillian froze with her coffee halfway to her mouth. "You mean someone could have my work now?"

Drake shook his head and took another sip of

coffee. "If there had been any break-ins, we would know about it."

"How?"

"Guardian. We have the best computer hackers in the world. I wouldn't be surprised if Jewell, the woman on the call we made, has a live video feed of the bank's security camera system."

"She can do that? Is that legal?" Jillian doubted it was. It just didn't seem legit.

"Guardian has federal law enforcement status, and as such we must abide by the law. If she has it, it is done within the general context of the law."

"General context, huh? That sounds like it has wiggle room." Jillian liked gray areas because they allowed her to think, create and invent. She wouldn't be surprised if the woman at Guardian used her gray areas for the same thing.

Drake smiled and winked at her. "I can neither confirm nor deny the presence of wiggle room in our operations."

Jillian tossed a piece of banana muffin at him and laughed when he caught it in his mouth. "If we take the faraday cage with us, will it present any problems?"

Drake shook his head. "Just another piece of luggage."

"Were you serious about going to Yellowstone?" She hedged her excitement at the idea just in case he'd changed his mind since last night.

"Yeah, of course. We can do Yellowstone and then head up to Jackson Hole in Wyoming, see Devil's Tower and then pop over to the ranch." Drake took a huge bite out of his last remaining muffin.

"How long will we be playing tourist?"

"Ha! You can pronounce it today. That word gave Drunk Jilly a rough time last night." Drake laughed at the finger she flipped him. "I don't know. I have plenty of vacation time due me." He shrugged. "Three weeks? A month? If we get bored or if things between us don't work out, we can go home early."

Jillian's mouth dried out in an instant. "You don't think we'll work out?" She picked at her piece of muffin as she waited for his response.

"I think we need to give ourselves the time to see what we are together. I know the sex we had today was phenomenal. I know I want to be with you and that for some reason no one else in my life to this point has had the ability to make me feel… hell, I don't know, selfish, maybe?"

"Selfish?" Jillian didn't understand how she made him feel that way.

"Like I'm guarding my time with you. I should be insane with worry about Dixon. And I am worried, he's always in the back of my mind, but I find that I'm also so drawn to the connection I feel with you that I'm willing to split time, still worried and concerned about Dixon, but focused on you and me. Does that make sense?"

She got up, walked over, and sank to her knees in front of him. "Yes, it makes sense, and I understand how close you and Dixon are. I watched both of you when I was playing wallflower, way back when. I know you take care of him. It's one of the things that drew me to you. You're selfless." He opened his mouth, but Jillian put a finger over his lips, moving in closer between his legs. His towel unraveled and fell open. She ran her hands up his thick, muscled thighs. She cupped his heavy balls with one hand and wrapped her fingers around his cock, not surprised they did not meet. She looked up at him through her lashes. "I'll gladly go with you for the next month, but you have to make me one promise." Their eyes met, and he nodded. "If you must go because he needs you, just tell me before you go. I'll be here waiting when you're done taking care of your brother. If that changes, I'll tell you."

She settled on her legs, stroked his cock once, and then lowered to lick the precum from the tip. She sucked the head into her mouth and swirled her tongue around the cap. Drake's hand went to the back of her head. Not pushing or forcing her down, but gently holding her. She tried to take more into her mouth and gagged.

"Use your fist at the base, take me as far as you can without gagging and use your fist to pump me." His words sent a thrill through her. He was telling her what he enjoyed, and she was determined to exceed his expectations.

Jillian stroked up every time she lowered her head. With his cock slick, it was easier to take more of him into her mouth. She pushed onto his hardness, impaling him against her soft palate and pushing him into her throat. She panicked and popped off, drawing an immediate breath of air.

Drake cupped her face, his thumb wiping away the saliva that had escaped her when she went down on him. "You are so beautiful, Jilly. So fucking beautiful." He lowered down to her, fused their lips together and then literally crawled over her, taking her backwards onto the floor. The plush carpet under her tickled, but that was only a momentary distraction. Drake flicked her towel open and descended onto her breasts, sucking, licking and even biting them. She arched into him, wanting more. He raised his knee spreading her open beneath him. "Get on your hands and knees for me." He maneuvered her so she was on her towel, and he centered behind her also placing his knees on the towel.

Jillian wondered for about a tenth of a second why he moved them so precisely and then the realization hit. Rug burns. She looked over her shoulder at him. His eyes were glued to her sex. She lowered onto her shoulders and waggled her hips with a moaned, "Please."

"Fuck, you will be the death of me." Drake leaned over, planted both hands beside her head and entered her. He was once again cautious and considerate, but Jillian wanted him buried deep inside her body. She rocked backward as he slid forward. They both groaned as he slid home. They set up a fierce rhythm. She rocked back on every thrust forward. The sound of their skin as it slapped together mingled with the staccato of their breaths and gasps. "More. I won't break. Fuck me harder," Jillian begged, needing his aggression as much as she needed his gentleness.

His hands found her shoulders, and he pulled her up off the floor. He shifted behind her, lifting a leg to give him more power. His grip tightened, and she reveled in the tingles of almost-pain that slithered around just underneath her skin. She loved the combined sensation of pleasure and pain—an impossible topic to broach with her other lovers. She needed to trust her partner to reveal her secrets. "Please. Please. Please." The word was on repeat in her brain and fell from her lips.

"What do you need?" One hand wrapped around her and snaked down toward her sex as his hips stilled. "Tell me what you want me to do."

Jillian dropped her head and pushed her hips against him. "Make it hurt a little." She whispered the words and waited. His hand stopped at the top of her sex, and he lowered his mouth to her shoulder. "Say the word, and I'll stop."

Jillian nodded, her heart pounded. Drake bit her shoulder, and the burst of pain vaulted her a thousand feet up as she strained to reach the top of the mountain again. He lifted away, and an open hand fell across her ass before he slammed his cock into her. She was in heaven! He set up a punishing pace, interspersed with hard slaps to her ass. He reached under her and slid his fingers through her sex while pounding his thick shaft into her. "Please. Don't stop. Don't stop." Her entire being centered on this man bringing her closer to something she desperately wanted and needed. "Don't stop!"

He curved over her closer and whispered in her ear, "I'm not stopping. I'll make you fly." His fingers found her clit and squeezed hard. Her orgasm hit her, and she screamed. Drake continued to power into her while his finger squeezed her clit, and she sobbed. The tactile sensations that crowded under her skin were too intense to understand. His hard body bent over her again, and he bit her shoulder, a constant pressure that built slowly but the stimulation was so unbelievably necessary. She strained against the demands of his body, against the will of his hands and his mouth until she came. Her body clenched so tightly she lost awareness. It was as if she'd exploded then remerged, debilitated and exhausted. Jillian felt him wrap around her and claim his finish. He pushed them both to the floor before he rolled onto his back and then pulled her into his body.

She drifted on the pleasure of the experience until she realized he was tracing where he'd bit her. She closed her eyes and drew enough strength to apologize. "I'm sorry."

Drake stiffened then lifted onto his elbow, so he could lean over her and see her face. She tipped her head toward the floor, not caring to witness the expression she knew he wore.

"What are you apologizing for?"

Jillian shrugged.

"I sure as hell hope you aren't apologizing for wanting a bit of pain with your pleasure." Drake reached for her chin and tried to bring her face around. She refused to move. "Don't ever apologize for what you want or need from me. Now that I know what you like, I can take care of you."

Jillian risked a look at him.

He smiled and dropped a kiss on her shoulder. "We need to talk about that, and about what you don't like, set some boundaries. We can have an agreed upon safe word before we get involved with anything more, but believe me, I want to give you what you need—unless it is another man. I won't share you."

Jillian rolled onto her back to gaze up at him. "Even if he was Dixon?"

His eyes clouded over, and he slowly shook his head. "Not even for him. Is that going to be a problem for you?"

Jillian shook her head, mimicking his slow back and forth motion. "I don't know what I like except a small amount of pain. It enhances or perhaps magnifies, everything. I don't like the idea of multiple partners. I don't want people watching us. I've read about people who like a lot of pain, but I don't know…"

Drake smiled and lowered for a slow, sensuous kiss. He pulled away and tucked her back against him. His hands cupped her breasts as his thumbs stroked her nipples. "We can experiment. I think nipple clamps would be the place to start." He gave each of hers a slight squeeze pulling a delicious sensation across her entire torso. He whispered in her ear, "There are so many toys that can enhance what we do together."

She lifted her hands to cover his, stilling his fingers from their erotic trail of ecstasy. "You don't think I'm weird?" Clay's mocking taunts skittered through her mind.

He kissed her shoulder before he replied, "I think you are beautiful, sexy and maybe a bit kinky." He chuckled and kissed the top of her head. "And I think we fit together perfectly."

She turned into him and sighed as she melted into his chest. This was bliss, heaven on earth, and she prayed when she opened her eyes that the euphoria still remained.

CHAPTER 13

Drake slipped his foot into his boot. Jillian's humming from the bathroom put a smile on his face. The woman was a hellcat in bed. They'd fucked in the shower, on the floor, against the window, on the bed, over the dresser, against the wall and she rode him while he sat in the excuse the hotel called a lounge chair. She was a bendy little thing, and he loved that she wanted to feel him. Some women he'd been with would complain he was too forceful, but not Jilly. She ticked every box he had or thought he had. Beautiful, fun, intelligent, sexy, wanton even, and fuck him standing, she liked to be spanked. His grin turned wicked. Naughty, naughty, Jilly.

She bounced out of the bathroom and smiled at him. "Ready?"

"I was ready a half hour ago." He popped her on the ass as he walked by to get to the suitcases.

"Bull. I believe you had me bent over the vanity in the bathroom thirty minutes ago." She swung her purse to her shoulder and lifted an eyebrow in challenge.

Drake scowled and looked at his watch. "You may be right."

"I know I am." She picked up the small tote she'd cleared out. They would put the faraday cage inside the innocuous looking piece of luggage and haul it with them on their drive back to South Dakota.

In between screwing each other's brains out and eating the buffalo wings and egg rolls they'd ordered in, they plotted the path for their adventure using his phone and maps.

"I never would have combined wings and egg rolls." He popped the last half of an egg roll into his mouth and crunched it down.

"Something about the crunch and sweet and sour sauce that goes so well with the heat of the chicken." Jillian acknowledged as she licked her fingers, cleaning the fire sauce from a wing away.

Drake followed the motion as she sucked her thumb into her mouth. His cock stirred against his jeans. He shook his head to clear it before he gazed over the mess strewn across the small coffee table. So far, they'd only succeeded in planning where they would stop tonight. He'd thought with their combined IQ's that they'd be able to plot the way easily, but Jillian had a serious attention deficit disorder working. Every time he tried to get her to look at the map, she'd find a way to distract him. Not that he was complaining, because her distractions were sexy as hell, but the tenacious way she diverted the conversation from the next leg of their journey hinted that something was off. After they retrieved her work, they'd have plenty of time to talk.

The rental agency met them with a pickup van and drove them to the office where Drake dropped his credit card and rented the largest SUV on the lot. Was it overkill? Maybe, but after being crammed into Jillian's nod toward economic and environmental salvation, he needed to once again exert his testosterone-fueled machismo. A black SUV, the size of an M1 Abrams tank, would suffice.

Jillian gave him directions to the bank, and they

were the first customers through the doors. Drake flashed the Guardian badge fixed on his belt. The light jacket he threw on disguised his shoulder holster where he carried his Glock. He'd be damned if he was going to fish in his boot for his weapon if shit went south. He didn't think it would. Whoever was looking for Jillian couldn't have found them and anticipated where they would go in the short amount of time they'd been in San Jose. Jacob agreed, but they decided on a show of force anyway. The PSO who'd been watching over them at night was outside the bank in case they needed help. Mark was at the airfield waiting for another pilot and clearance to fly Gracie back home.

He assumed they waited for the office workers to finish coffee. It was the only reason he could think of to make them wait twenty minutes when there were no other customers. Especially since they knew Jillian had a protective detail with her. She provided her identification to access her box while he hovered. He followed her like a sentinel, drawing several glances from the tellers. He could tell he was worrying the mousey man who escorted her into the room, not a vault, where her deposit box was located.

"The number?" the man asked, as his eyes darted toward Drake for the tenth or eleventh time since they'd started this short walk.

"Three-seventy-seven." She glanced at Drake and smiled.

"Of course, ma'am." The man produced a ring of keys and thumbed through them until he reached the one that would work with her key. It took a moment because the man dropped his key ring and had to go through the process again. Finally, he inserted his key, unlocked the drawer and pulled it out. "Do you require assistance?" he asked, lowering his hand to lift the lid off the interior compartment.

"No," Drake spoke for the first time and with crisp authority. Both Jillian and the bank officer jumped. Jilly put her hand over her heart and laughed, almost falling on top of him. Once again, her laugh encompassed her entire being. The mousey man smiled and chuckled when Jillian snorted. Her hand flew to her face, and she started laughing harder. Drake shook his head at the antics of his woman. His. Woman. His feelings of possession were something of a revelation, and he wrapped an arm around her. She waved at the banker as he left and lifted the lid to the box.

"You get to lift this out since you told him I didn't need any help." Jillian held the security deposit box to keep it from lifting as Drake gripped the handle of the case. It was wedged in pretty tightly, but he managed to extract it with minimal effort. The case weighed twenty to twenty-five pounds. He set it on the table and waited for her to open it. She entered a five-digit code at each clasp and then slid the bar under the clasp to release the airtight seal.

Jillian lifted the lid and smiled. "Drake, I'd like to introduce you to my best work to date. Meet Delbert." She slipped on a pair of white cotton gloves that were stuffed into a small compartment of the case and lifted a photovoltaic cell. "With a little electromagnetic radiation, this guy will produce as much electricity as forty, five-foot by three-foot, solar arrays."

The idea behind the mechanism impressed him more than the device itself. He couldn't wait to see it in action. "Delbert. You're sticking with that name, huh?"

Jillian dipped her chin and waggled her eyebrows. "Yup."

Drake chuckled at her antics. "Alright then, I want you to walk me through the science you put into Delbert once we get clear of here." He dropped a kiss on her upturned lips. "You're brilliant, Doctor Law. Brilliant and beautiful and a sex fiend."

∽

They missed most of the traffic on Interstate 280 South although there was a slowdown where South Seventh Street merged in. Drake set the vehicle's GPS once they merged onto 680 and relaxed into the seat. No one followed them that he could see.

The vehicle's phone system announced an incoming call. Drake hit the button on the steering wheel to answer.

"Hey! I got you on GPS. Why are you going north?" Jewell's voice filled the vehicle.

"We are heading to Yellowstone." Drake glanced at Jillian. Was it his imagination? No, she looked upset. He gave her a questioning look. She cocked her head at him like he should know why she was pissed.

"No way! I so want to go to Yellowstone! Can I join you?"

"Sure, anytime." Drake jumped at the punch in the arm he received. "Shit!"

"Shit, what's shit? Do you have problems?" He could hear Jewell's fingers scrambling across the keyboard.

"No, just something unexpected." Drake cast his eyes toward Jillian. She was not happy. What in the hell. Oh. *Oh!*

"You need to bring Zane to Yellowstone with you. You know, your husband…the big handsome guy you're head-over-heels for." he glanced at Jillian and lifted an eyebrow, "He'd love the area."

"Ha! He is so busy with his side of the job that a vacation won't happen for at least a year, but take pictures. I'll live vicariously through your adventures. I have Doctor Law off the grid. Completely. Her credit cards, cell phone, hell even the GPS on her little car is turned off. Anyone looking for her will find nothing but a big black hole where she once existed. I'll turn it all back on or uncover it once this shit is over, but for now, there is absolutely no reason to stress. You are free and clear. Say hi to Yogi and Boo-Boo for me."

"That's Jellystone, Jewell, not Yellowstone."

"Yeah, I know, but it's gotta be somewhere up there. Hey, Jade also wanted me to tell you that she is repeating the last message she sent you as of ten o'clock this morning. I do not know what that means, and I forbid you from telling me."

"Roger that. Thanks, Jewell."

"You got it, D. Take care of her and have a great time."

"Affirmative. Let me know as soon as you figure out who was after her, and the threat is neutralized."

"Will do, buckaroo." Jewell sang.

Drake disconnected the call and looked over. "She's very married."

She crossed her arms over her chest and looked out of the window. "I didn't know that."

"You didn't ask that."

"You were flirting with her."

"No, she was flirting with me, but she doesn't get that is what she's doing. It is the way she talks to everyone." Drake pulled over on the side of the road, killed the engine, took off his seatbelt and turned to face her. "Something we need to get out in the open right away. I want to get to know you. Only you. If this isn't an exclusive thing for you, too, then we need to reevaluate and head straight for South Dakota."

"What? Wait, you were the one who was flirting, and now you're asking me if I'm the one who is serious?" Jillian closed her eyes and shook her head. "Did I get a smidge jealous? Yes. Do I consider this between us exclusive? Yes, yes I do, but I had no idea you did! Communication works both ways. I am brilliant, but I can't read your flipping mind, Drake. I'm not Dixon."

Drake blinked back his surprise and scrubbed his face for a moment. "Fair enough. Communication. We should probably work on that as we work on getting to know each other."

"You think?" Jillian nodded toward the vehicle's dash. "Is the other one, the one who sent you the message, married?"

"Jade? Committed, engaged and totally in love. She is sneaking me updates on Dixon. Against procedure but much appreciated."

"You have some good friends." She glanced at the highway and nodded her head that direction. "Do you need me to drive?"

Drake chortled and strapped back into his seat. "Another thing you need to know about me. I'm not a good copilot. I always sit on the left."

"Oh, a control freak? I'm intrigued." Jillian batted her eyes at him.

"I am. Tell me why you wouldn't look at day

two of this trip." He checked to make sure he could merge safely and pulled back onto the interstate.

"Honest communication?" Her voice was very low when she asked.

He checked her quickly and noted that she was very interested in her fingers again. "Between us, always. Full disclosure and honesty. We both deserve that." He accelerated to pass a semi in the right-hand lane.

"I didn't want to talk about it because I was afraid to jinx what is going on between us." She peeked at him and then dropped her eyes again.

"Jinx? You're shitting me, right? You hold a doctorate in mechanical engineering, and you believe in jinxes." He openly gaped at her.

"I do! Stop looking at me like that. Jinxes happen." She snorted and then giggled after he barked a laugh.

"No, they don't. Circumstances happen. Events happen. There is no harbinger of bad news or misfortune that will appear out of thin air. Giving in to those superstitions robs you of the happiness you could have at that specific moment." He reached over and threaded his fingers between hers and squeezed her hand. "Jinxes aren't real. Don't allow anything to stop you from finding joy."

He could see her nod with his peripheral vision as he drove. She gave his hand a small tug, and he glanced at her.

"It's hard. For a long time growing up, everything good got ripped away. My parents, my grandpa, Matt. You learn to be afraid of being happy because being happy meant something could be taken away from you to make you miserable again."

He glanced from the road to her. He'd suffered loss and abuse as a child, but not loss after loss after loss. Placing himself in her shoes, he could understand her hesitancy in admitting she was happy. He lifted her hand and kissed the back of it. "I can't promise you bad things will never happen, but I can promise you it won't be because you jinxed yourself by allowing yourself to be happy."

"Logically, I get that." She gave him a sad smile. "And I promise to try."

Drake threw her a wink. "That's a start."

CHAPTER 14

Road Trip, Day One - Reno, Nevada

"I like this one." Jillian pointed to the tent that was on display.

"I don't think we will need that much room." Drake nodded toward the small tent at the other end of the mock campsite. "Something like this, maybe."

Jillian pursed her lips. "You wouldn't fit." She made a show of pacing off the length of the tent. "Lie down."

"Why?"

Well wasn't it obvious? "Because I'm going to see if you'll fit."

Drake laughed. "No, I'm not going to lie down." He folded his arms over his chest, making the seams of his t-shirt scream for relief. Jillian faced him and mimicked his stance down to the tilt of her head. He did nothing but smile at her.

The standoff lasted for about thirty minutes. Okay, more like thirty seconds before she pointed to the two-man tent. "There was no way that thing will hold both of us. We are going to spend every night in it, right?" Drake lifted an eyebrow and nodded.

"I don't know about you, but no matter how much we snuggle, someone is going to end up with a black eye from elbows and your feet are going to stick out of the door flap thingy." She stepped over and shook the tiny little flap to accentuate her point.

Drake looked at the tent again and then at the one she'd pointed out.

She moved next to him and whispered conspiratorially, "You have to admit my pick is a better option."

"No. I can't see it. We don't need a screened in patio and a fourteen by thirty main room. Tent, not palace, Jill." Drake drew a deep breath and pointed to a light tan tent with dark brown accents that sat in the middle of the two extremes. "Compromise?"

Jillian ambled over to the tent. It was tall enough for her to walk into. She glanced back at Drake. He'd have to stoop when he was in the tent. She unfastened the zippered door and stepped inside. Drake followed her. She drew a breath and tried to picture it. "I suppose if we opened up one of the sleeping bags and used the other as a cover we'd both fit. But that would be the extent of the available room."

"What else were you planning on having in here?" Drake dropped to a knee and looked up at her with a smirk.

"What about the other stuff we're buying?" She glanced out the little mesh window to the flatbed cart that had two coolers, a small rectangle grill, two sleeping bags, and a foam liner to go under them.

"We will arrange all of that in the SUV, so we can access them, but we won't have to pull it out every time we make camp." He laid down and stretched an arm behind his head. "See, I fit."

"Catty-corner. Where am I going to sleep?" She dropped down to her knees and looked at the available room beside him.

"Right here." He pulled her down and tucked her against his side. "See, perfect."

Jillian sighed. Camping was a foreign concept to her, but Drake made it sound fun. As Katy Perry roared over the speaker system, Jill realized that he was right, spending time alone together, learning about each other, was pretty close to perfect. A small boy with a mass of red hair opened the flap. His mouth dropped open, and he pointed at them. "Dad, this one's gots peoples in it!" The flap dropped. They could hear the little boy running away and shouting for his father. "Daddy, come see, this one has peoples."

"Well, that's our cue to leave." Drake released his hold, and she sat up.

She leaned on her hip, propped up with her arm. A wave of her hand motioned around the interior of the tent. "Okay, this one will do. What else do we need?"

She pushed open the flap and crawled out of the door before she stood up.

"Backpacks, some waterproofing spray and then we'll stop by a grocery store on the way out of Reno." Drake followed her out of the tent.

"Where are we camping tonight?"

"A place called Battle Mountain. It is another

four hours from here." He pushed the flatbed cart toward the back of the store. "What do you want for lunch?"

Jillian rolled her eyes at him and groaned. "Uh...the breakfast burritos, hash browns, and coffee we had a couple hours ago?" She was still full and wouldn't be able to eat anything. The burrito was easily the size of her head, and she'd almost finished it.

"That was four hours ago." Drake stopped the cart. "I'm a growing boy."

"You are a bottomless pit! Two burritos and two orders of hash browns. No wonder you're the size of a mountain." She stepped up on the flatbed and sat down on one of the coolers. "Forward, Jeeves."

Drake snorted out a laugh and pushed the cart. "Okay, we'll go grocery shopping, and then I'll hit a fast food place before we head out."

Road Trip: Day Two - East of Battle Mountain, Nevada

"So, do you think we could make a detour on the way to Yellowstone?" Jillian peeked over a road map she had unfolded when she asked.

"A detour? Why?" Drake darted a glance over her way.

"Because I want to see the EBR-1 Museum." She glanced at one of several tourist books that she'd picked up at a bookstore next to the grocery store where they'd stocked up yesterday. She held her hand over her mouth and yawned until her body shook. He may have been the reason she was tired today, but in his defense, she was irresistible. They'd field tested the foam matting underneath their sleeping bag last night. It passed. Twice.

"What is the EBR-1 Museum?"

"Oh, it is so cool! I saw a special on it on television, it had to be a couple years ago. I think it was the History Channel or something like that, but it is the Experimental Breeder Reactor Museum. It is the first power plant to use atomic energy to produce electricity."

"A museum dedicated to an atomic reactor?" Drake let out a low whistle. That was some cool shit.

"Not any reactor, the first one built to produce electricity in the United States." Jillian pushed the map in her lap away and picked up the tourist booklet. She thumbed through it before she thumped it with her finger. "It says here that it is open all summer from 9 a.m. to 5 p.m. and admission is free. Can we go?"

He sure as fuck was heading that way. "Hell, yes. The original breeder reactor. Making nuclear fuel by introducing a neutron to a uranium-238 atom." It had been a while since he'd read any articles on the origins of nuclear energy production, but that shit stoked his science geek like almost nothing else.

Jillian almost danced in her seat. A small squeal erupted before a flurry of words headed his way. "I know. It is amazing what they were doing back in 1956. When that atom absorbed and changed into plutonium-239, which became another fissionable atom. Can you imagine having a chance to work on a project that was not only producing electricity but also making more plutonium-239 atoms? They had to have believed they were on the cusp of miraculous things."

Drake loved her excitement, because he shared it, too. "They were. Their work set the stage for the nuclear power plants that are in production today. Where is the Museum?"

"Idaho. If we take this road...ahh...Interstate 80 until we need to go north." She put the map on the dash and traced her finger. "Yellowstone is here, so I think it's only a little bit out of the way if any."

Jillian's smile blazed across his heart. God, he'd give anything to keep it there. He reached over and squeezed her thigh. "I don't care how far out of the way it is. We have nothing but time."

Road Trip: Day Six - Beartooth Roadway, Montana

"Drake?" Jillian's soft voice from where she snuggled against his shoulder drew his attention away from the multitude of stars that blanketed the night sky.

"Hmmm..." A light breeze moved the hair on his forehead and cooled the evening, making the moment damn near perfect.

"Do you think the people who've never lived anywhere other than the city could believe this?"

"I don't know if they know what they're missing. In New York, you're lucky if you see a handful of stars." He gazed at the Milky Way and the abundance of beauty that filled the heavens. His mind drifted to Dixon. Was he able to see the stars? He lifted a lock of Jillian's hair and let it drop strand by strand.

"I've never seen them this clearly." She twisted and laid on her back. "Have you?"

Drake nodded. "Afghanistan, Kashmir, Chile, and South Dakota all have places like this." He rolled his head to look at her. "Dixon and I have seen some wondrous sights."

Jillian ran her hand up his stomach and laid it over his heart. "I know you miss him." She turned and lifted up on her elbow looking down at him. "Wait, that's wrong. I don't think anyone can fully comprehend the dynamic between the two of you, but I am aware of how much you miss him. I understand that a piece of you is absent when you're not together. " She leaned down and placed a soft kiss, one of comfort and support, on his lips. "I'm here for you if you ever want to talk."

He enfolded her against him when she relaxed. There weren't many who understood the bond they shared. If anyone could, he'd bet Jillian would be the one. A shooting star flashed across the sky. Jillian's hand shot up pointing at it. "Make a wish!" She tensed up for a moment and then sighed.

"What did you wish for?" Drake adored her childlike exuberance. Her personality was a multifaceted swirl of brilliance, science geek, sensuality, and innocence. The resulting mixture enthralled him.

"Probably the same thing you did. That Dixon would come home safely."

Drake lifted, letting her head down gently onto the sleeping bag they'd been lying on. "Most would wish for money, fame or love." He ran his nose up the column of her neck and nipped her ear.

"I have money. I don't want fame and love? Well, I've learned that love comes when it comes. If my wish in any way manifests in you and Dixon reuniting, then it was a wish well spent." Her hands threaded under his t-shirt and fanned up his back, pulling him down on top of her.

"Thank you for the wish." He acknowledged her gift without telling her the wish he'd cast into the universe; it was too early to acknowledge the feelings that had penetrated his consciousness.

Road Trip, Day Ten - Dunraven Pass, Yellowstone National Park, Wyoming

"You said six miles." Jillian pulled on his belt loop. The whine in her voice was atypical of her usual zeal for backpacking in the park.

"I did." He looked for a handhold and lifted

himself up a three-foot drop, turning to help her scale the small obstacle.

"You didn't tell me the path was six miles straight up!" She took his hand and scrambled up the limestone and granite outcropping. Her hair was damp around her face, and her cheeks were crimson red. It had been an athletic climb, but she'd done well.

He reached back and pulled out a bottle of water, handing it to her. "We're almost there."

She snorted into the bottle, which produced an inelegant grunt that Frank Marshall would have been proud to deliver. It told him exactly what she thought of his 'almost there' comment.

"Admit it. You love this." He motioned toward the expansive view. Jillian turned and gazed out. She leaned into him, and he wrapped his arms around her.

"Okay, so maybe it was worth it." She shielded her eyes as she looked out and sighed. "I wish I had my phone or a camera."

Drake took in the panoramic view. They were about a half mile from the top and about to emerge from the tree line. The deep green of the pine forest in the valley below was interspersed by the lighter green of summer grasses in meadows. A canyon in the distance slashed through the woods with jagged edges. Shadows plunged cliffs into ominous and foreboding darkness. Beyond the canyon was miles upon miles of forest and at the edge of his vision was a grassland that held a shimmering body of water. A lake or a river, from this distance, he couldn't tell which. The view was magnificent. He scanned the range and finished the water. He put the trash into his backpack. Having photos to remember the trip was a great idea. No cell phones for her until they'd ascertained who was after her, but a digital camera...

"If you want one, we can pick up a camera when we restock." He tugged her ponytail. "That and a backpack for you so I don't have to carry all the water."

She swiveled toward him and beamed a smile. "Deal! This is so–" Her eyes focused past him, and her face fell. "Drake."

He glanced over his shoulder and immediately reached around and slowly guided her behind him as he turned. She grabbed his arm and peeked around. "It's a bear."

He wanted to laugh at the obvious, but instead, he nodded. "Shh...stand perfectly still," he whispered to her as he took in the unexpected visitor. A small black bear was on the next slope over, about one hundred yards away. He knew males were larger, so the animal was a female or a very young male. If that was a female, he hoped they were not in between that momma bear and her cub. At least she'd had a couple months to forage and wasn't straight out of the den with her cubs.

He kept one eye on the animal who had yet to spot them and canvased the terrain, trying to determine if the bear was alone. They were downwind, which was an advantage he'd take. He had his forty-five and his 9-millimeter, but shooting a bear with a smaller caliber weapon would just piss the damn thing off. A flash of movement on the pine-dotted slope above the bear caught his eye. Two black balls of energy and fur tumbled down the hill. The mother bears bawl made it to them when one of the cubs tried to tackle her. She rolled onto her side and swatted at the rambunctious cubs who took turns harassing mom and each other. Drake carefully lowered, bringing Jillian down to the ground with him. When they were on their knees, he whispered, "Carefully and quietly back down the trail."

He held out his hand so she could use it as an anchor to lower over the three-foot drop they'd just scaled. He'd give her credit, she was quick, and she was quiet. Drake dropped over the shelf of rock and motioned down the trail. She grabbed his hand, and they worked their way back down the path, leaving the bears unaware of their presence.

"Now I know we need a camera! Was that a black bear? Of course, it was. She was too small to be a grizzly, and they are brown, right? She had twins? Is that common? Are they aggressive? What do black bears eat? How old do you think those cubs were? I need to find a book about bears. How long is the gestation period do you think?" Jillian skipped down the path shooting her comments over her shoulder. She spun around and raced up to him. Grabbing the back of his neck, she pulled him down for a kiss. It was hard, fast, and brief, leaving him wanting more. She laughed. Her face was radiant. "I saw three bears, in the wild!"

"I know you did."

He laughed when she danced a little jig, turned and started to jog down the trail. "Come on! Camera, backpack, and a trip to the library!"

Drake shook his head and started jogging after her. Hell, he'd follow her to the ends of the earth.

CHAPTER 15

Drake sat on a large boulder and watched as Jillian scrambled over a pile of stones heading for what she deemed was the best vantage point for a picture. The camera he'd bought her had cost two arms and a leg, but it was worth it. They'd revisited their favorite sites and found new ones throughout the national park. Old Faithful and Mammoth Hot Springs were marked off the to-do list in one day, but Midway Geyser Basin's Grand Prismatic Spring held her interest for two days, specifically the pigmented thermophilic bacteria that produced the colors. Together they delved into the science behind the phenomena and once again drove over ten hours to get to a decent sized library for reference books. The journey was for naught because they ended up logging on and anonymously accessing the internet to search for their answers. Drake smiled. That was okay because they spent hours looking at the old books, especially the ones that held hand-drawn diagrams and personal notes made by people who'd lived in a different time. Yes, they geeked out. It was awesome to be able to share a part of himself that, up until now, only Dixon had appreciated—or understood.

Today they were taking a day trip, backpacking through the Grand Canyon of Yellowstone. He carried her invention and hard drives in his pack, plus a few snacks and bottled water outside the waterproof, zippered compartment where Delbert rested. She carried a jumble of random items in her pack. Drake glanced at the vivid pink nylon. Pink. Jillian saw it at the sporting goods store and had to have it…and, of course, he bought it for her. It wasn't practical, but it made her happy. He reached over and lifted it to keep it out of the direct sun. The last time she'd left it, her chocolate bars melted and coated the jumbled mess at the bottom of the pack. A raccoon tried to make away with it when she was cleaning it out. Jillian was having none of it and chased the animal off even after it turned and hissed at her. He'd have given odds that Jillian would have tucked tail at the sight of an angry coon, but nope, she chased after it, banging a flashlight against an aluminum plate. The coon was the smarter of the two involved in the tussle. He scampered up a tree and disappeared. Drake had laughed until he cried.

He palmed his cell phone to check his messages while Jillian impersonated a mountain goat. They got decent reception at the campground, but none this deep in the canyon. He didn't have a Sat phone, nor did he need one. As long as he could check his messages once a day, he was content.

"Hey, look up!" Drake shaded his eyes and smiled at her. She was hanging off the edge of the plateau she'd been aiming for when she started the climb. "You should come up here. It's beautiful."

"Be careful," he warned. The woman had an inner daredevil lurking, and he loved it.

"I am being careful. Come up here. The view is fantastic."

"Nah, I'll see your pictures when you come down. Besides, I like the view from where I'm standing." Her breasts swelled over her bra and gravity helped to display her assets in a fascinating way. Jillian looked down at her chest and threw back her head, laughing as she rolled back onto the plateau.

Dixon checked his phone out of habit. Jade hadn't contacted him since she'd sent the message via Jewell three weeks ago. That meant Dixon was either unable to contact Guardian without breaking his cover or had nothing to report. At a minimum, Drake assumed Dixon somehow managed to ingratiate himself with that fucker the world called their father. It was better than the alternative that lurked in the back of his mind. One he refused to let see the light of day. The lack of information or updates bothered him more than he'd let on to anyone, even Jillian, and he'd bared his soul to the woman over the course of the last three weeks. He glanced up at her. She was kneeling down taking a close up picture of some wildflower. Tonight she'd use the books he'd bought her to identify the species of each. Those she couldn't find in her books, she tagged, and they'd look them up the next time they surfaced in a town with a library.

Since they'd purchased sleeping bags, a tent and

a small camp kit, they rarely went to town except when they needed food or supplies. Or trips to the library. He chuckled to himself as he watched her. Jillian was not a diva in any sense of the word. She'd jog with him in the morning. He'd let her drop off and then run the circuit again—full out. She was getting stronger and faster as she tried to do his sit-ups, pushups, and pull-ups routine with him every morning.

She started her trek down the wall of the canyon, hopping from one ledge to another and laughing when she tripped over her own feet. She smiled at him and jumped again. That's when the quiet whisper that had been haunting him strengthened to a voice, and the voice spoke words into his heart. *You love her.*

She scrambled over the rock pile and practically ran down the other side. From where he sat he reached out and caught her, stopping her forward momentum. She wrapped her arms around his neck and leaned down for a kiss. He pulled her down on top of him and lay back on the flat boulder where he sat.

Pushing off his chest, she broke the kiss, moved her camera from around her neck and set it to the side. "What brought that on? I thought I used you all up this morning."

And she had. Twice. Jillian was damn near insatiable, but he was definitely up for that challenge. They'd explored what they both enjoyed, and while she enjoyed the occasional spanking and flirting on the edge of pain when they had sex, she wasn't into the hard-core things he associated with masochism. Which was fine by him. He'd make several purchases when they got back to the ranch, oh, and hopefully soundproof their room before Dixon got back because Jillian was loud. Drake loved it though. He did that to her. He made her lose her fucking mind, and it fueled the side of him that needed to be everything to her.

Today, his life had changed. Irrevocably. Yes, there were indisputable portions of him that only his brother's presence in his life could fill, but there had also been fragmented pieces of him that had weighed him down and had left him to drown in an abyss of ancient memories and horrific childhood fears. Those burdens had lifted. Jillian had done that. She'd cut the tethers that fettered him to a past he'd longed to bury. He'd mourned that history for far too long. He was done with it. Forever. This was his time to live, to live in the love of this woman. This was a moment he'd remember for the rest of his life. He pulled her down again and kissed her, kissed her with the knowledge he'd fallen in love with her.

"Wow." She breathed the word as she lifted away to breathe. "What got into you?"

Drake smiled and pushed the hair that escaped her ponytail out of her face. "I've made a shocking discovery."

She smiled and planted her elbows on his chest, so she could look down at him. "Do tell."

"I love you." He gazed up at her face, framed by the beautiful azure blue of the sky. Her big brown eyes misted with tears and a brilliant smile spread across her face.

"You know I love you. I have loved you in one fashion or another since I was sixteen." She lowered down so he could kiss her. His fingers grasped the hair from her ponytail and tangled in the silky tresses, tilting her head so he had better access. When they finally parted she narrowed her eyes at him. "You know you could have picked a more convenient place to tell me."

Drake laughed and swung his head to the left and the right, making an exaggerated gesture looking at the canyon walls. "It's beautiful here!"

"True, but also inconvenient. There is literally no place to make love to you at this moment." She glared off into the distance. "And it is at least five miles back to the campsite and the vehicle."

Drake pulled her down for another kiss. "I've heard stories about people having wild sex in remote areas of the world. Outside, under the stars."

Jillian shivered, "Eww! No, thank you. The wilds of our sleeping bag inside of our tent are as wild as this woman gets."

"Well then I better get you back there, hadn't I?"

"I think you'd better."

He sat up, dropping her into his lap. She wrapped her arms around his neck and tucked her head under his chin. "Say it again?"

He belted his arms around her and held her tight against his chest. It felt so right, so natural. "I love you."

She sighed into their embrace and whispered an echoing response, "I love you, until infinity."

He smiled and whispered, "Forever."

There was a small huff of laughter before she replied, "Forever, plus one."

He kissed her hair and breathed her in, wanting this feeling to invade the DNA of every cell in his body. She was right. They needed to take this revelation back to their campsite. He stood and dropped her to her feet, snatching a long, intoxicating kiss from her before he grabbed his backpack and shouldered it. The trip back to camp was going to seem far longer than the trek to the canyon.

∽

The sun dropped behind the canyon walls, draping the campsite in premature dusk. They collected dried sticks and small logs on the way back. He dropped his load off beside the fire pit and brushed off his shirt. Jillian dropped a smaller stack beside his. She turned into him and linked her arms around his neck.

"Fire, food, sex. In that order, Mr. Simmons." Jillian lifted to her toes, and he dropped his head as she pulled him down. "Don't keep me waiting." She kissed him soundly with a close-lipped kiss. She dropped her arms, twisted away and grabbed the backpacks. The sassy sway of her hips as she walked to the tent didn't help the perpetual hard-on he was rocking.

He built the fire quickly and copped out on the

meal. He didn't want to waste any time, so he opted for canned stew with plenty of crackers and shaved cheddar cheese. Over the last three weeks, he discovered Jillian had exactly two talents in the kitchen. Microwaving frozen dinners and warming canned soup. She was a willing, if hapless, student, and while she'd attempted to master a few of the techniques he used to cook over a campfire, if he wanted sustenance that wasn't raw, burnt into a charcoal briquette, or torched on the outside and raw on the inside, he'd have to cook. Hell, the woman had just mastered roasting a marshmallow without nuking it into oblivion. He chuckled as he stirred the stew and added a few of the spices he'd purchased the last time they were in town. Thank God for Miss Amanda and Aunt Betty. They'd never starve.

Drake knew they ate, but honestly, he couldn't tell what the food tasted like or what, if anything, they talked about as they inhaled the calories. She washed the camp dishes, and he put away all the food so no scavengers would be drawn to their campsite. By the time the first stars started to twinkle in the heavens, Drake was zipping them into the tent.

He turned on the battery-operated lantern.

"Why the light?" Jillian reached for him.

"I want to remember every detail." Dixon moved against her, lowering them to the sleeping bag that covered the tent floor. Clothes disappeared, minor distractions in the face of overwhelming need. Drake rolled them until she was on top of him. He could see the outline of her face and her beautiful brown eyes. He pushed back her hair and stared up at her. "How did I get so damn lucky?" He had no idea what he'd done right to have Jillian back in his life. But he'd take the gift and treasure it.

"We both got lucky." She straddled him and ran her hands up and down his chest. "I love you, Drake. The man inside this sexy body is different from the boy I used to adore. He's older, more experienced, and yet still the same, loving, caring person who set aside his desires so others were happy. I don't deserve you."

"I didn't really see you when we were younger. I wish I'd paid more attention." He ran his hands down her back and rested them on her hips. She rotated her hips, and he groaned when she pushed down onto his rock-hard cock.

"Make up for it, stud. Pay attention to me now." Jillian's pet name sent a charge through him, and she didn't need to ask twice. Drake rolled them over and consumed her with a kiss as he centered over her. Her desire eased his way as he entered. She was always so fucking tight. He pulled out and thrust forward, working his way inside her. Breaking away from the kiss, he worked his way down to her breasts as he slowly opened her to take him fully. He sucked her nipple into his mouth and used his teeth to tease her with small nips, sending her glimpses of sensuous pain. She arched into his mouth and grabbed the back of his head, holding him to her breast. "Yes. Like that."

Drake feasted on her while driving them both higher. Needing more, he lifted away from her body. God, she was remarkable. Her honey-hued skin displayed small rose blossoms where he'd nipped her flesh. Her nipples were peaked and hard, her face flushed, and her eyes had darkened with desire. She was simply the most exquisite woman in the world, and she loved him. "I'll never let you regret loving me." He lowered for a kiss.

She pushed on his chest stopping him. "I could never regret you. I've been in love with you forever, and I've never regretted a single moment of that time."

Drake froze over her. The sincerity in her eyes nearly killed him. "I was so blind."

"I was invisible, and we weren't ready for each other." She lifted a hand and traced his lips. "Stop thinking so hard. Make love to me. Make me scream your name."

Gladly. He grabbed her behind the knee and lifted her leg, giving him more room and better leverage to thrust. Her body writhed under him and each desire-filled sound she released spurred him on. He lifted her other leg, just enough to…

"God! Yes! Please!" Jillian's fingernails dug into his arms where she braced herself. Drake slid one hand to her hips, and with the other, he found her sex. Jillian chanted words like *more, harder, don't stop*. Hell, Drake couldn't stop now. He prayed he'd be able to last until she finished. His own release was poised and ready to strike him with a billion joules of electricity. He was too close. His fingers found her clit, and with confidence, he worked her body like an instrument. She stiffened as her body clenched around him. Her release rippled through her, stroking him and shattered them both. Jillian screamed his name, and he thrust one, two, three more times before he emptied inside her.

He fell over her, landing on his elbows to keep

the majority of his weight off her small frame. He dropped his forehead to hers, sharing their breath as easily as they shared each other's bodies. Drake finally rolled to his side and pulled his lover into him. He needed to take her home. Take her to meet his family, the people who mattered. He was in love, and he wanted the world to know it.

CHAPTER 16

"Thank you for that. I've seen *Close Encounters* twenty times and…wow, it just didn't register how big Devil's Tower actually is."

"Twenty times?" He stuck his hand out and mimicked the music on the movie.

Jillian laughed and pushed his hand away. "Stop, you dork. A foster parent had it on VHS and watching it gave me an escape."

Drake pulled her into him, draping his arm around her shoulders and kissed her forehead. "You're welcome."

Jillian threaded her fingers through his where they dropped over her shoulder. He squeezed her hand, and they ambled slowly back to the SUV.

They'd piled their camping gear into the back yesterday and driven to Gillette, Wyoming where he'd rented a hotel room for them. Almost a month of solitude had come to an end. She was amazed at how much she'd enjoyed camping. Exploring the country with Drake as a guide became an adventure. She loved photographing nature.

They'd always planned on seeing Devil's Tower before he drove her to the ranch. It signaled the conclusion of their seclusion. Jillian mentally laughed at her rhyme. She was such a putz. Two more days and they would arrive at the ranch. She was meeting "the family" as it were, and she was intimidated. What if they didn't like her? She gave herself a mental shake. It didn't matter if they didn't like her. Drake loved her, and she was a nice person. This would work. It would be fine. She hoped. "You think they'll like me?" She twisted and looked up at him as she asked.

"I know they will." He stopped and turned her into him. "They are my family. Those people are the salt of the earth, and they will adore you as much as I do. Stop worrying."

"I can't help it. I've never met anyone's family. I mean as a…girlfriend?" She didn't know how else to label herself.

"Hmmm...well first off, girlfriend isn't going to cut it. You're more to me than that."

Jillian leaned into his chest. "You're more to me, too." His arms tightened around her, and she closed her eyes, wrapping her arms around him and sliding her fingers into his back pockets. "Where are we going now?"

"Well, we have two options. We can drive down to Rapid City and get a room. We'll drive through the Needles and see some of the Black Hills tonight, and I'll take you up to the Faces in the morning. You'll need several hours to make it through the walking tour and see everything."

"The faces?" Jillian pulled back and blinked, putting him in focus. *God, is that what he called his family?* "Is that some kind of movie reference?"

Drake laughed so hard he shook. "Ah...no, the Faces are what the locals call Mount Rushmore."

She gave him a little shove, "Stop laughing! How was I supposed to know that?"

The country was beautiful but in a different way than Yellowstone. As they drove south from Hulett, they traveled through small towns like Pine Haven, Upton, and Osage. They ate lunch in New Castle, Wyoming. She sat in a diner on Main Street and watched the local people come and go. Not one vehicle was locked. Windows were rolled down, and rifles hung in racks along the back windows of the trucks. Men wore the same thing Drake wore, boots, jeans, shirts and cowboy hats or ball caps. The women's fashion interested her more. Jeans, boots and tank tops were the norm. Occasionally she saw dresses, but the women wore cowboy boots instead of heels. She'd seen that fashion on television but didn't actually believe people dressed that way. The open-faced roast beef sandwich that Drake ordered arrived on a platter that should have been reserved for Thanksgiving. Rich, dark gravy soaked the beef, bread and covered the mound of mashed potatoes that had somehow been wedged onto the side. The waitress plopped her cheeseburger down and then added another platter of onion rings and French fries.

"I didn't order these." Jillian pointed to the plate.

"Comes with the meal. I'm sure your man can help you finish them." The waitress pulled a bottle of catsup out of her apron and plunked it down on the wooden table top. "Need anything else?"

Jillian shook her head.

Drake lifted her hamburger bun and removed the three slices of dill pickle from her burger. She shuddered as he ate them. He slid his side dish of carrots toward her, and she pushed the stack of onion rings and fries towards him, so she could get to the carrots. It was as if they'd been together forever. Neither had much to say as they happily stuffed their faces with food. She slowed significantly when she'd eaten all her carrots and was halfway through her burger. Drake continued to attack his plate of food until the plate was clean of all but a small amount of gravy.

Drake pushed his empty plate away and leaned back in the booth. "The ranch is just east of here. If you want, we can be there by nightfall."

Jillian paused as she set her iced tea down. "Oh." She glanced back at him.

He lifted and eyebrow and leaned forward. "What's wrong?"

She shrugged. "Nothing, it's just that I'm…okay, honest communication, right?"

"Absolutely." Drake nodded.

"I want this last night. I'm afraid of meeting your people, and I want one more night of just you and me." She shrugged again and lowered her eyes to her half eaten meal. "I'm being selfish."

Drake reached across and lifted her chin. "I

understand. I gave you the option in case you were tired of sleeping bags and hotels."

"As long as you're with me, I'm fine." She could feel her face flush, and the cocky smile on his face told her he saw it, too.

"Then south it is."

Drake dropped his black credit card on the table for the waitress. Between them, they'd paid cash for most of their purchases over the past month, the exception being her camera, the occasional hotel stays and this meal. They waited for the receipt. Drake tipped the waitress, and they headed south out of town.

~

Jacob, Justin, and Jared King sat with Nic Demarco and Zane Reynolds in one of Guardian's secure briefing rooms. Jewell was at the computer console when Jade flew into the room. She sank into the seat next to Nic. "Did I miss anything?"

"No, we are waiting for contact," Nic replied in a hushed whisper.

Jade glanced at Justin. "Do you know what this is about?"

He shook his head. "We received a coded transmission from Chief."

"I have them." Jewell put the call through to the briefing room speaker. "Go ahead, Tatyana."

"There is a threat to Guardian. Mike and I were working a lead that we were given on my sister's location. I used some old contacts. They had other information." Taty's voice was rushed and whispered, almost... afraid.

Jade's eyes shot to Jacob who'd sprung to his feet. "Are you safe?" He blurted out the question on everyone's mind.

"We are. For now. Please, I don't have much time." They could hear Chief's voice in the background although what he said was indistinguishable. "The Russian Mafia was alerted to the Guardian operatives in their organization who work undercover. I know several high-ranking members who were not arrested during the international sweep. Chief has questioned one that we have...borrowed, yes?"

"What information do you have for us?" Jason leaned forward in his chair.

"They have pictures and names. Mike, Dixon, and Drake. The doctor...um...Blue. The pictures were taken when we made the exchange in the warehouse in New York."

Jade's gut clenched hard. "How? Who is distributing the information?"

"Stratus." Tatyana's word froze the room.

Jade felt a hand tighten around her heart. The name had been whispered for years, but only recently had there been proof of the organization's existence. The groundswell of evil around this organization made any of the fuckers they'd taken down before seem like toddlers. Shit was about to get real.

"The man we have said he was contacted by a person who claimed he worked for Stratus. They paid the Bravata to go after us, and they have moved extensive assets into the United States to that end. Assassins and teams. The Bravata does not know where we are based. They search, monitor airports near New York and D.C. They weren't looking for us here, it is how we were able to gain access to our asset. The twins are in danger."

"Send us your location. I'm sending a team after you to get you out." Jason stood up and started pacing.

"It will be in the dead drop email as soon as we can get to a computer. It could be days. The man we have will need to come back with us. We believe he knows more than he's saying. I must go. We have to move." The line went dead.

"Jewell, get Drake on the line."

"Assassins monitoring airports in the New York and DC area," Zane said as he turned to Justin. "The sniper. He could have been targeting Drake, not the professor."

"Doctor." Jewell corrected.

"Right. But think about it. If that assassin were after Drake, it would make sense of the lack of any connection, intent or indication that Doctor Law had been targeted. She isn't the target. Drake is."

"What about the emailed threats against her?" Jared posed the question.

"Scare tactics, maybe? There is absolutely no connection between those emails and any threat that I can find, and believe me, I've searched. The only connection that makes sense is the one to Drake." Jewell stared at the men as she finished, "The police in San Jose arrested the people who broke into her apartment, they admitted to seven other breaking and enterings in the local area."

"The mugger?" Jared shot back.

"Again, a man matching the description that Doctor Law gave the campus police was arrested and charged with petty theft. Purse snatching." Jewell pulled a pencil out of her messy hair and bit down on it several times. "A threat against Drake makes sense."

Jason wiped a massive hand over his face and blew out a large breath. "Fuck me. They've been mostly off the grid. Jewell, get his electronic profile and shit can it. Make him disappear."

"On it."

"Jared, where is Dixon?" Jason's words cut across the room.

"Detroit the last time we had eyes on him. His father's a slimy son of a bitch. He's got Dixon working in Detroit. He's not going to trust him right away. This operation could take months and based on what we know about the fucker, Dix may never get in a position to take him down. It was a shot in the dark."

"One we couldn't afford to pass up. If he gets in, we will have our first look into an organization that could be connected to the people who control Stratus."

Jade sat forward. "Wait, someone controls Stratus? We didn't know that. Did we?" Justin sent her a look that would have normally cautioned her to tread lightly, but what the fuck?

"You think Dixon's father is mixed up with Stratus?"

"We don't know." Jared shared a glance with Justin.

"But if Stratus knows Dixon and Drake were working with us during the takedown of the Russian Mafia, then they *have* to know Dixon is a plant."

"Holy fuck. When was the last time he checked in?" Jacob spun and pointed at Jared.

Justin put a hand on Jacob's shoulder. "Believe it or not, we want Dixon's father to know he worked with Guardian. *Worked* being the operative word. Dixon's assignment is to crack open a foothold for us, to get a look into Stratus. He knows the risks. We talked about it at length. It was his decision."

"Jason, you sent him in as a fucking sacrificial lamb?" Jacob roared.

"No, I sent in a trained professional to get us information and access. Information we can use to fight a battle that has been swelling off your scope. You have no idea what is coming down on top of us." Jason shook his head and reiterated with a murmur, "No idea."

Jared put his hands in his pockets. "Then tell us,

Jason. Tell us what the fuck is going on. We've all seen the pressure you're under. We can tell something is happening, but none of us are involved. What's happening? What is keeping you here, away from your family, away from us?"

"I can't. Not yet." Jason rubbed the back of his neck. "Jewell, do you have Drake?"

"Ummm...yeah, on it." Jewell turned back to her systems.

CHAPTER 17

Drake smiled because he was fucking happy. The windows were down, the music throbbed over the stereo and Jillian had her hand stuck out the window bucking the wind. It was a perfect day. They were singing the chorus to an old Guns N' Roses song when the phone system in the SUV activated, cutting off the music. Jillian giggled when he belted out the remainder of the chorus and hit the button to accept the call.

"Alpha-Five prepare to copy." Jacob's voice shattered the lighthearted mood. Drake took the vehicle off cruise control and pulled over.

"Go ahead."

"A threat has been identified. Your identity was compromised. We have reason to believe you were the target at MESE, not Dr. Law. What is your exact location?"

"What the fuck? Who? Why?"

"Russian Mafia were the actors. You were identified and targeted by Stratus."

Drake gripped the steering wheel and held on. His thoughts spun as he tried to wrap his mind around the implications of that statement. "Stratus. Why me?"

"Not just you, Chief, Maliki Blue and…"

"Dixon." Drake shot a look over at Jillian. "Have you made contact with him?"

"We're working on it." Jared's voice broke in. "Where are you?"

"They are sitting on 141 South of Sundance, Wyoming." Jewell's voice answered for Drake.

"How close is that to the ranch?" Jacob fired the question.

"Four, maybe five hours? There is no straight way there from here." Drake considered which roads to take.

Jewell broke in. "Joseph's place is closer."

Drake blinked and looked at the surrounding area. They were maybe an hour away from one of Joseph's safe houses. He'd flown there, but that was years ago. "I'll need landmarks, I flew in last time."

"I'll get that information," Jewell confirmed.

"Jewell, I've used my credit card, recently. How good are the people tracking me?" He needed information. The transition from staying one step ahead of an unknown threat to becoming a defined target marked by a known assailant required him to use every asset he had, and Jewell's information was vital.

"I don't know the answer to that. I'll clear your electronic history. If they are sophisticated enough to track you, nothing I'm going to do after the fact will prevent them from finding where you've been. It's where you are going we need to protect." He could hear her working the keyboard.

"Can you disable the GPS system on the rental?" Drake glanced at the white button with the blue star on it. The rental company could track him, and any college-level hacker could find a backdoor into the GPS system. Hell, he'd done it with Dixon just to prove the detailed process they found on the internet to hack the system was accurate. They'd been bored, and it had been a distraction.

"It's on my list. Working it, I promise." He could hear her fingers flying over the keyboard. "I've dropped the directions to the safe house to your cell. Memorize them. I'm turning your service off in five minutes. You know what to do with the brick."

"Roger that. Archangel, if they come after us, I'm taking them out." Drake wasn't looking for permission, rather clarifying tactics.

"Of course, authority granted." He heard Jason's acknowledgment.

His phone vibrated in his hand, and he glanced at the incoming text from Jewel. "I have the directions. Skipper, you've got to find Dixon."

There was a pregnant pause before Jacob answered, "I will do everything I can to make sure Dixon stays as safe as possible. I'm not going to try and sell you a line of horseshit. He's pretty much on his own, and he is looking over his shoulder already. He's one smart son of a bitch. Smarter than you."

Drake huffed, "One fucking point, Skipper."

Jacob's voice mellowed as he took over. "We'll do what we can without putting him at risk. Let us worry about that situation, D. Get your ass off the grid. Joseph has a secure Sat link. Let us know when you're bunkered in."

The music blared back over the speakers when the phone link disconnected. Drake reached up absently and turned it off. His focus remained on the phone. He looked up, got his bearings and re-read the directions again. He handed the phone to Jillian and paused. Her face was ashen, and her huge brown eyes had tears in them. "Are you all right?"

"No." She whispered.

Drake checked his six and made sure there were no threats. He reached out and cupped her cheek with his hand. "What's wrong?"

"They want to kill you. They were shooting at *you*, not me? The things that happened on campus and at my apartment...that was just, what...random shit?"

He could see the confusion in her expression. "It would seem." He had to admit it looked exactly like random shit. Drake scrubbed his face with his hands. He needed a minute to figure out the shift in the dynamics because he was flying by the seat of his pants right now.

She grabbed his arm and then threw up her hands in a frantic motion. "Okay...okay... How do you stay safe? Who protects you? Why aren't your people coming out here to protect you?" Each question got louder and the pitch higher. The last word verged on hysterics.

He reached out to her trying to calm her down. "Hey, sweetheart, listen, this isn't as bad as you think—"

She batted away his hand. "Isn't as bad as I think? Didn't he just say someone was trying to kill you? That you were too far away from your home base? That you couldn't drive five hours? That the threat was real? That's what they said, right? Did I get this wrong?" Her voice lifted to octaves he hadn't heard before.

Okay, so maybe not the right thing to say. Drake lifted his hands and spoke like he'd talk to a skittish colt. "A couple things I need you to understand here. First, if I was capable of taking care of you when we believed someone was after you, then I am by default capable of taking care of both of us if someone is coming after me. Second, we don't know how sophisticated or well-funded these goons are. They could be muscle-headed numbnuts who couldn't find their asses with two hands and a road map." The corner of her mouth lifted. "Now get to memorizing these directions. We have," he shot a quick look at the clock on the dash, "three more minutes, then that thing becomes a brick, and I toss the battery."

"Why toss the battery?"

"Because there are programs that can track any inactive cell phone regardless of the service connected to it. Guardian has such a program, and we work under the premise if we can do it, our enemies can. Watch your six. Always."

"Six?" Jillian echoed.

"Think of a clock face. If twelve o'clock is straight ahead, then six o'clock is directly behind you. Keep looking behind you."

"Oh." She took the phone but placed a hand on his before he could start the car. "Promise me you won't let the directionally challenged, muscle-headed numb nuts kill you."

Drake winked at her. "I'll do my best." Drake opened the back of the phone, pried the battery out and chucked the pieces out the window. He made sure the road was clear and headed out, hyperaware of the vehicles meandering down the scenic roadway. He found the turn off he needed and watched for anyone tracking him. There was no threat from behind, and Joseph's safe house was off the grid. The only coms he had were a secure Sat phone and a computer linked to a secure Guardian system. If the house was found and the computer compromised, the hacker would run into Godzilla. Jewell's pet would hand them their asses, and then Guardian would start tracking them. All precautionary measures, but necessary when dealing with the shadow world.

"Turn right, up here. That's the junction we're looking for, isn't it?" Jillian pointed to the road sign. It looked like someone had unloaded a shell or two of buckshot at it, but it was the sign.

"Yep. Okay. Seventeen miles. We're looking for a red reflector on a pine tree and a ghost of a road somewhere off to the right."

"You've been here before?"

"Yeah, flew a helicopter over. The guy who owns the place was in a bad way. Another friend of mine, Chief, took a bullet that was meant for Joseph's wife. The Cartel was tracking her because she had information they didn't want made public. Do you remember hearing about the Morales Cartel?"

"Vaguely. They were involved with dirty politicians, money laundering and drugs, right?"

"Yeah. Joseph's wife was the one who got that information to us." Drake painted a broad picture because he couldn't share the details.

"But your friend was shot at this safe house?"

"Yeah. An assassin was up on the ridge behind the house."

"So this safe house isn't really safe, is it?"

Drake glanced over at her. "That guy is dead. The way he tracked Joseph was identified, and we've taken precautions to ensure none of our people are ever traced that way again. I believe the house has been vacant since that time. No one will know we're there."

The odometer clicked sixteen miles, and he slowed down, checking his rearview mirror for any indication of movement.

"There." Jillian pointed to a reflector that was almost consumed by the bark of the towering pine tree. Drake couldn't slow down fast enough and had to back up. "That's the road?"

Drake nodded and thanked God Guardian was going to pay for any damages to the rental. He made one final check in his mirror and pulled off the road. He parked about ten feet off the hardened surface.

"What are you doing?"

"Just making sure our tire tracks are covered. Stay here for a minute?" He waited for her to nod and then headed back to the road. He could see a truck traveling behind them. It was about five or six miles back. Drake bent down and grabbed several handfuls of dirt and rock sifting them over the obvious impressions in the dirt before he scattered pine needles on top of that. If someone looked hard, they'd be able to see the tire tracks, but it was the best he could do. He sprinted back to the vehicle and put it into drive, pulling it farther onto the trail. He couldn't see the vehicle passing on the road, but that meant they couldn't be seen either. They drove slowly along the trail and found themselves outside a barbed wire gate. He put the vehicle in park. "I'm going to need you to drive this through the gate when I open it. I'll close it behind you."

Jillian jumped out of the truck and jogged over to his side of the vehicle. "You know if this didn't scare the crap out of me, it might be fun."

"I like your sense of adventure." Drake dropped a kiss on her upturned mouth before he opened the barbed wire gate. He dragged the wire out of the way and closed it again after she drove through, using the bar and chain that was attached to the fixed fence to tighten it enough to slip the wire loop over the anchoring fence post.

He waited for Jillian to get back in her seat before they rumbled and bumped down the rutted access route. Drake would never call this glorified goat path a road. He wondered how the hell Joseph got the materials and equipment back here to build the house.

Drake pulled up in front of the safe house. For a one-hundred-foot radius around the dwelling, the ground had been cleared of all large trees and bushes. The property had been vacant for a while as the grass stood a good foot high and lay over due to its weight. A path of quarry stone wandered back to a shed behind and to the right of the building.

"This is beautiful." Jillian's apparent awe forced him to look at the structure again as they got out of the SUV. It was a nice house, but Jillian wasn't looking at the house, her eyes were glued to the meadow behind the cabin. Wildflowers grew in a profuse explosion of rainbow colors.

"About four or hell, even five years ago, Joseph's brothers had given him a rash of shit about ordering over five hundred dollars of wildflower seeds. I think I know what he did with them." Drake smiled to himself. Joseph idolized his wife. He wondered what the story was behind the flowers. Drake disarmed the alarm system with the code included at the end of the directions and entered the cabin.

"Cabin" was not technically the correct term

for the two-bedroom, three-bath home they entered. Drake could tell it had been built with an eye towards old-fashioned craftsmanship. Every room had windows that showcased the beauty outside. The furniture was brown leather, sturdy and sparse. Jillian peeked into the rooms. "Bedroom and en-suite here."

"Perfect. I'll get our stuff as soon as I check in." Drake moved toward the roll top desk that sat in the corner. He lifted the top and flipped on the power to the Sat phone. It would need to warm up and link up before he could use it. He followed Jillian into the kitchen. Yeah, getting marble countertops up here had to have been a royal pain in the ass.

"Look," Jillian whispered as she pointed out the back window. At the edge of the meadow browsed a small herd of deer. Their tails twitched as they grazed. This far from a town and backed up against a national forest, man wouldn't be much of a factor. They probably had few predators.

The Sat phone beeped, and he made his way back to the device and placed his call.

"The line is secure, the transmission location is scrambled. No one is going to be able to pinpoint your location. Did you have any issues?" Jacob immediately questioned him.

"No. What's going on, Skipper?"

"I'm not sure. I'll let you know as soon as I figure it out. We sent a message to Dixon's dead drop. We've weighed the pros and cons of going in after him."

"And?" Drake dropped his arm around Jillian as she came to stand next to him.

"And the cons won. Hands down. We don't know what your old man is capable of doing."

Drake tensed, speaking through his clenched teeth. "Dixon and I knew. We knew what he was capable of doing."

"I'll do everything I can, D. Whatever it takes, my brother."

"For as long as it takes, Skipper. Does Jewell have any more information?"

"Not yet. Once she turned your cell off and got you headed to safety, she worked on reinforcing the veil around Dixon, trying to bolster the cover story he was supposed to give your dad. We consulted our engineer and shored up a few premises should those bastard care to look."

"The next check in?"

"Twenty-four hours."

"Roger that."

Drake dropped the phone into its holder. He cut the power to the device and drew a long breath before he pulled Jillian into him and held her tightly. Even with everything spiraling out of control, her presence grounded him. His concern for Dixon's predicament hadn't lessened, but Jillian's presence balanced him and drew him out of the oppressiveness that would normally consume him.

She pressed into him and turned her face into his neck. "I'm scared."

"I know. Try not to worry about it too much. We'll make plans for the worst-case scenario and pray we never have to use them."

"No, you don't get it. I'm not afraid for myself. I'm terrified someone is going to hurt you, that they could take you away after we just...I'm scared to think about a future without you, and I'm sorry if it's too soon to talk about being together forever, but I do want that, and that scares me too..."

Drake held her as she sobbed the words. Stress, no doubt. He rocked her back and forth and rubbed her back as she cried. She'd been such a trooper for so long he'd forgotten she wasn't used to the insanity he'd lived in for most of his adult life.

He lifted her and carried her into the bedroom and placed her on the bed. He lay down next to her and wiped the tears from her cheeks before he kissed her softly. "We are going to be fine." She opened her mouth to say something, but he stopped her with his finger to her lips. "But to make sure you know, in here," He put his hand over her heart, "that what I'm telling you is the truth, I am going to let you help me design our exit strategy to avoid anyone who might decide to come after us."

She stilled and locked her eyes with his. "Design?" He nodded. She smiled. "Can we blow things up?"

"Those are the best kind of designs." He chuckled until her eyes widened and her smile slid away. "What?"

"I was trying to be funny." She blinked owlishly at him.

"There aren't any innocent bystanders in this scenario. If someone comes this far to pursue us, they are our enemies. No exceptions. If the exit strategy we utilize to get away from these bastards causes collateral damage," Drake shrugged away his indifference, "I'm not going to lose any sleep over it."

She stared at him for several long minutes.

"What?" Drake could see her mind working.

"I...well, I'm wondering what horrible things you've been through. Collateral damage, enemies that pursue you, exit strategies..." Her head shook slowly back and forth. "You've had a hard life, haven't you?"

"In a way, but it is my reality, and if you want a life with me, it will be your reality, too."

"But you said you ran a training complex." She lifted up and propped her head on her hand.

"I do, now. I'm also a team member who deploys on occasion in support of my company and my family. I used to do that job full time. For years I worked in foreign countries, always in high-risk situations. The mission that Jacob talked about on the phone earlier?" He waited until she nodded. "We rescued young women who were being sold as sex slaves. Even if I knew then that doing so would put me in the same position today, I would do it. Those women had no one else to help them. There is so much unopposed evil in the world. My work with Guardian mitigates some of the despair."

Jillian leaned over him as he rolled to his back and smoothed his hair away from where it had flopped over his eyes. "You are a good man."

Drake made a strangled sound before he replied, "No, I'm not, but I am a man who tries to do good things."

"Is that so?" Jillian's hand trailed down to the snap on his western shirt. Her finger wove under it and pulled, prying the fastener apart. She slid her finger down to the next one and repeated the movement.

Drake put both hands behind his head and stared, transfixed, as she unfastened his shirt and pulled it out of his pants, undid his belt and unzipped his jeans. She smiled up at him as she released his cock. She licked her lips and bent down, taking him into her hot, wet mouth. His eyes slammed shut, and he sucked a harsh breath. Fuck, what her mouth could do to him. She could reduce him to a mindless madman within minutes. She popped off him and moved, straddling his knees, getting into a better position to take him down her throat. She bent down again and did exactly that. Drake's hands found her head, and he wove his fingers through her long blonde hair. It was all he could do not to hold her and thrust into that beautiful warmth. He tugged on her hair. "Close." It was the only word he could force out of his mouth. She looked up at him, his cock still in her mouth and hummed.

His eyes rolled back in his head. His hips thrust forward on their own accord. What little control he had melted out of his ears along with his brain. She took him deep again and once again hummed around him. Drake clenched his fists in her hair, holding her as he used her throat and chased his release. White hot pleasure shot through him as Jillian swallowed and swallowed again. He loosened the grasp he had on her hair, and she released him to lick the length of his shaft. Drake used what was left of his highly dubious muscle control to pull her up his body.

Their kiss was slow and languid. He needed his actions to tell her how much he loved her and needed her. He slowly removed her clothes and then his. He loved the woman under him and yet his words failed him. They couldn't convey the intensity of his desire, the depth of his love or the expanse of his need. Instead, he let their union speak for him. Of necessity, to give his recently sated body a chance to recover, he prolonged her arousal until she writhed underneath him with whimpers of desperate need. When her whimpers turned to mindless begging, his indefatigable lust for her had done its job, and with his body pressed against her from head to toe, he made them one. He held her with a reverence he'd never given anyone else, kissed her with the unquenchable desire she alone had ignited, and prayed she would understand the love he offered, without reservation.

CHAPTER 18

"Here." Jillian pointed toward a jutting, jagged corner of rock that would impede their speedy exit from the back of the house.

Drake looked up from where he was working. "Good. Mark it and then keep going. I'll be over there in a minute." They were clearing the pathways they could use for an escape route. According to Drake, they needed to be able to sprint from the house to past the tree line. His words this morning did another lap through her cranium. *We can ghost it from there, but this is where they'd have the best chance at a kill shot.*

Best chance at a kill shot. The specter of fear traced her skin, raising gooseflesh once again. She stuck a stick in the ground and wrapped a small piece of cloth around it. Rational thought had ceased about thirty seconds after that conversation. She worked, doing what he asked, but she was terrified, too stunned to be panicked. The calm manner in which Drake detailed people shooting at them, described clear fields of access, and how they would impede the enemy alarmed her.

A low shrub overgrew the path. She knelt and pulled a small hand saw out of the backpack she'd lugged up the sharp incline. She held the closest branch down and started sawing where it joined the bush to remove the tripping hazard. "You know last night when I asked if we could blow something up?"

She glanced over her shoulder. Drake was shirtless and digging up the rock she'd marked. He stood, arching his back in a stretch. "I recall something about it." He smiled and winked at her.

"It was a joke. You know the concept, right? LOL, laugh-out-loud-funny, ha-ha, can we blow something up. Wile E. Coyote and Acme-mail-order type of funny."

"I understand the concept of a joke. Your suggestion was a good idea, nonetheless." Drake bent down, and with both his gloved hands grasped the mini-boulder she'd identified. Drake lifted the rock and tossed it away from the path. It rolled down the hill, crashing through the small trees and underbrush before it lost momentum and settled out of the way.

He strode up the incline and sat down beside her. They'd worked hard all day. The first thing they did was bury Delbert. They'd marked his resting spot so they could find it again, but if she hadn't witnessed Drake dig the hole, she probably wouldn't have been able to point out where it had been buried. He'd camouflaged the ground so well, the site looked undisturbed. She was exhausted, and she'd only done the light lifting. She pulled out a bottle of water from her pack and handed it to him. He drank it down in one go.

"Tell me what you see." He gestured down the steep incline toward the house.

"A beautiful meadow. Beautiful flowers. The house, a shack, the SUV." She pointed towards each as she spoke.

"Do you see any easy way out?"

"No, but we've cleared pathways."

"Best guess, how long would it take you to run from the house up to where we are now?" Drake crunched the empty water bottle in his fist and capped it before he returned it to her backpack.

Jillian scanned the area. From the house to the meadow was maybe thirty feet. They'd have to sprint through knee-high grasses and flowers to reach the slopes that enclosed the meadow. That was at least...oh six hundred feet. The paths up into the trees? The three that they'd cleared were straight up in some places and at least a quarter mile to the tree line. The distance was even farther on some of the paths they'd cleared. She shook her head. "I don't know, a couple minutes, maybe." She could run fast. Terrified, she could run faster.

"Right, let's say you could make it from the house to where we are sitting in two minutes. How many times do you think I could pull a trigger in two minutes?" Drake put his arms back and rested on his hands as he stretched out his legs.

She swiped at the gooseflesh that rose on her arms. "Too many."

"Correct. Now take that scenario and add confusion, surprise, and disorientation into the mix. Not yours, your attacker's. You know where you are going. You know what is happening, what is going to happen. The people coming after us have no idea how we will react. How many shots do you think they'll get off at you?"

Jillian turned to look back at him. "Hopefully, none."

"See? Blowing up shit has its place."

"But won't your friend be upset?"

"I think when it comes down to it, if it is a choice between our lives or some minor property damage, he'd be okay with the decisions we made." Drake chuckled and dropped his head back, so he was looking at the sky. "At least that's what I'm banking on. One never really knows with Joseph."

He laughed at something, and she nudged him. "What?"

His eyes flicked towards her. "Joseph is very efficient at getting rid of things that irritate him." He closed his eyes and mumbled, "Please God, never let me irritate that man." He opened his eyes and drew a deep breath. "I still need to find something to make into a detonator and a substance to explode."

"We could use Delbert." She leaned forward and pulled her knees close. "If we use it as a way to build a charge without giving it a release point…it would make one hell of a bang."

Drake sat up and brushed off his hands. "I

won't destroy Delbert. We can rig something from the equipment Joseph has around. He has an arsenal under the floor in the shed. I'll get the combination. If he doesn't have anything stored that's useful, there are common chemicals we can combine and then use manual ignition points or perhaps rig timers."

"That panel can be rewired. I have all the tech data and schematics in the hard drives. It is still in development, and I need to refine the processes and procedures anyway. We can rig it and use it if necessary. Like you said, this all may be for naught." She bumped into him with her shoulder. "Right?"

He nodded and looked away. His failure to look at her and reassure her all this work was just a precaution amped her apprehension. He stood and brushed off his jeans before he extended a hand to her. "It's about time for us to check in. In another few minutes, it will be too dark to work, and I'm starving." He grabbed her pack, the shovel, and his pick before he started down the hill.

~

Drake could hear the shower running. He downed another bottle of water as he waited for the Sat phone to acquire the satellite connection it needed. He dialed into the secure connection and waited.

"Alpha."

"Hey, Skipper." Drake sat down and leaned forward, staring at the floor as he held the phone to his ear.

"Standby." Drake waited for the link to secure from Guardian's end.

"The line is secure," Jewell confirmed.

"Hey, girl." Drake acknowledged her.

"Hey yourself. You enjoying the cabin?"

"Haven't been in it much. Working on egress paths to the tree line." Drake glanced toward the front of the house and the bedroom he shared with Jillian.

Jared announced himself. "Dom Ops online."

Jacob started, "Okay, Archangel is unavailable. Bring us up to speed from your end, Jewell."

"Roger that. Electronically, I have swept what I could under the carpet. Your rental vehicle has been out there for almost a month. Tatyana said the remnants of the Russian Mafia were given resources they'd mobilized in the US to track down you, Maliki, Chief, and Dixon. I'm working on the assumption those resources include someone who can gather and filter information. Based on that, I think we should work on the theory they know where you were up until I disabled the GPS in your vehicle outside of Newcastle."

"You can go with that assumption, but why wouldn't they have gone after Drake while he was tromping around out in the wilds of Yellowstone?" Jared interjected.

"Well, I'm looking at the map I pulled from the GPS. There is no signal for days. Then a bleep and then nothing. I'm assuming the mountains blocked it. In that time, Drake and Jillian moved, popped up somewhere else, and then moved again. They could have been tracking them, but thanks to Mother Nature, Drake was always one step ahead. *Or*, the more believable assumption would be the assets were on the east coast. Hence the attempt when Drake landed in New York. Dixon disappeared in the city." Jewell cleared her throat. "Drake went to the college and stayed in the engineering building, giving them time to set up. He literally dropped into their lap. When the attempt failed, and every cop in the state converged, they had to regroup. They could have been localized and needed to pull in more assets to deploy."

Drake shook his head. "What about now? If we work on the assumption they were on the East Coast, I can get us back to the ranch."

"No," said Jacob. "We had a long conversation about this with Archangel last night. While Guardian is hiding in plain sight at the ranch, we don't need to intentionally lead anyone into our safe haven. There are women and children at the training complex, plus the people at the hospital rehabbing."

Drake leaned back in his chair and stared at the wall. "So the question is, do they know where I am?"

"I don't know." Jewell sighed. "My best hypothesis is they probably know where you were when I killed the GPS. Do they know where you went after that? No way, unless they have satellite imagery and have the resources to scour eastern Wyoming looking for your SUV. If we work under the assumption that Stratus is funding this event…"

"We have to assume Stratus is backing this event. We don't know the extent of, or what, is at their disposal, but based on some information uncovered in Colombia, their resources could be vast." Jacob's voice trailed Jewell's. "I would assume they know your location. Do what you need to do to protect yourselves. Have you located Joseph's arsenal?"

Drake cleared his throat. "I'm assuming it's the vault under the tool shed. Unless he has a fallout shelter hidden under the damn thing. Either way, I need the combo." A fucking fallout shelter would be amazing at this point.

"Standby," Jewell said.

"So, no bullshit here...how fucked am I?"

"Jared?" Jacob prompted.

"We have no domestic intel on the Russian Mafia's fairy godmother we can validate. Stratus, which has been rumor and myth for the last fifteen years, has suddenly appeared and become a reality. We believe we have credible international intel found during a recent operation in Colombia. No matter the locale, what we do know from this event is they have global reach and more than enough money to buy the people and assets to do their bidding. Elite professionals. Watch your back."

Drake's shoulders dropped at Jared's words. "Okaay...well and truly fucked, then." He flashed a hard glance toward the bathroom where the sound of Jillian singing in the shower posed an innocent counterpoint to the gravity of the phone call. The thought he endangered her was intolerable.

"I can send a team, D. We can get you out of there, but if they are watching you, Chief, Maliki, and Dixon, we can't take you to the ranch or the complex in Arizona. We'd have to get you to a safe house. It would further expose you and Doctor Law."

"Jillian is not part of this, Skipper. I can send her out." Hell, he'd been a sitting duck before, and he could deal with it, it was part of the job, but Jillian didn't sign up for his bullshit.

"No, that won't work. We're assuming they have a description of your vehicle. If they see her driving it, they'd take her and use her to get to you. The safest thing for her is to be right next to you." Jacob countered.

"So we wait."

Jared cleared his throat before he spoke. "No. You wait. We work. These bastards are fallible. We just need to find their weakness."

"I can send a team." Jacob offered the lifeline again.

Drake ran a hand through his hair as he

thought. Sending a team would do nothing but put them on the map and then paint a target on their backs. They had food, water, and seclusion, and he was more than capable of taking care of his woman. "No. Get me the combo to Joseph's arsenal. I'll take care of us."

"Roger that. Jewell is calling Joseph."

"Skipper, give me a Sit rep on Dixon, and I'd appreciate it straight. No filter." Drake heard the shower cut off in the silence that followed.

"It's a Dom Ops mission. You aren't on the 'need-to-know' list," said Jared.

Drake ground his teeth but maintained control. He fucking hated Guardian's compartmentalization sometimes, but he understood why it was done. "Jared, consider me on the fucking 'I-need-to-know-he's-alive list'."

After a momentary pause, Jared sighed. "He hasn't checked in, which is nothing unusual for an undercover operation. We have some street camera images of him as recently as yesterday. That's all I can tell you." Jared's voice trailed off.

Drake closed his eyes in relief. Dixon was alive and walking around on the street, not being held in some fucking dungeon. He'd take it.

"Thanks."

"You're welcome. Dom Ops out."

"I can't reach Joseph. Power up in three hours and I'll give you what I have." Jewell sounded distracted.

"Roger that. Thanks, Jewell."

"You bet, D. CCS out."

"Alpha out."

Drake ended the call, set the phone back on the desk, and considered what he was and wasn't told. Stratus, an underground organization once considered a myth, was now, apparently, a fact and had given the Russian Mafia his name and identity. Subversion, corruption, duplicity, and graft not associated with the usual scum of the earth had been thrown under Stratus's banner for so long that the world accepted the entity's presence although no one could prove such an organization actually existed. Until now. It seemed either Stratus did exist, or someone had decided to use its mythical cloak to further their own cause.

Either way, the organization had one common thread that Guardian would and could exploit. The scum who came after him had no idea what this Guardian was capable of doing. Drake lifted his head and rolled his shoulders. They had no idea what he could do or would do to protect the woman he loved. As much as he wanted to avoid the situation, he'd be prepared if the bastards found them. A sneer pulled up his lip. *God pity the souls after him because he'd fight like a rabid animal to make sure Jillian remained safe. They had no idea who they'd cornered.*

CHAPTER 19

"What's in here that you need?" Jillian held onto Drake's belt as he moved in the pitch dark towards the small tool shed.

"Joseph has some items cached. They may be useful." He pulled her into the little building and shut the door behind them before he used a flashlight to illuminate the area. "Here," he handed her the light, "shine it down here." He dropped to his knees and pulled an old dilapidated trunk piled with stacks of random items on it away from the wall. Jillian moved the flashlight and directed the light toward the floor where the trunk had been. Drake tugged on a big metal D-ring that sunk into the floorboards. The entire three-foot-by-five-foot portion of the floor lifted.

Jillian hopped out of his way and banged into the trunk with her shin. She hopped up and down rubbing the spot that would no doubt become a bruise the size of the state of Rhode Island. "You okay?" Drake's hand was at her elbow steadying her as she bent down to lift her jeans. There was a good-sized mark, but no blood, which was a miracle because it felt like she'd amputated her leg from that point down.

"I'm fine. Just not channeling my inner grace at the moment." She pushed her jeans over her hiking boots. "What's under there?"

"That remains to be seen. Knowing Joseph, it could be anything. You okay to hold the light?" Drake pushed her hair away from her face. The space between them vanished as he bent down and brushed his lips over hers.

"I am now." She sighed the words as he lifted away. Drake chuckled and moved to step over the trunk and went to his knees. Jillian made note of where the trunk was and carefully navigated her way around it. Drake pulled a piece of canvas away. "Wow." She whistled and cocked her hand, putting all the light on the gun safe that someone had buried in the ground. "Your friend's afraid the zombie apocalypse is happening soon, isn't he?"

Drake laughed as he spun the dial. "Honestly, the zombies would be afraid of Joseph."

The more she heard about this guy, the less willing she was to meet him. He had a cabin in the middle of nowhere, enough canned food and bottled water to last six months, and a weapons safe. *Can you say 'prepper'?* Jillian snorted at her own Discovery Channel driven hypothesis until Drake opened the door. "Holy Shit."

"Yeah. Good ol' Joseph." Drake grinned up at her. "Give me the light." Jillian handed it over, and Drake positioned it on the small ledge of the safe.

"Those are military guns." Jillian had seen them in movies.

"No, not really. They are military grade weapons, but none of these were purchased by the Department of Defense." Drake stood and looked around the shack. "Could you take that canvas and spread it just outside the door? I'm going to use it to drag all this down to the house."

Jillian pulled the thick canvas through the door and flattened it before she walked back in and closed the door behind her. Drake held out a rifle toward her, and she took a step back. "What if I hold it wrong and it shoots?"

Drake laughed and pulled the weapon back. "Here, look. See, this is where the ammunition goes." He pulled back a little handle and a hole just above the part that was supposed to hold the bullets opened up. "It's empty. It's smart to always assume a weapon is loaded until you know for a fact it isn't. This one is clear." He slapped the side of the gun, and a loud metal clank sounded. "I just put the bolt forward. It is safe for you to take. Just hold it here," he showed her with his own hand, "and here. Then walk it to the canvas and lay it down."

It was heavier than it looked. Jillian made the trip, laid the gun down and went back in. Drake handed her three more of the same type rifle, several wrapped packages, a small duffel and two containers, each the size of a shoe box. When he finally shut the door on the safe, he wore a shoulder holster with a handgun in it and had two others laid on the floor beside the safe. She bent over to pick them up.

"No! Don't touch those."

Jillian jumped back and tripped over the chest, falling over the top. All the random crap stacked on top of the trunk scattered across the floor and into the hole where the safe was located. She banged her elbow as she fell and hissed a string of cuss words that would make Cliff so proud of the woman she'd become. Not.

"Shit! Jilly, are you okay?" Drake helped her sit up. He tried to examine the arm she was holding. "Where are you hurt?"

Jillian turned so he couldn't touch her elbow. "No! My pride's destroyed. Any hope of showing you I'm useful has been brutalized beyond repair, and I hit my funny bone, which I guarantee you *isn't* funny. Plus, I'll probably have a black and blue mark on my butt!

Drake dropped beside her and started chuckling.

"This is *not* funny!" Jillian smacked him with the hand cradling her wounded funny bone. He turned away, but she could see he only laughed harder. "Stop!" She pushed him, and he flopped onto his back and literally howled. Damn it, his laughter was contagious. "This isn't funny!" Her reprimand would have been much more believable if she hadn't been laughing, too.

Drake pulled her into his chest and hugged her

against him. He kissed her hair in between aftershocks of laughter. "I'm sorry."

"No, you're not." *Yes, she was pouting, and yes, it sounded pathetic, even to her own ears.*

His huff of laughter moved her hair. "Yeah, I am. The pistols were loaded. I didn't mean to scare you." His chest rumbled under her. "You were so…"

"Pathetic. Go ahead, say it." Jillian flopped onto her back and covered her eyes, but she couldn't stop laughing. The damn man was irresistible.

Drake rolled to her and lifted up on his elbow. "You aren't used to my life, Jilly. You aren't pathetic, you're adorable."

She lifted her hands and blinked up at him. "An adorable klutz it would seem."

He nodded once. "Well, there is that." He lowered and brushed his lips against hers in a sweet kiss. "Seriously, are you okay?"

"I'll be fine. Battered but not broken."

He stood up and extended his hand to her, helping her to her feet.

Drake helped her out the door before he went back into the shack to retrieve the other weapons that still remained in the pit under the floor. He shut the door and grabbed the two front corners of the canvas. "Walk behind me and let me know if something falls off, please?" He turned and pulled the laden tarp with long easy strides. Jillian followed along behind, rubbing her elbow. "You know the series of events leading up to this are highly improbable. I mean, think about it."

Drake glanced around at her. "I agree." He tugged the canvas wide to round the corner to the house. "Highly improbable."

Jillian watched as he dropped the corner of the material and stooped over to grab two rifles, taking them into the kitchen. There were no lights on in the house. Jillian wasn't going to risk face-planting in the unfamiliar surroundings, so she sat down on the stairs and watched as Drake made quick work of taking the equipment inside. It took less than five minutes for him to clear the canvas and sit down next to her. "Are you regretting it? Being here, with me?"

Jillian leaned into him and dropped her head on his shoulder. "I don't think I could ever regret spending time with you. I do suggest, however, the next time you take me on vacation, we eliminate the guns and bruises."

He put his arm around her. "For future reference, guns and explosives are kinda my thing.

They are my primary training blocks. The bruises, I'll try my hardest to avoid."

She closed her eyes and gave a small chuckle. "The bruises were my fault, I'll admit it. Future vacations, however, must be gun and explosive free or I'll make you pay."

He squeezed her closer to him. "Just how would you require payment?" His voice dropped as he placed a breath-stealing kiss on her lips.

"Oh, that and more." Jillian wrapped her arm around his neck and urged him back toward her waiting lips.

"Then let's relocate so I can start accumulating credit for whatever vacation screw ups I happen to commit in our future." He stood and offered her a hand.

"I don't think it works that way. You can't bank credits." Of course, that didn't stop her from holding his hand and following him through the darkness.

"Then we'll consider this a trial run, so we both know what is expected when I really need to suck up and get back in your good graces." Drake stopped and spun her around. She felt the mattress against the back of her legs and his fingers at the hemline of her shirt. Without a second thought, she lifted her arms over her head and waited as Drake removed the shirt.

His hands traveled down her arms and caressed her sides before they rose to cup her lace covered breasts. His thumbs caressed her nipples, sending tendrils of desire through her body. She shivered at the warm breath he blew across the fabric before he kissed the exposed skin above the lace. "So sensitive."

Drake's mouth continued to tease as his fingers unfastened her jeans. His hands delved into the fabric and pushed the denim down her hips. She toed off her shoes and stepped out of the jeans while pulling his shirt up and over his head. The button fly on his denims lasted two seconds after his shirt became a pile of material on the ground. Locked in a kiss, she could feel him trying to toe off his boots. He lost his balance, and they both landed on the bed in a heap of entwined legs and arms.

Drake growled and sat up. He stripped his boxers, jeans, socks, and boots off in one fluid movement. Twisting, he pounced on her. Jillian's surprised shriek echoed in the quiet of the house. She cupped his cheeks in her hand and lifted his head away from her neck where he was tickling her with his whiskers. In the muted light coming into the room from the moon, she could just make out his features.

"I'm not going to be an easy man to love."

He shifted and rolled her on top of him. His fingers popped the hooks on her bra. Jillian sat up, straddling him while she slipped out of the confining lace. She leaned forward, running her hands up his chest, feeling the plates of muscle under her fingers ripple. "I don't recall asking for easy." She lowered to kiss him but stopped before their lips met. "I've always worked hard to get what I want, and what I want is you. Don't worry about me giving up on us. I'm not going to run away because you like to play with guns and things that go boom." She dropped the fraction of an inch required to join them together. His hands traveled the length of her back and found the thin lace of her thong. She squirmed, trying to move, but he gave a quick tug, ruining another pair of underwear. "Again! You're impossible!"

"Don't worry, I'll buy you a truckload of new ones. I like the 'ease of access' feature." Drake ran his hands over the cheeks of her ass and gripped them, pulling her closer to his erection.

"That isn't a feature. You just like to play He-

Man and ruin them!" Jillian sat up and undulated her hips over his cock, now pinned under her.

"Is that a problem?" Drake asked, as he lifted his hips and pushed up when she moved down. Moans mingled in the dark. His hands traveled the length of her waist, rising to cup her breasts as she lifted and lowered again.

"No." Jillian couldn't manage more of an answer. His hand drifted down to his cock. As she rose, he centered his hard shaft at the entrance to her core. She leaned forward and braced herself on his shoulders before she lowered her hips and took him into her body; his size, no longer a shock, just so damn perfect. She loved riding him, listening to him as her body drove him to abandon his quiet reserve. Having him at her mercy was a new and rewarding concept for her. If she worked her hips just right, she could make him beg, and that power thrilled her, but it was a privilege she'd never take lightly. Jillian knew few, if any, had ever seen this man vulnerable. It was a gift she'd always cherish.

His hands blazed a trail across her skin as she lifted and settled, moving her hips just enough to gain the growls and curses that told her he was ready to take over. Like breakers cresting on their roll toward shore, the pleasure of their union pushed forward, building in intensity. Jillian gasped when Drake pulled her down and ground up into her.

"Yes!" The jolt of pleasure/pain stoked the banked heat at her core, building the smoldering fire into a raging inferno. He lifted her and held her hips, staying any voluntary motion on her part, and then he began to thrust. Each sharp, powerful push edged her closer to an explosion that threatened to consume her. One of his powerful hands reached up and found her breast and teased her nipple into a hard point. He ran his callused finger over the tip, and she shuddered as his hands triggered wave after wave of climactic ecstasy. Mindless, she writhed on the hard organ splitting her into a thousand shards of ultimate gratification. She sensed rather than knew when Drake found his release, her mind and body utterly focused on her own orgasm.

His hand stroked her hair. The repetitive motion grounded her, slowly bringing her back to their reality. Still, with all the unknowns and danger that surrounded them, she allowed herself to float in the aftermath of their lovemaking. Sated, she fell asleep, cradled in Drake's love and strength.

CHAPTER 20

Using a pair of tin-snips, Drake cut the wire and finished the last of the explosive triggering mechanisms he'd built. He could wire these devices in his sleep, and on one or two occasions while on deployment with Alpha Team, he'd swear he'd actually done so. He glanced over the equipment they'd pulled out of the weapons safe Joseph had hidden under the tool shack. He released a long breath and glanced toward the bedroom where Jillian slept.

As much as he wanted to stay in bed and hold her close, necessity had forced him from her warmth. The two small bricks of C-4, eight hand grenades, ten blasting caps, three timers, and remote activation devices had come in handy. The M-4 semi-automatic rifles, three forty-five caliber automatic handguns and two full ammo cans would be placed strategically around the house and outbuildings so he could access them. The C-4 and hand grenades would be rigged into the lines of defense he'd plotted around the area. The wired detonations would be placed far enough away from the cabin to give them a running start should they be activated. He could cover the most obvious routes to the cabin with the snares but would use the timers to annihilate the enemy should the need arise. He wouldn't take any chances. Unwittingly, he'd been the one to bring Jillian into this mess. He was damn sure going to make sure she got out of it.

The latest intel on the movement of the threat, or the lack thereof, would be available soon. He glanced at the clock over the door. It was just after six, so seven in the morning on the East Coast. Jewell would be at work by now. He powered up the Sat phone and poured another cup of coffee while it acquired the secure link. The summer air bordered on hot, but there was a nice breeze through the high meadow valley behind the house.

Drake closed the door behind him as he went outside. He didn't want to worry Jillian, but his gut told him something wasn't right.

Jewell's voice floated across the connection. "Good Morning, Drake. The line is secure. Alpha is already in the office, he'll be on soon."

"Okay, and good morning, Jewell. I need some good news."

"I wish I could give you some. There has been zero for us to trace. I honestly don't know if we are being played, if someone in Russia is messing with Tatyana, or maybe they were fed the wrong information. I have zero; I mean absolutely zero to go on. Everything leads to dead ends and brick walls."

Drake gave himself a minute to digest the information. "Thinking outside the box, could they be good enough to move on us without being seen?"

A long sigh preceded Jewell's reply. "Yeah, they could be. We're damn good, but that doesn't mean someone couldn't be better. I learned that lesson the hard way when Zane went after our last Russian hacker."

"Okay." He took a sip of his coffee. It was tasteless.

"Alpha has just signed on, his line will go secure in just a minute, and D?"

"Yeah?"

"I'm sorry. I just can't validate this threat, one way or the other." Jewell sounded utterly defeated. It was something he'd never heard before.

"Girl, you can't be expected to pull a rabbit out of your hat on every case. We'll hunker down and wait it out. Sooner or later they will make a move. If not against me, then…"

"Yeah. At least we got ahold of Maliki. Like you, he's gone underground and holed up. Tatyana and Chief called back in. They will be making their way back to the States."

"So, Dixon is the only one who doesn't know to watch his six." Drake closed his eyes and shook his head. Dammit, he knew he should have stopped Dixon from taking this damned assignment.

"That's not true. He's undercover. He's watching and vigilant." Alpha chimed in.

"Skipper, what's your gut telling you on this one? Do you think there is a threat?" Drake respected the fuck out of his Skipper's intuition.

"Yes, although I don't know to what extent. Too many things have surfaced too close together to think it is anything but a coordinated effort. You need to dig in, fortify and keep your head *and* your ass low to the ground."

"Roger that."

"Did Jewell brief you?" Jacob asked.

"Yes, I did," Jewell cut in. "Fat lot of good that did anyone."

"Jewell…" Jacob's long drawn out release of her name provided the subtext. She was beating herself up. The woman was damn near an IT goddess, and if she couldn't find anything, then the people after him were actual deity or Guardian was chasing ghosts. Either way, apparitions, and immortals were fucking impossible to track—or he assumed they were.

"I'll do as you suggested, Skipper. Jewell, stop worrying about us. I'm prepared and ready for them if they come. Do me a favor and concentrate on Dixon and the others."

"Roger that." Her confirmation lacked the enthusiasm he'd hoped for. "CCS out."

Jacob sighed. "Zane is at the ranch working a situation that developed on the heels of a Shadow operation down in Colombia. I don't think Jewell has slept since he left. I need to head over to her section and check up on her."

"Roger that, Skipper. I'm here for the duration."

He chuckled humorlessly. "For as long as it takes." People who hadn't walked a mile in a Guardian's shoes had no idea the gravity those words held. The words weren't just a motto. They were indicative of a way of life. Sometimes, those in Guardian's employ tenaciously clung to those tenets as they struggled to survive.

"Just another fun-filled day at the office." Jacob sobered suddenly. "Seriously, D., do you need anything?"

The unease in Jacob's voice did little to settle the anxiety the lack of information caused, but he heard the concern and that mattered. "I need intel, but sans that, I've used the C-4, grenades, and armament Joseph had buried to make sure if they come after me, they have to go through hell first."

Jacob coughed as if he'd choked on his morning beverage. "C-4?"

Drake took a sip of his own coffee before he chuckled, "Roger."

"Damn, brother of mine uses a fucking knife, and yet he buried C-4 and hand grenades? How does that make any sense?" Drake smiled at the humor in Jacob's voice when Jacob quipped, "Do not blow yourself up."

"Not what I'm planning on, but thanks for the

vote of confidence." Drake took another swig of his coffee and gazed out over the pasture.

"Oh, I have every confidence you'd be able to level the entire mountain." Jacob laughed before he reminded Drake, "Check back in twelve hours."

"Roger that."

CHAPTER 21

*J*illian watched the sun set behind the mountains. The summer evening held the warmth of the day, but a gentle breeze made the profusion of cornflower blue, vermillion and lemon-yellow wildflowers in the field behind the house bob and sway in a gentle dance. From the swearing and sounds of rattling, Drake played hot potato with the pots in the kitchen. It was his night to cook. It was amazing the recipes they'd concocted using the canned food they had available. The stew simmering in the kitchen smelled heavenly. Her stomach rumbled in agreement with her nose.

Six days had elapsed since they'd pulled into

the small valley. She could sense Drake's growing frustration at the stasis they found themselves in. It was obvious Drake needed to meet a challenge head-on. He didn't fare well with the directives his employer had put in place. Reacting to the threat coming after him was his natural inclination. He tried hard to keep his concerns to himself, but for the majority of her life, she'd been a wallflower. She was an old pro at watching and learning. What she'd learned about Drake could fill volumes.

Two important aspects of their enforced hiatus in the safe house nestled in this snug little valley hit her immediately. His past had more than adequately prepared him for what they faced, and hers had not.

She glanced to her right. The pathway leading away from the house to the right was twenty-three running strides from the bottom of the porch stairs. She could make the tree line in less than forty seconds. The two pathways to the left were thirty-seven and forty-three strides, and both, because of the terrain took her just under a minute to clear. Drake had made her run the paths repeatedly. She'd counted each step. At twenty-three, thirty-seven and forty-three steps, depending on the route chosen, she shifted off the track and then back on to avoid a trip wire. To miss the jag in her mad dash to the top of the trailhead meant her body parts would fertilize the wildflowers. Furthermore, there were three remote activation devices, one at the top of each trail. If she reached the top of the trail and Drake signaled her, she was to push the switch on the detonator—an innocuous looking, dull, scratched, aluminum lever that would result in three separate explosions, one near the house, one near the shed and one near their vehicle. She had no way to gauge the size of the explosion, but Drake said they'd be "big enough to distract the bad guys."

Jillian glanced down at the dirt under her feet. She'd practiced and had assured Drake she'd understood. What she didn't tell him was she wasn't sure she could push that button. How could she when he could be in harm's way? A snort of derision escaped as Drake's words echoed through her thoughts. *"I need to know you'll do exactly what we've practiced. Knowing you'll follow the exact steps we rehearsed will enable me to do what I need to do, and it will give me an advantage because I know what's coming. The bad guys don't. It will also tell me you've escaped and you're safe."*

She told him what he wanted to hear—that she

understood and would implement his instructions. She just didn't know if she could. How could she? If he wasn't clear of the blast zones before... She'd never be able to live with herself if she was responsible for his injury or death.

"That is a somber expression for such a beautiful night." Drake walked across the porch and dropped down beside her.

She nodded to the trails on her left. "Running the routes in my mind." She could run those trails in her sleep, but it was a likely excuse and the first thing she'd been able to come up with. "Do you think they are out there?" She leaned over and dropped her head on his shoulder. He wrapped his arm around her as they sat together.

"I do." The answer was solid and sure. She lifted her head and glanced at him. "Something has happened. What?"

He stared at the wildflowers just as she'd done and shrugged. "The position of another Guardian target who'd gone 'dark' for the same reason we have done was compromised, and he was attacked. He was able to escape, but not before he was injured.

Jillian jumped to her feet, spinning as she demanded, "Who? Not Dixon?"

He shook his head. "A friend. Doctor Maliki Blue. Guardian has sent a team to extract him from his fallback position. He's injured, so he'll be taken to the complex in Arizona. There are no families there. It's bare bones, and all non-essential personnel have been evacuated."

Jillian rubbed her arms, warding away the gooseflesh that rippled over her. "Will we need to go there?"

Drake's gaze continued to study the distant horizon and shook his head. "If we are detected, there will be nothing left of the people who come after us. Maliki is a doctor. He wasn't prepared to fight his way out. He's trained in self-defense and weapons only as a precaution, but…" Drake stood and wrapped her in his arms. "If they come, the only place we are going is home, because I am trained to eradicate the threat. There won't be anyone alive to follow us home."

Jillian calmed in his arms. "I'm still trying to wrap my mind around the fact that you kill people," she murmured. "It's not easy."

He spun her around, so she faced him. "They will be trying to kill me. I'm a federal law enforcement entity. I have the right to defend myself and to defend you against their use of deadly force. I'm not telling you this to frighten you. You need to know what is happening so you can be mentally prepared. If they found Maliki, it is only a matter of time before they find us."

Jillian blinked back tears. "If we kill them all, they'll just send more. How is your ranch safe then?"

"Because nobody knows I'm there. We're hidden in plain sight. For the bad guys to find the physical location of the ranch, they'd need a reason to examine hundreds of hours of satellite footage of an obscure part of South Dakota. Guardian has never given anyone a reason. I've never been on the grid. Like everyone else, the majority of my pay goes to a bank account offshore. Most of the staff and personnel at the complex are paid in cash. What they don't need is banked in masked accounts that are untraceable. No one there has a digital footprint. No internet presence whatsoever."

No internet presence? In this day and age, that was ridiculous. "How do you buy things online?"

"Other than the secure link we have with Guardian, we don't, but nobody has complained about the lack of internet. It actually became a challenge to see how we could adapt and live without being plugged in 24/7. We do a weekly run to Rapid City. We take a van. Anyone who wants to go shopping can go. Once a month, we fly those who want a weekend away to a major city. Usually, we vote on where we are going. New York, Chicago, Denver, San Francisco. There isn't anyone who suffers from the lack of an internet presence. All phones are Guardian issued and secure. Guardian also has a logistics branch specifically created to provide undercover and covert operations with needed equipment. When we opened the complex, the division expanded to take care of the day-to-day needs, like medicines for the hospital and staple food supplies for the dining facility. They fly it in on the weekly supply plane. That flight plan is not filed. It never has been, and it never will be. If we are asked by any local people, we say we are employed as hands on the Marshall Ranch. The people in Hollister know Guardian has a presence, but to the last man, they keep it quiet. Guardian has helped everyone in that community, from free energy, to bringing in feed for their cattle or even helping to rebuild a barn that burned down. The people in that little South Dakota town are hard as nails and true patriots. They won't talk to strangers about us."

Jillian stared up at him. The steps the organization took to keep the complex off the grid were remarkable. "What exactly does this complex do?"

"I've already told you that it started as a rehabilitation site. A safe place to send our people when they needed time and safety, so they could concentrate on getting back on their feet. It has morphed over time. Now it is a training branch, and it is home base for a few."

"Like you and Dixon."

Drake nodded. "And a few more."

He lowered and kissed her softly. "You don't need to worry. We'll be…"

Jillian gasped as a small herd of deer in the meadow bolted as one and leaped out of sight into the tree line.

"Run, now!" Drake spun her to the right as he barked the command.

Her arms and legs pumped as she flew up the path. She hopped over the small rock and pivoted, missing the trip wire, before she pounded up the trail. Her breaths came in huge ragged gasps that were ripped from her chest. She pulled up and dove under the bank of cover they'd built. Scared hands gripped the straps of the backpack that had been prepositioned, and she put it on before she grabbed the detonator and put it within a moment's grasp. Her heart pounded, and she sucked in air, but the raw, intense burn meant nothing because her eyes were focused on the house below. She had an idea where Drake would be, or rather where he needed to go to gather weapons. The kitchen light shone through the window over the sink, and in the twilight, a pale-yellow light had started to filter onto the porch.

Jillian clasped her shaking hands and stared at the detonator she'd laid carefully on the branches before her. She prayed some animal had spooked the deer. There were predators in the Black Hills, coyotes, wolves, big cats and the occasional bear. Drake had made sure she knew what to do if she came across any of the apex animals while she was working with him in the hills.

Quiet blanketed the valley. Well, that wasn't true, she heard the nighttime bug songs start up. As the light crept out of the valley, a layer of dread settled around her. She focused her eyes away from the house as the light from the inside would hamper her night vision, or at least that was what Drake had told her. She shook her head. So much information in the last week was about survival—her survival. She hugged her legs to her chest while scanning the area.

A movement toward the back of the meadow caught her attention. Something was out there. Jillian slid a few inches down the steep incline while still sitting on her butt so she could see past a branch that blocked her view. She couldn't see exactly what, but something was parting the grasses and flowers on the valley floor. Something big.

Another dark mass entered the meadow from the right. She jerked her head to the left below her position, looking for another entity, but saw nothing. She grabbed the detonation device. Her eyes bounced from movement to movement before she scanned the area immediately below her. A sound at the base of her trail froze her momentarily. As if Drake was standing beside her, she followed the steps he'd trained her on all week. *One*: slip off the backpack. *Two*: open the front zipper pouch. *Three*: take out the handgun, keeping her finger *off* the trigger. *Four*: lay the gun down, zip the compartment and put the backpack back on. *Five*: Pick up the gun. *Six*: Breathe. She gulped air, realizing she'd actually stopped breathing. *Seven*: Acquire a target.

Step eight was to grip the handle of the weapon tightly when she picked it up. That would disable the safety. Step nine was to point at the target once she validated it wasn't Drake. Step ten was to pull the trigger. Five times. Not once. Five times, all with her eyes open and while she was pointing at the target. *Ten steps and she'd accomplished six. You can do this.*

She glanced back at the meadow. It was so dark now it was almost impossible to pick out the forms that moved in the grasses. They were still there. She knew it even though she couldn't see them. She sent a prayer up as she shifted her attention to the trail she'd just climbed. Drake had told her to trust him to take care of himself while she was at the top of the ridge. She'd be doing that now because she needed to safeguard his escape. She grabbed the detonator in her left hand and opened the flip top. The questions she had earlier evaporated like rain on a sun-baked sidewalk. Gone in an instant. She'd follow Drake's instructions to the letter. When the cards hit the deck, she'd call. She wasn't bluffing, and she had the winning hand. She had Drake and a wildcard in her left hand. It was something they'd worked on together. Jillian lowered her finger to the first switch and flipped it because it was only a matter of time before Drake would be powering up that incline. The last card was about to be dealt.

CHAPTER 22

There. Drake used his middle finger to spin the focus on his ten-by-fifty binoculars. Two men. He noted their armament. Although he couldn't see much detail in the dark, they each had a rifle, which made them a long-range threat. Where the fuck was Asp when he needed him? That son of a bitch could shoot a gnat off a mosquito's ass at two thousand yards. What Drake needed was to pull them closer. He was a marksman, but not a sharpshooter or sniper. He preferred to fight his battles close up and in person.

He swept the meadow and let out a low curse. Two more, similarly armed. Were they the totality of the team sent after him? He shook off that hope.

Four men on the frontal. If they were trained, and gauging them by the divided approach, they must have had some training, there were more out there. He swung his binoculars to his left and... bingo. He dialed his focus in. He couldn't see her, but he could see the straps of the prepositioned backpack. Drake dropped the binoculars and lifted them immediately. If she wasn't wearing the pack... He scanned the area but saw nothing. He swung his glasses back to where the strap had been. It was gone. She had it back on and probably had the handgun out. His mind flew through the drill he'd made her repeat a hundred times a day for the last six days. *One, two, three, four, five, breathe, baby.* Drake chewed the inside of his cheek for a moment. He allowed himself ten seconds before he exited the darkened room by dropping out the window. He'd needed the elevated position to see through the meadow, but he knew where the primary attack was coming from so he had a plan of action. With one rifle slung across his back and another in his hand, he landed on the soft dirt and dropped down, crab walking away from the house.

Drake pulled out the handguns he'd stuffed into his boot and belt on the way through the house. He'd also pilfered an Interceptor 911 out of

Joseph's bedroom. He'd found the wicked blade under the mattress along with three throwing stars. The assassin loved his blades.

Drake moved into a defensive position against an outcropping of granite. No one was going to come up on his six, and he had a clear field of vision to the front of the meadow while still being able to protect the path where Jillian had fled. He lay down on his stomach, minimizing the target he'd make when he started firing at the bastards who were after him.

Drake tucked the stock of his weapon against his cheek and aligned his weapon sights. He drew a deep breath and let it out, forcing the tension in his muscles to relax. Habits forged through years of training and more real-life experience than he cared to examine kicked in. He wondered fleetingly what it said about him that he was almost inured to circumstances such as these.

He opened both eyes and waited. The songs of the night creatures ebbed and crested, and still he waited. Moving or exposing himself wasn't an option. He kept his focus on the mission at hand by scanning the area where the four must appear. It was only a matter of…

Drake closed his left eye and aimed. Two of the

four men were in the clearing by the back porch. He needed the other two to expose themselves before he attacked. The men advanced on the porch keeping out of the light cast from the kitchen. A third man appeared in a rookie mistake. He squeezed the trigger dropping that man and one of the other two before his targets vanished.

Drake scrambled from his location a split second before a barrage of bullets rained down on where he'd been. He wiggled through the small depression to the right and sprinted to the next outcropping of granite and limestone. An explosion made him jump, but he didn't move. They had more than four men. Hopefully, the trip wire took out the motherfucker trying to creep up on them. A low call for help was all he needed to hear. Drake spun, planted his hand on the top of three fallen logs and dropped behind them. He followed the cleared path to the right, soundlessly and with speed. The man moaned again and said something, but it wasn't in English. That stilled Drake. It could be a setup. He dropped behind a large pine tree and closed his eyes, listening intently to the sounds around him. He cursed his haste, because now the house was between him and Jillian. A small distinct snap of a branch directly behind him catapulted him into action. He palmed his handgun, spun out from the trunk of the tree and fired. Two men. He dropped one, the second one bolted toward the house with Drake in pursuit. The man threw his hand back and fired with a handgun Drake hadn't noticed, but the shot was a wild-assed attempt and was only meant to slow him down. Drake pumped after the bastard, throwing himself at the man's knees before he got to the house.

The force of his hit sent the man face first into the dirt. Drake scrambled up at the same time as the motherfucker under him punched back with his left hand. The knife he was holding sliced through his jeans and found purchase in Drake's calf. Adrenaline and pure unadulterated stubbornness kept him upright.

The sneer of satisfaction on the bastard's face lasted the two-tenths of a second it took Drake to lift his weapon and put a bullet through the man's brain. Motherfucker! He limped toward the trail Jillian had taken. Blood pooled in his boot, saturating his sock, and with every step, burning pain reminded him of the presence of the blade, but taking the damn knife out wasn't an option. He'd end up bleeding more.

He started for the path he'd directed Jillian toward. He'd eliminated all four of the bastards he'd seen in the meadow, and the tripwire-activated explosion had injured or killed another. Drake hobbled past the house, one rifle still slung across his back, a forty-five in his hand and a fucking knife still stuck in his damn calf. He glanced up just as the lights in the house went out. *No!* Drake lunged forward. The percussion of the blast lifted him off his feet and propelled him through the air towards a stand of pine trees. Splintering pain careened viciously through his head and shattered the darkness with red and white brightness. He felt the impact as he was thrown into an immovable object and was plunged into darkness.

~

Jillian watched in horror from her protected position as a fireball flew into the sky. Pieces of the house fell halfway up the mountain trail. She dropped the detonator and covered her ears when a secondary explosion rocked the small meadow. The rental vehicle went next followed by the small shed. *Why had Drake signaled her to blow it all up? Where was he?*

She wrapped her arms around herself and rocked, trying desperately to contain her hysteria. It was there just under her skin. If she allowed it to escape, she'd be useless to Drake when he reached the trailhead. Random fires burnt in the small meadow below, the largest engulfed the framing, which was all that remained of the house. The SUV and shed smoldered but she saw no movement. *Where are you?* Her eyes scanned the lower trail. *There!* She could see a tall shadow climbing up the trail. She held her breath as the form stopped at the tripwire and carefully moved around it. Strange that he'd stepped in that direction. He'd used the opposite side when they'd cleared the path. A sub-zero chill of apprehension ran up her back. That wasn't Drake. She could tell by the way the man moved.

Jillian reached down and grabbed the weapon. *Five*: Pick up the weapon. But this time she put the pad of her index finger on the trigger. *Six:* Breathe. Jillian tried to inhale. She forced herself to slow down, to exhale, and then her lungs functioned, taking in the air and releasing it. *Seven*: Acquire the target. The man wasn't Drake. She knew this for a fact. *Eight*: She lifted the weapon and squeezed the handle in her fist, deactivating the safety. Jillian cupped the hand holding the weapon in her other hand. She was shaking so badly she couldn't raise the weapon without steadying it. She waited until the man drew closer. Dark hair, short and holding a rifle. He stepped over a rock she'd used as a stepping stone. Jillian resisted the urge to close her eyes and pray the man walked past her. She'd be seen, and he'd kill her. No, she wasn't going to go without a fight. *Nine*: Jillian lifted the weapon. Her action caught the man's attention. He froze and then an evil laugh drifted on the smoky night air.

The suddenness of the gunfire seemed to play in slow motion in her mind. Jillian recognized what was happening as the man's body jerk repeatedly. She saw his flesh tear away. She witnessed his shocked expression and then the look of terror. She observed him fall toward her and land face-first in the dirt, leaves and pine needles that littered the hill. She still held the gun, pointed in his direction, but she hadn't fired a single round.

Jillian lifted her stunned gaze from the dead man in front of her to the trail behind him. A bloody and battered Drake leaned against a pine tree. His right arm hung at his side. In his hand was a 45-caliber handgun.

"Jilly, lower your gun, hun. You're pointing it at me." Drake's voice snapped her eyes back to the weapon in her hand. Her shaking hand. "Just point it toward the ground." Drake's voice was closer. Jillian lifted her eyes. She couldn't see him very well through the tears. "It's okay. It's over, babe." She stared at him as he approached. Shallow cuts all over his face oozed blood. His shirt hung off his torso in pieces, and he held his left arm awkwardly. He did something to the .45 in his hand and then tucked it in his belt by his left hip. He reached out and placed his hand on the weapon she held. "Let it go, Jillian." She glanced from him to the weapon and back again. "I've got you, babe. It's okay. Let it go."

CHAPTER 23

Drake pushed the barrel of her handgun to his right, removing his heart from point-blank range. Being stabbed and damn near blown up was enough excitement for one night. He didn't need the woman he loved to make him into a pin cushion. Her finger was still on the trigger, and she was shaking so badly he could feel the tremor through the weapon. There was nothing good about the situation. She was in shock. He could tell by the way her pupils were dilated, the shallow, jagged way she was breathing and the pallor of her skin.

"Okay, sweetheart." He winced as he moved his left arm. He'd dislocated his shoulder in the blast, and he hadn't wasted time trying to put it back in the socket. Because of that, he had no strength in his hand to pry her fingers away from the trigger. "Baby, I'm injured. You have to help me. Take your finger away from the trigger."

"You're hurt?" Her eyes seemed to focus as she looked at him.

Thank God. "Not bad, but I need you to help me, okay?"

She nodded. "Okay."

"Let go of the gun." Drake had a solid hold of the barrel. He wasn't going to get shot, but he needed to get them both out of the area in case these goons had back-up.

Jillian looked down at the forty-five and blinked, then pulled her hand back as if she'd been burned. Drake put the weapon in his belt at the small of his back, between his jeans and the leather. It was less than perfect, but without his left arm, he had to improvise. He just prayed he didn't somehow end up shooting his foot, or worse, his ass, in the process.

After shoving the metal into place, he reached for her and pulled her into him. "I need you to be strong for me, Jilly. We need to get out of here. Can you walk with me?" Drake held her to his chest as his gaze swept the ground below. Nothing moved, but God only knew how long that would last. He felt her nod and kissed the top of her head. He needed to get her going before reality bit her in the ass, and she lost it. He grabbed her hand and pulled her up the hill. It would be a long, long fucking night.

∽

Drake stumbled over a small rock nearly going down to his knees. "We need to stop."

"I've been saying that for the last hour," Jillian snapped at him. "You're bleeding."

He glanced down at the bandage he'd tightened around the hole in his leg. They'd stopped after they stumbled down the ridge in order to relocate his shoulder and pull the fucking knife out. It wasn't a long blade, but it still did a job of messing him up. His calf had a puncture wound a couple inches deep. "Yeah." Drake glanced around and nodded toward an outcropping of granite. "Over there." He hobbled to the V in the rock. "Wait here. Let me go back and make sure nothing is sleeping back there."

He pulled his handgun from his belt and moved

forward. The only thing he was worried about was rattlesnakes. They'd be tucked up against the rock keeping warm. He put the weapon in his left hand and grabbed a stick that had a small fork at the end with his right.

"What are you doing?" Jillian whispered right behind him.

He turned his head and narrowed his eyes at her. "What part of stay there didn't you understand?"

She straightened to her full height and pointed at where they had stood moments before. "The part that would leave me alone. In the dark... without you!" Her voice held a hysterical edge to it.

Drake closed his eyes and gathered his waning strength. He nodded. "Okay. Keep me in sight, but stay behind me. I'm going to check the crevices for rattlers."

"Snakes?" If her voice wasn't bordering on hysterical before, it was firmly on board the freaked-out train now.

"Just stay here. It won't take me long, and you can see me. Okay?"

The rapid up and down movement of her head should have been comical, but he'd lost his sense of humor recently. Drake limped forward and proceeded to shake the bushes and prod the crawl spaces. He made a complete sweep of the small area. Thankfully, nothing there needed killing. He dropped the stick and extended his hand to Jillian. It took two seconds for her to skitter to a stop at his side.

"I need the pack." He waited as she slipped it off. It took several seconds of groping in the dark before he found what he was looking for. Two small, hand-sized packets. He pulled the plastic bag apart and unfolded an emergency Mylar blanket. "Spread that on the ground." As she worked, he opened the other pack so they would have something to put over them. It wasn't cold, but they were both exhausted, and the mosquitoes would drain them given a chance.

"I need to take a look at your leg." Jillian patted the blanket next to where she knelt.

Drake leaned over and set the backpack down. He extended his leg in front of him and controlled his descent to the ground as much as he could. "You can't see anything in the dark. If I stay still, it should clot and stop bleeding."

"And if it doesn't?"

"I'll know because the blood will pool on the blanket." He wrapped his arm around her with his good arm and pulled her into his side. Offering her the other Mylar blanket, he waited until she'd covered them. "We need to get some sleep."

She pushed away from him. "But what if someone comes?"

"I'll wake up. It is what I'm trained to do, but if they can track us in the dark, over foreign landscape, and through a forest, then they deserve to get the drop on us." Drake realized his joke had backfired when she tensed in his arms. He chuckled and rested his cheek on the top of her head. "Silly Jilly." She elbowed him gently at his comment. "I didn't mean to scare you. We are in a protected location. The shelf of rock protruding above us will block us from view if they have satellite coverage. They won't even get a heat signature. We are as safe as we can be. If we are exhausted, we are at a disadvantage. I wouldn't tell you to rest if I thought you were in danger. Now close your eyes and sleep."

Drake closed his when he felt her snuggle in and get comfortable against him. His shoulder ached like a bitch. He felt like he'd walked a mile-long gauntlet without armor and his leg throbbed with each beat of his heart. He'd had a few bouts of vertigo while they were climbing, so he probably had a concussion, but he hadn't been nauseous, and he'd known who and where he was when he'd come to at the base of the trail. His exhaustion was physical, of that he was sure. He turned his head and kissed Jillian's forehead before he closed his eyes and allowed his body to rest.

Drake woke with a start. The sun beat down from high in the sky. It was at least ten, if not later. Not moving, he listened. A red squirrel chased another along a long pine branch. Several birds flitted through a small open area off to the right of their position. Drake slowly tensed and relaxed his muscles, grimacing with each movement. He winced and sucked in a breath when he moved. The dried blood around the bandage on his calf pulled and that fucking hurt like a bitch. He could feel blood seeping from his wound again. Damn it.

Drake looked down at Jillian. She'd somehow managed to rest with her head in his lap. The position seemed awkward as hell, and he had no doubt the woman was going to be stiff and sore when she woke. He shifted and planted his arms beside his butt, pushing himself back up against the wall he'd used as support throughout the night. Jillian bolted upright, her eyes wild and searching. "What? What is it?"

"Nothing. We're fine." Drake rolled his shoulders and watched her gather herself.

Jillian rubbed her hand over her face and yawned. "I need to…" She searched the area and then pointed. "Is it okay to go?"

"Yeah, just a minute." He pulled himself up and tentatively put weight on his leg. The dull ache ratcheted up about ten notches, but it wasn't so bad he couldn't deal. He adjusted the weapons in his holsters and grabbed the handgun he'd laid on the blanket beside him last night. "Okay, you find a bush. I'll keep an eye out." He needed to figure out where the hell they were. He knew they'd started to go south and if he'd followed the ridge like he believed he had, then they should be able to reach a branch of the eastern slope of the Black Hills.

He waited for Jillian and then took his turn before he ushered her back under the rock overhang. His hastily picked defensive position was actually a damn good spot. He lowered himself back down on the blanket.

"I need the first aid kit." She motioned toward the backpack. Drake opened the thing, grabbed the white box, and handed it to her. "And that little bottle of whiskey."

"What for?" Drake blinked at her.

Her brow furrowed, and she cocked her head at him as if she was examining a bug. "To disinfect this wound, of course."

Ahh...no. "How about you use the alcohol wipes instead." He motioned to the first aid kit.

A single eyebrow arched up at him, and she extended her hand. "The whiskey."

Drake opened the pack and pulled out four bottles of water, and two MRE packets. There was a flint and a steel striker, waterproof matches in a plastic sealable bag, and two chemical sticks that glowed when the capsules inside the plastic were broken and the elements mixed. "Sorry, no whiskey." Drake held up his hands like a dealer in a casino.

Jillian reached toward the pack. Drake moved it just out of her reach. She laughed and crawled over him grabbing the pack. She gave it a good yank, but his grip wasn't budging. "Okay. How about I promise not to use all of it." She tugged the bag again.

He shook his head. "Only if I pour it."

She sat on her butt and stared at him before a wide smile split her face. "That works."

Drake glared at her, the minx was up to something. He pulled the small flask of whiskey out of the pack and held it next to his chest. He didn't necessarily like whiskey, nor did he want to drink it, but he'd been on the receiving end of Doc Cassidy using vodka to clean out a wound once. That shit stung and not just for a little while. He'd rather be the one in control of his torture. Maybe.

Jillian used his knife to cut the old bandage off. With care, she unwrapped the wound. The bandage released from his leg without too much trouble because it had started bleeding again this morning. He watched as she cleaned his leg and then glanced up at him. "The wound is clotting, but there is still a deep puncture, here. Please give me the alcohol so I can pour some into the wound. I don't know enough about field care to know if I need to pack the wound or not."

Drake leaned over his leg and glanced at where the knife sliced through his muscle. There wasn't a lot of swelling, nor was there any extraordinary redness around the puncture. "If I keep it elevated a bit today, rinsing the wound out with alcohol should suffice."

"Had a lot of knife wounds, have we?" Jillian extended her hand, and he made a reluctant act of handing over the small bottle.

"Not personally, but in my line of work, you see

a lot of wounds, see how the medics and docs care for them in the field. This is one I need to stay off of and keep clean." He winced, and his entire body tensed as she poured the liquor. It stung like an entire hive of wasps were buried inside his wound. The bastards were pissed, too.

"Are we safe here?" Jillian looked up from unwrapping a clean pad to cover the hole in his calf.

"As safe as can be. Guardian will be sending people from the complex." Drake mentally fingered through the list of people that resided at the complex. Fury, Asp, Anubis, hell any of the Shadows. He tried to remember the training schedule. Were there any teams due in? Possibly, but he wasn't a hondo on that recollection.

"Why?" Jillian picked up the trash after taping the gauze wrap liberally coated with antibiotic gel securely around his leg. "I mean why now? I thought the idea was to make sure we couldn't be traced back to the complex. Sending someone now would do that, wouldn't it?"

Drake patted the ground next to him and waited for her to move up beside him. "When I didn't check in today, it pushed the situation into another response level. There are specialists at the complex who…well trying to track them would be like trying to track a ghost. It is impossible. Knowing my bosses, they will have dispatched those assets, and they've probably already tapped into a satellite to get a visual on the safe house." Drake turned to her. "And while we are on that subject, why did you blow up the house?"

"What do you mean why did I blow it up? You said to watch for the signal. I did. The lights went out." Jillian turned and drew her arms across her chest and mimicked him, "There is no reason the lights would go out unless I turn them off."

"Well, I did say that."

"Yes, you did. You said that meant you were at your fallback position, the tool shed and you'd cut the power."

"Right." She'd followed directions. Once he cut the power, he'd have ten seconds to haul ass away from the shack before it blew. Instead, for some unknown reason, the power had gone out, and he was standing too damn close to the first and largest explosion. "I have no idea what caused the power to go out."

"You didn't do it?" Jillian popped away from his side and stared at him, mouth agape.

He reached over and put his finger under her

chin, closing her mouth. "No, but it worked out." He pointed to one of the MRE packages. "Let's get that open, get some calories into our systems, and then we'll be lazy and rest." He planned on keeping them quiet and still for the remainder of the day. People who aren't moving don't leave tracks. Fewer tracks, less chance of becoming prey. She continued to regard him with a horrified expression for a long moment, before, with a shake of her head, she did what he'd asked, muttering to herself the entire time. She didn't elaborate. He didn't ask.

Drake helped Jillian figure out the cooking tabs for the field heater contained in the kit. He moved his weapons, setting them where he'd have instant access, and he scanned what he could see of the ridgeline they'd followed last night. Yes, they were holding up, yes, they were concealed, but no, he didn't believe for an instant the danger to them had passed.

～

Drake glanced over at Jillian as she slept. There was a reason he'd dozed off and on during the day. If someone had located them during the day, a night-time attack would put

Drake at a disadvantage. When they hadn't been resting, they'd collected sizeable rocks and built a stone wall about three feet high. Jillian now slept behind it. Would it stop a bullet? God, he hoped so.

Drake shifted carefully and leaned back against the mountain. He was tired, sore, and pissed. A small clattering to his right brought his rifle up, although he swept to the left first. A large shadow stood on the trail. The man's arms lifted slowly until they rose over his head. He stepped forward, and Drake moved his thumb, switching the selector from safe to semi. The loud metallic click stopped the man in his tracks.

"Blowing my house up wasn't enough? You figure to shoot me, too?" Joseph's low, evil growl felt like a warm fucking hug.

Drake lowered his rifle and eased the safety back as Joseph approached the entrance to the space he'd claimed. He rolled and winced, allowing his brother-in-arms to sit down next to him.

Joseph scanned the area, including the rock overhang. He reached in his pocket and tossed a bag toward Drake. "Antibiotics and mild painkillers."

Drake lifted his eyes from the pills. "Walking pharmacy?"

Joseph growled, "Getting to be a habit."

"Being a pharmacy?" He pulled the antibiotic pill bottle out and popped two, swallowing them dry.

"No. Pulling Alpha Team's asses out of the fire." Joseph huffed out a lungful of air. The sound said more than his words.

Drake laughed quietly and shook his head. "Been a hot minute since I've been on Alpha Team."

"Doesn't mean y'all don't still fuck up by the numbers, does it?" Joseph relaxed back against a tree. "Asp has the high ground, and we are covered until we start down in the morning. She injured?" Joseph nodded in Jillian's direction. Her feet were visible from behind the wall he'd built. The woman was mentally and physically exhausted, as was he. It didn't surprise him that she hadn't heard their conversation yet. Hell, if he didn't have to be vigilant, he'd sleep through an earthquake. The last week of sixteen-hour days had depleted both their physical and mental stamina.

Drake shook his head as he spoke, "No. She's not injured."

"You going to live?" Joseph taunted.

He reached for the bottle of water that remained and took a swig, dislodging the pills that were stuck in his throat. He put the cap back on and shrugged. "Probably, unless you kill me for blowing up your house."

"Jury is still out on that, and thank you, motherfucker, for destroying the one safe house in the continental United States that had any sentimental value."

"Shit, man, sorry, and I was unaware you possessed the ability to be sentimental."

"Not for me, fuckwad. Ember liked that little place."

"Is that why you seeded all those wildflowers?"

The look Joseph gave him could peel paint off a wall. He chuckled and held up his hands in surrender. "I won't tell a soul. No one will ever know what a romantic you are."

"Tread lightly," Joseph growled.

Drake stifled all the laughter that bubbled up. He needed to change the subject, and quickly, before the big teddy bear in front of him grew fangs and decided to kill him. "Noted. What's the status?"

Joseph shifted and shook his head. "Impossible to say. Jason and Gabriel have been unreachable. Jacob and Jared are chasing leads that vanish as quickly as they appear. Jewell has gone off the deep end. Zane had to head back to D.C., and he dropped a fucking shitball in my lap." He pinned Drake with a cold, deadly stare. "Whoever is fucking with us needs to die. Now."

"For once, I concur with every word that just came out of your mouth."

"For once, huh?"

"Yep." Drake darted a glance toward Jillian who was snoring lightly. His woman. "I'm in."

"Whatever it takes," Joseph ground out.

Drake swung his gaze to the assassin. The words he'd uttered so many times, the ones that he and Dixon lived by, morphed in that instant and took on an entirely new meaning. Joseph lived those words, lived them not only for his family in Guardian but for Ember and their son, Blake. Drake nodded. Once. He got it. Message received. "Yes. Whatever it takes."

Joseph moved a finger indicating Drake and Jillian. "I'm taking you both back to the ranch."

Drake shrugged. "I figured."

"You're both dead. Officially. Lycos is planting the evidence."

Fuck him. "Her father? Brother?"

"Can't be helped right now. Need to make sure no one is coming after you. Can't risk it, not with non-combatants at the ranch. You explain it so she understands."

"She understands. She doesn't like it. At all." Jillian's voice rose from behind the rocks.

A ghost of a smile traced Joseph's lips. "She should know it won't be forever and her father and brother will be watched to make sure they are safe."

"She appreciates the effort," Jillian said as she sat up and blinked toward the darkened corner where Joseph sat. "Who are you?"

Drake offered, "Joseph, meet Doctor Jillian Law. Jillian, this is Joseph King, the man whose house we just blew up."

Joseph dipped his head in acknowledgment.

"Oh. I'm so sorry about your beautiful house. I can pay to have it replaced." She pushed her hair out of her face. Drake knew the offer was sincere.

"No need." Joseph stood and rolled his shoulders. "You two get some sleep. Asp and I have you covered. We leave at first light."

Drake watched him drift back into the darkness.

"He's kinda intense, isn't he?" Jillian asked. A low, evil laugh floated back to them. "And he obviously has excellent hearing. Who is Asp?"

Drake smiled and moved beside her. "Yes, he is and that he does...and you don't want to know who Asp is."

"Okay." She snuggled into him as he lay down beside her. "My dad and brother are going to be devastated. I can't..." She sniffed and wiped at her cheeks. "I can't do that to Cliff or Matthew. Please, don't make me put them through this." Her voice cracked as she turned into his chest and sobbed.

Drake kissed her hair. "I wish there were another way, but Joseph is right."

"No. It isn't fair, they wouldn't tell a soul. You know that. You know they wouldn't jeopardize my safety, or yours." Sobs laced Jillian's words.

Drake ran a hand down her hair and played with the ends. He was in a fucking no-win situation. Maybe Jacob or Jason would understand. Hell, he'd ask if they'd do the same to Tori or Faith. He couldn't believe Jacob would have allowed Frank to think his daughter had died. He had to hope that Dixon would realize what had happened. Maybe he could get word to him at some point. "I'll talk with the bosses and try to make them understand. If they do agree to let Cliff and Matthew in on what is going on, it will have to be after whatever type of memorial service is arranged for you and me. These people are deadly. If they believe for a second that things don't add up, they will come after me again."

Jillian sniffed and hiccupped, "You mean us."

Drake closed his eyes for a moment. "If they knew what you meant to me, they'd come after both of us. Or they'd try to use you to get to me." That thought sent a cold shiver of apprehension down his spine.

"You understand, don't you? Why I can't..."

Drake could tell she was trying to compose herself. He drew a deep breath. "I do. I'll do what I can." He wondered if Jewell would be able to do something, make contact in a way that was untraceable. The woman was a digital genius.

He felt her head move as she looked up at him in the darkness. "What evidence are they going to plant?"

He shook his head and snuggled her back against him. He had a good idea about what would happen. A John and Jane Doe would be planted out here in the hills. The bodies would be similar in size, but there would be no way to identify them. The corpses would eventually be identified as Drake and Jillian, but she didn't need to know anything about that. Ever.

He knew the moment she succumbed to sleep. Her body relaxed against him, and he thanked the heavens that she was able to rest, despite the shitshow that was happening around her. Drake closed his eyes and allowed himself to completely relax for the first time in over a week. Worrying about what would happen tomorrow wouldn't do anything except deny him the rest he needed. With Fury and Asp watching over him, he'd sleep like a baby. God knew he needed it too because walking down this mountain was going to hurt like a bitch.

~

Jillian glanced at the men that flanked them. The one from last night hadn't said more than three words. The big guy with the rifle that looked more like a science fiction weapon than the guns she saw on television was polite but spoke maybe three words more than the other man. That was okay because she had more than enough to think about.

She was dead to the world. Her father and brother would be told she was alive, according to Drake, but not until after the memorial or service or whatever Cliff and Matthew decided.

A cold chill raced through her. Fear and anxiety formed in the bottom of her stomach. Every instinct told her to trust Drake, that he would do whatever it took to keep them all safe, but putting her family through the pain and suffering, even for a small time...Jillian snuffed back tears and wiped her cheek again. Drake squeezed her hand. She glanced at him, and he lifted an eyebrow in silent question. She could only shrug. No, she wasn't okay, but she'd have to learn to deal with the circumstances.

The big guy pulled a handkerchief out of his pocket and handed it to her. She tried to smile but wasn't sure she managed. She was mourning her family's reaction to her 'death.' She was allowed to be sad. And tired. She was so damn tired. The trail narrowed, so they had to travel single file. Drake went before her so the big guy could help him through the rock-strewn path.

"Just a little bit further." Joseph's voice was low as he stepped up. "It's hard, what you're going through."

Jillian shook her head. As if this guy would know. "They'll never forgive me."

"Not your fault, not your doing. You want to protect them, right?"

Jillian spun to look at the man. He was big, greying black hair and green eyes. His eyes were...hell, haunted, maybe? She turned back around, trying to absorb the intensity of the man behind her. "Of course I want to protect them." Of that, there was no doubt.

She watched Drake's leg buckle. The guy with the rifle grabbed his arm and kept him upright. "Drake is a good man. He's family."

Jillian turned around. "That sounded like a threat."

Joseph leveled a stare at her. "Did it?"

She nodded and held his gaze. It was hard, but she wasn't going to be the one to look away first.

A smirk spread across the man's face. "You'll do."

Jillian frowned at the man. "I'll do? What does that mean?" She crossed her arms over her chest, ready for a fight. Tired, angry that she couldn't change her situation, and thirty seconds away from sitting down and crying, she threw caution to the wind and faced off with the person who had come to rescue them. Stupid, mainly since he was as big if not bigger than Drake.

A full smile transformed the man's features. "You have spirit, and instead of breaking down into a blubbering mess you bucked up. " He nodded down the trail. "We need to keep moving."

Jillian blinked at him before turning on her heel. "That was a compliment, right?" She shot that comment over her shoulder as they started down the path.

Low laughter, the type that sent chills down your spine during a horror film, floated toward her before he answered. "Yes, yes it was."

Jillian suppressed a shiver as the events of the last forty-eight hours flashed through her mind. Thank goodness this guy was on their side. She doubted things would have turned out as well if he wasn't.

She scrambled down after Drake, and as the path widened into a small meadow, she ducked under his arm and allowed him to put some of his weight on her shoulders when they traversed uneven ground. The terrain was grueling to travel with two good legs, she could only imagine how much pain he was in.

"Thank you." She whispered the words to him, not intending on letting the other men hear her.

He glanced down at her. His face was drawn, and there were circles under his eyes. "For what?"

"For taking care of me. For doing what you can

for my family. For loving me." Tears fell from her eyes as she looked up at him.

He stopped and swiped his thumb over her cheek, wiping away the moisture. "I'm sorry that you, Cliff and Matthew have to endure the coming weeks, but I promise I'll do everything I can. I love you." He leaned down and kissed her forehead.

"I know," Jillian answered. At the bottom of everything, all the swirling, chaotic mess of events, that very truth was her foundation. "I love you, too."

Joseph walked by. "About a half mile more." He continued on without looking back.

Drake drew a deep breath. "Come on, babe. Time to go home."

CHAPTER 24

Drake sat with his injured leg propped up on the railing as he sat with his ass planted in one of the oversized rockers he and Dixon had built for the wraparound porch. Cat, the animal that had adopted him because he made the mistake of feeding it, jumped into his lap. He was exhausted, but he knew he'd have a visitor, sooner rather than later. Drake stroked the short mousey-colored fur of the scraggly-assed cat. Cat wound up her Briggs and Stratton motor, but the damn thing had a hitch in her get-along. Every so often Cat squeaked in the middle of her purr and then had to start the motorboat going again. She was a pathetic excuse for a cat, with a bobtail that had a kink in it and half an ear missing, but she was a good mouser. He'd actually bought the damn animal food—expensive, canned, brand-name-type, cat food, but she preferred the mice and bugs she caught.

A few low cattle calls punctuated the quiet of the night. Drake closed his eyes and listened as he thought over the last fourteen hours or so. He'd been proud of Jillian today. She'd been a trooper. Throughout the trip down, she'd stayed with him, side-by-side, following Joseph without complaint. She sat through the video link debriefing and gave her statement to Jared. Jillian even stayed by his side while Doc tortured his wounds and examined his shoulder. After declaring he'd live and slapping a Band-Aid with hearts on it over a minor abrasion, Doc got a meal sent to Drake's house and drove them down in his truck, which was cool—although now that he had time to think about it, climbing into that beast may have been harder than walking the distance to the house would have been. They ate in near silence. Not that there was any strain other than exhaustion. He showed her the bedroom and en-suite. Jillian moved like she was a zombie, showered and then immediately face planted in the bed. He'd lay odds the woman was asleep before she hit the sheets.

He couldn't blame her. It had been an exhausting day.

Drake had just finished talking with Jacob. The obituary for Doctor Jillian Law would be published tomorrow. Cliff and Matthew had been notified by state police of Jillian's death. Drake hated putting them through the pretense, but when Guardian explained why perhaps he'd be forgiven.

He closed his eyes and shook his head. *"We will reach out to them as soon as we can, they will understand why. I'd go myself, but we can't send anyone that could tie Jillian to you or to us. There are ways, shadows if you will, that can get to them without being seen. I'll let you know when we've reached out."*

"Thank you." Drake would be able to let Jillian know when her father and brother were notified. It wasn't much, but it was something.

"We also put a notice in Dixon's dead drop. We don't know if he's been able to check it."

"Have you heard anything from him?"

"Not directly, but we have a...resource who has seen him. He's doing what he needs to do."

Doing what he needs to do. Jacob's words echoed in his mind. Dixon had done what he needed to do the last time he'd been trapped with that son of a bitch. The ramifications had lasted years. He prayed Dix was checking his electronic dead drop. The rat-bastard of a sperm donor would use notification of Drake's death to hurt Dixon.

He heard the footfall before the familiar form came into view. Drake smiled into the darkness.

Frank dropped into the other rocker and pushed off, sending his chair into motion. "Heard you blew up Joseph's cabin."

"Yup." It wasn't a cabin; it was a house. A damn nice one, and yeah, they'd blown it to smithereens. "Pretty sure I'm never living that one down. I could find the cure for cancer, and my headstone will still read..." he motioned with his hand, "...he blew up Fury's cabin."

Frank gave his "no shit, stupid" grunt and Drake chuckled. The man could say more with a grunt than most people could say in two minutes of talking.

"You and your woman are invited to dinner tomorrow night. Amanda wanted to give you today to settle in." Frank reached into his shirt pocket and pulled out two pieces of taffy. He offered one to Drake.

"Appreciate that." He took the candy and

unwrapped it while Cat investigated it. Frank shook his head as Cat's motor hitched and squeaked. "Never figured you for a cat person."

"Ha, well neither did I." He bopped her in the nose with the wax paper, and she took offense, promptly showing them her tail as she left. Drake popped the candy into his mouth and started refolding the wrapper.

"Dixon?"

Frank's one-word question opened the box he'd tried to keep a lid on since he'd asked Joseph for a status update. Hell, even Jared had nothing more to give him. The not knowing was chipping away at him, leaving him feeling hollow, empty and more than a bit worried. But, that was his battle, no one else's. Drake shrugged and replied as emotionlessly as he could, "Nothing direct. He's alive and still undercover."

Frank looked out into space and then let out a sound that Drake did not want to hear. "Huh."

Drake knew that comment always had something behind it. Getting Frank to voice the words might take a miracle, but he knew the man had something to say. "Huh, what?"

Frank sent him a sideways look. "Seems strange, that's all."

"Care to explain?" Drake took his leg off the porch railing, so he could turn and face Frank. "They tried to kill you, twice. Tried to take out Chief and Taty."

"Maliki, too," Drake added.

Frank turned his attention back to Drake for a moment. "That so? Have I ever met him?"

Drake shook his head. "Don't think he's ever been to the ranch."

Frank nodded and returned gazing out into the darkness before he continued, "Right. Anyway, from what I've overheard, they see Dixon on them street cameras. Makes me wonder. If we see him, wouldn't you assume whoever's hunting you sees him, too?"

Drake nodded. Of course, they'd see him, but he grasped at a straw. "Maybe they don't know where he is. He's changed locations." It seemed like years ago since he'd been told that his brother was no longer in New York. Hell, maybe he was back. Drake shut down the supposition before it started to repeat through his brain in a sadomasochistic mantra.

Frank gave another grunt. This one told him he was a dumbass. He shook his head and smiled.

He'd been on the receiving end of that grunt a few times.

"Asked myself, why would they be staying away from Dixon?" Drake waited, his mind spinning with possibilities while Frank seemed to consider his words. The older man turned his eyes to Drake. "Been pondering that some. In my mind, comes down to one conclusion. Someone's protecting him. Someone connected to whoever is after you."

His father. The man loved Dixon, in a fucked up kind of way, but Drake never doubted that his sperm donor loved Dixon as much as said sperm donor hated him. *The bastard*. Drake clamped his jaw shut and ground his teeth together.

Frank sat forward and turned his head to Drake. "I took a liberty. I called Jason and told him what my doddering old mind had spun together. Wanted you to know."

Doddering old mind, my ass. Frank was a fucking genius. One that spoke in grunts and would rather deal with animals than humans, but a genius nonetheless. Drake nodded his head, silently thanking Frank for his incentive.

Frank stood and stretched. "You head on in now. Get into bed with that filly and get some sleep.

Heard there is a mountain of paperwork waiting for you." Frank stepped off the porch but spoke over his shoulder, "Dinner's at six. Don't make me wait."

"Like that has ever happened," Drake spoke louder at Frank's retreating back.

"There is a first for everything, son. Don't get uppity or I'll take you down a peg or two."

Drake laughed, "Yes, sir." He had no doubt Frank could still do some damage. The man was on the near side of sixty, and he was tougher than a wolverine protecting her den.

Drake stood slowly and tested his weight on his leg. He limped a bit, but it wasn't too bad. He walked into the house and back to his master suite. When he and Dixon had built the house, they took into account that one day they might both have significant others or that they would share someone but still need their own space. The right side of the house was Dixon's. The left was Drake's. They had identical master bedrooms, en-suites, and office areas. They shared a massive living room, plus a kitchen and theater room. Drake made his way back to the bedroom. He shucked his clothes and slipped into bed.

Jillian rolled over and snuggled up next to him.

"What took you so long?" Jillian purred, as she trailed a hand over his abs and then traveled lower.

Drake's body took immediate notice. Making love to her might be a test in ingenuity, though. His leg was out of commission for at least a couple days, but he could think of several ways they could enjoy the comfort of his California King bed.

He turned to face her as her hand found his cock. Her grip tightened, and his eyes may have rolled back into his head for a moment. She pushed him onto his back and lifted up, sending the sheets cascading down along with her thick fall of dark blonde hair. "You, Mr. Simmons, were told by the doctor to rest. I believe his words were, 'exert no effort'." She leaned down and licked a strip up his cock. Drake bucked into her hand and groaned. He didn't remember Doc saying any such thing, but he wasn't going to say a fucking word. He was a genius after all.

Jillian's hot breath along the side of his cock sent a shudder of passion through him. He clutched the sheets in his fist and tried desperately not to come within two minutes, like some pimple-faced teenager during his first sexual encounter. But her mouth…holy fuck, her mouth and tongue were enough to break a man. Drake swore and groaned as his hips bucked up into that beautiful suction. He was so fucking close. Jillian must have sensed it, too, because she popped off and straddled him. At this rate, he wasn't going to last, and he would be damned if he came before her. He grabbed her hips and lifted her up over his mouth. His arms circled her thighs, and he pulled her down. He felt her body jerk when his tongue made contact. Drake loved the taste of her, loved how responsive she was to his touch, how she chased her own pleasure. He held on, finding her clit and teasing, sucking and licking her into a frenzy as she moved her hips against his mouth. She gripped his hair, and her thighs tightened around his head as she climaxed. Drake groaned as he lapped up her release. She gasped and lifted away when he assaulted her clit with his tongue.

Just when he thought the woman couldn't get any sexier, she lowered and kissed him, licking his lips and delving into his mouth. The taste of herself obviously turned his little minx on. Fuck. He reached behind her and grabbed his cock, squeezing the base to give himself some time.

She looked behind her and then returned her gaze toward him. "I want to ride you."

Drake held her waist with one hand and his

cock with the other. "You like that, huh? Being in charge and riding your man?"

Her grin was the stuff of wet dreams. She sat back and arched as he slid into her tight, wet, heat. Jillian dropped her hand to his chest and draped them in a shroud of blonde hair. "Yee-haw and giddy-up, big boy."

His hand snaked up from her waist and twisted in her hair as he gently tugged her down for a kiss. He released her as he thrust up, their breaths mingled as she held herself just above him. He retreated and thrust again. Drake waited until she focused on him. His hips continued long, languid strokes that propelled him toward release. "You overwhelm me."

He was lost in her. He was never supposed to find this part of himself. Yes, he was a bastard for falling in love when his brother was in peril. Yes, he was a bastard for pulling Jillian into his world, and yes, he was a bastard for wanting a life with her, but he didn't care. He couldn't. Not when his life had been rearranged on an existential level.

"I love you, Drake. I love the man you are, the wonderful brother you've always been, the strong guardian you've become and even the part of you that is my nerdy friend. But *I* don't want to talk right now." She ground her hips down on him before she whispered, "Giddy-up, horsey."

Drake threw back his head and laughed as she moved to brace herself on his shoulders. "Yes, ma'am." He grabbed her waist and obeyed her command. He was so fucking owned.

CHAPTER 25

Jillian hurried across the hard-frozen ground. Even in her down-filled coat and lined boots the cold November wind sliced through her. She loved the ranch and the complex, and since she'd arrived four months ago, she'd kept busy working on perfecting Delbert. Joey had gone back to get it for her. Joey… she smiled into the thick scarf that kept the biting wind from lashing at her face. Ember called her husband, Joey. Nobody else did, at least not to his face. Ember, Keelee, Jasmine, Sky, Lyric, Amanda and Aunt Betty had adopted her. She'd learned that each one of them had arrived at the ranch in different ways, but for each of them, love kept them firmly planted in the South Dakota soil.

It was Winchester Wednesday. The social event of the week. The ladies drank wine and watched Sam and Dean while they gossiped about the happenings around the ranch and complex. The men had childcare duties. They swapped responsibilities on Thursdays, so the guys could play poker, drink single malt and do whatever it was that men did when they bonded. She was late. For some reason, Jason King, the brother who was the CEO of Guardian had a scheduling conflict and needed to discuss the status of her miniaturization of the power pack for the long- distance coms units. It was going well, and she sent in weekly updates to the logistics branch chief. Why Jason King needed a personal briefing was beyond her. He kept her until she knew she was late. Hopefully, the ladies waited for her to start the episode. It was the second part of a two-part thriller that had Dean in purgatory...again.

She stomped her boots off on the front porch and opened the grand door to the 'big house' where Frank and Amanda lived. It was the ranch version of a mansion. Huge, but warm and inviting with a massive fireplace. She unwrapped her scarf and hung it on one of the many pegs that lined the wall, calling out as she stripped out of her coat. "Please tell me you didn't start yet!"

"No, I didn't start."

Jillian spun at the sound of Drake's voice. "You're here!" She leaned around him to look into the great room. A hundred candles twinkled on every surface. She stood straight again and spun to her left, looking into the dining room that was dark and deserted. "Where is everyone? Why are you here?" Drake laughed and rubbed the back of his neck like he did when he was embarrassed. "What's going on?"

Drake extended his hand to her, and she took it. *Oh...no, no he couldn't be...*Drake bent one knee and kissed her hand before he looked up at her. "Jillian Allison Law, I'm in love with you. Because you are in my life, I can breathe. You are my happiness and my sanity. You're the reason my life makes sense. I don't want to live without you. Will you marry me?"

Jillian realized her hand covered her mouth. Tears filled her eyes. "I love you so much. You are everything to me, you always have been."

Drake smiled. "Is that a yes?"

Jillian shook her head. "Yes, I mean, maybe, but right now? No?"

She heard a gasp and looked up. The entire balcony was lined with the people she'd grown to love. She returned her gaze to Drake. "I can't marry you, now. Not until Dixon comes home."

"When Dixon comes home?" Drake parroted her words. "He hasn't been seen in three months."

Jillian dropped to her knees in front of Drake and touched her hand to his chest, covering his heart. "And yet you know, here in your heart that he is still alive. Don't you?"

Drake nodded.

"I've watched a little bit of you fade each day that he's been missing. Do I love you? Yes, without reservation. Do I want to marry you? God, yes, desperately, but will I accept your proposal while you fight a battle between your love and loyalty to your brother and the love we share? No. I won't. When we find Dixon and bring him home, I'll marry you."

"And if we never find him?" Drake covered her hand with his.

"I'm not going anywhere. I'll be here. I love you, but I know your heart is divided between your obligation and relationship with him and your love for me." He started to speak, but she covered his lips with a single finger. "I know you have room for both of us. That has never been a doubt for me, but you need him as much as you need me. Differently, of course, but the need is just as important." She leaned in, and he wrapped her in his arms.

"Thank you." He kissed her temple.

She chuffed out an emotion-filled laugh. "For saying not now?"

"For seeing and understanding what I couldn't express. I love you so damn much."

"And I love you."

"Did she really say no?" a voice blurted out above them.

"Jade!" At least ten voices shouted the name at the same time.

"What? She said no! How fucking epic is that?"

A litany of voices rose. Jillian looked up at the people who were gathered at the railing. Drake's chest started moving under her hands. She glanced back at him in time to see him throw back his head and laugh. He rose to his feet and pulled her up with him. "You better say yes the next time I ask you." Drake grabbed her face and kissed her. Jillian melted into his embrace. *Of course, she'd say yes, as soon as Dixon came home. Alive. She wouldn't accept anything less.*

CHAPTER 26

Zane Reynolds walked into the room beside his wife, Jewell. They'd been summoned into the main conference room not more than three minutes ago, but already seated at the table were Jason, Jared, and Jacob. What really stood out in Zane's mind was the presence of Gabriel, the former CEO of Guardian Security. "Close the door and put the room into privacy mode, would you, Zane?" Jason didn't look up from the stack of papers in front of him.

"Where are Jade and Nic?" Jared asked as Zane did as he was bid.

"I didn't invite them. Jade is a wild card who breaks rules she doesn't like. I believe if Nic is made aware of what is going on, it would only be a matter of time before Jade knew. They are a team, I get it." Jason leaned back in his chair and took off his glasses. He looked at each of the people sitting around the table. "Frank Marshall called me a little over four months ago. He had a theory. So, I discussed it with Gabriel, and we put out some covert feelers through the business community. Nothing that could be traced back to us, yet the information that started to come back seemed to validate our suspicions."

Jacob leaned forward. "Well, that's cryptic as fuck. Care to put it into words us less educated folk can follow?"

Jason glanced at Gabriel who nodded.

"We've been gathering intelligence through both of your units, covertly."

"You mean without our knowledge." Jewell slapped her tablet down. "I knew it. I knew there was a leak of information." She turned and glared at Zane. "You were funneling them information from my section. Weren't you?"

Zane nodded. He hated doing it, but as it was explained to him, he didn't have an option.

Jewell launched into a tirade as Jared exploded,

"Motherfucker, why in the hell?" Jacob sprang up demanding who in his section was working against him.

"Shut up!" Jason roared. "Sit your asses down and shut your mouths, now!"

He pointed at Jewell who'd opened her mouth again. Zane put his hand on her leg to quiet her.

Jason stared at each one of his siblings. "I don't want another word breathed in this room until I finish this briefing."

"We have confirmed Stratus is a real entity." Jason passed out a sheet of paper. Zane knew what it said. He'd given the list of six names to Jason this morning. The workers did the background searches as required. None knew why they were gathering the intel. As a ruse and to confuse any attempts to determine the 'why' of the assignment, each person in each section was given seven names. So, seven backgrounds were completed by each section, and for the first time in Guardian's history, the right hand was purposely blinded from the left hand. Five names filtered to the top of each search. It was incredibly easy to check and double check when they found the common key. Five names were mined, new players in the game. One additional name was known. He glanced at the names on the list Jewell held. Five names were printed, the sixth position remained blank. He understood the reason for that, too.

"These five people have a common link to each other. Flowers, or the man known to us as Flowers, was the secret decoder ring we used to find the other six."

"Six?" Jared looked from his list to Jacob's then to Jewell's.

"We'll get to that. We are assuming each of these five has taken a blood fealty oath to the organization that operates Stratus. We bore witness to that in Colombia when Flowers killed himself before he let Asp bring him in."

"Stratus works for someone?" Jacob asked.

"So much for not asking any questions until I finish." Jason leveled his gaze at his brothers. "We reached out to some of the underworld contacts Chief made when he was posing as David Xavier. The information we got back was patchy at best, but we have enough now to go forward. There are supposedly three women who run the Stratus Seven—now, with the loss of Flowers, the Stratus Six. Some of our contacts called them, 'The Fates'."

"You mean like the Greek mythology Fates? Cutting the golden string of life and shit like that?" Jewell grabbed Zane's hand, and he curled his fingers around hers.

He'd get thoroughly thrashed by his wife for the role he'd played in this intelligence gathering operation. He deserved it. He'd been placed in a no-win situation. Zane also knew she'd soon understand why.

"Who knows. That's as good a theory as any at this point. While we don't know why they are called The Fates, we do know they are well funded, well organized, and they are building up," said Jason.

"Have we identified the members of Stratus and which of them are called The Fates?" Jared asked.

"These are the members of Stratus who we believe are funded by The Fates." Jason handed a small booklet to each of his department heads including Zane.

Zane glanced down and read the first name on the list. Beside it was listed background information, businesses owned, shell companies, and monetary net worth.

"This doesn't show their connection to one

another," Jared grumbled his observation.

Jason glanced at Gabriel again. The man nodded once. Jason sighed and rubbed the back of his neck before he hit the button that would drop the monitor from the ceiling. "This is a graph showing each man. If you look back through their pasts, there is one central link. It also links the person we believe is being groomed for the seventh position. The intelligence we gained from Chief and Tatyana's not too willing companion when we got him back to the States was shocking. He knew more than we believed. After countless interviews, we've found our link.

"What do you mean? I've read every interview. I've gone through them with a fine-tooth comb. There was no indication of a link to Stratus or a link between these men." Jared lifted his confused gaze to his brother. "Who tipped you off they were connected?"

"They did."

"How?"

Jason pointed to the monitor and clicked his pointer. "These men all started their life of crime in an unusual way. Franco DeYoung was an aspiring ADA in New York City. He fell off the map almost seventeen years ago." Jason listed the other four members. All were lawyers.

"The last in this series of five is someone we know." Jason hit the remote in his hand again.

It took a second, but Zane saw the instant Jewell recognized the name. She spun to him and then to her brothers. "You're shitting us, right?"

"No. Consider the information in its entirety. He has had a meteoric political rise to power that has concerned many on the council, especially when the monetary support is being funneled from overseas assets through shell companies and then into his bankroll."

"That explains Flowers working the Colombian connection and bankrolling the FARC remnant to... Hell, that is why they used Flowers as a cover name. They were trying to undermine the President's closest adviser and cast a hell of a shadow on the President." Jared turned toward Gabriel. "That simple connection could cost the President the next election."

Gabriel nodded. He leaned forward and linked his fingers together. "There was an economist that was assassinated years ago. He wasn't just a simple professor. He'd published a theory in an obscure academic periodical. In it, he theorized that if a core few held the world's money and that same group controlled the world's most formidable military, the entire globe could be ruled within two years if specific economic actions were put into play. We've seen two of the steps he listed within the last five months."

"So what…what are they going after? The Presidency? The world's economy?" Jacob sat back as he asked.

"I agree with Jacob, we need to know what their end game is. We can't plan a defense unless we know where they will focus." Jared shook his head and closed the cover on the dossier he'd skimmed through. He pointed to the name on the board and then tapped the brown pressboard cover of the dossier. "The background on him isn't included."

"I've got that here." Jason indicated the stack of papers beside him. "Before I give you this, I can tell you what their end game is." He pushed the remote one more time.

Zane heard the collective inhale of breath.

"No." Jewell turned toward him.

He nodded. It was true. He'd validated every shred of information, and he'd had Moriah insert herself into the equation to verify it.

"Oh, my God." Jacob's whispered words had been the same words that had echoed in Zane's mind for the last eight hours.

Jason tossed a thick folder on the table in front of each person there. "Their end game is us."

EPILOGUE

The desk phone rang, interrupting Drake as he scanned a new blueprint of Jillian's building. He ignored it until it rang again and then grabbed it without looking at the caller ID.

"Go."

"Hey. Glad you're not dead."

Dixon's voice struck him like a bolt of lightning. He straightened and grasped the handle of the phone with a death grip as if that would keep his brother from disappearing again. "Me, too. Are you okay?"

"I am, for now. Out of the fucker's grasp for the moment and I needed a sanity check. How're things at the ranch?"

"Fuck, everything is good here. Dix, there is a new threat." Drake had to warn his brother since no one at Guardian had been able to ascertain if Dixon was getting the dead drop communications.

Dixon sighed, "Stratus. I know."

"How?"

Dixon spoke in a flurry of words as if pressed for time and looking over one shoulder. "Look, I don't have time to go into it. I couldn't respond to the dead drop, they watch me, monitor me all the time, but I was able to buy this burner cell. I accessed the internet, and I've opened a new email account. Tell Jewell it is under our mom's maiden name. She'll find it. The information I could validate is in the draft message folder. I'm destroying this phone as soon as we finish talking so there will be no way for them to trace that action. Are you okay?

Drake glanced out the window toward the ranch side of the complex. He thought of Jillian. Things were better than okay. "I am. Lying low after a minor run-in with some goons put into motion by the Russian Mafia and backed by Stratus. When are you coming home?"

"I don't know. There have been…complications. I'm working on it." Dixon sighed.

Fuck, it was good to hear Dixon's voice. It had been over five months since he'd been gone. Christmas was in two weeks.

"What are you working on?"

"I can't say, and you wouldn't understand. Besides, you knowing what I'm doing wouldn't help." Dix countered.

"I...fuck, Dix. I miss you."

"I miss you more."

"Ha. Semantics." Drake fell into the banter that eased both of their minds. It was good to get out of his head and play word games with his brother. No matter how briefly.

"Bullshit. There are no semantics. What you're doing is shading your own reality. Our own truth." Dixon countered.

"I miss you. Period and full stop." Drake flipped the words out as they came to him.

"Still shades of your truth." Dixon mused.

"Define truth." Drake countered.

"That for which there is no alternative but to believe as an absolute," Dixon retorted without delay.

"Is there such a thing for us?" Drake asked as he looked out of the window. He saw Jillian, bundled up and heading his way. He glanced at the clock on the wall. He fucking loved that woman, that truth was absolute.

"Yeah." Dixon was silent for a moment before he answered. "I think love is the absolute truth."

"Love for your family?" Drake asked.

"That is one type," Dixon responded, but his voice had changed.

Drake tore his eyes off Jillian and focused on his brother's voice. "You've met someone?"

"I'm not sure, but...it's complicated," Dixon answered.

"Grab onto it, Dix. Hold on tight." Drake pleaded with his brother. If Dixon had someone, then he wouldn't feel as guilty about his feelings for Jillian, and fuck him, those feelings grew stronger with each passing day.

"What about you?" Dixon's voice hardened.

"I've found someone, Dix. She's amazing and ... just, fuck…take care of yourself and simplify those complications. Without you here, I'm as happy as I can be. I miss the fuck out of you." Drake closed his eyes and prayed his brother would listen.

"I'm happy for you, D. Take your own advice and try to grab onto that reality. It won't last. Good things never do."

"Dix what are you trying to tell me?" Drake could swear his brother was talking in riddles.

"I...nothing, man. It's just fucked up here. Nothing is solid. Everything is so mired in lies, half-truths, and innuendo that I can't trust anyone. Hell, half the time I'm not even sure what I feel is real."

"Trust your gut. Don't take any chances." Drake dropped his head to the desk. He hated that he couldn't see his brother, be with him.

The laugh he got was dark and bitter. "Yeah, making a leap of faith could get me killed. Better to put my head down and do what I need to do, right?"

Drake bolted upright. "Walk away, Dixon. Get the fuck out, now." Fuck, he didn't need Dixon endangering himself.

"I can't." The words sounded distant as if Dixon had turned his head away from the phone.

"Dix..."

"Yeah man, I know. Listen, I need to go. I'm safe, for now, and I'm being maudlin. Feeling fucking homesick, maybe. Keep your head down and protect what's yours."

Drake blinked hard. Fuck him, he didn't want

to say goodbye. "I will. Take care of yourself. I love you."

"And I love you. Later, D."

"When? When's later, Dixon?" Drake clawed at an opportunity to know more.

"Got to go. Merry Christmas, Drake. Whatever it takes."

"As long as it takes, Dix. Merry Christmas, little brother." Drake put the phone down and held his head in his hands. His gut churned, and acid rose in his throat. His pulse pounded as he set the phone in its cradle. A sense of dread washed over him. He closed his eyes and said a silent prayer before he picked up the phone again. Even if it took his resignation, he refused to stand on the sidelines any longer.

To read the next in the Kings of Guardian Series, Dixon, click here!

The End

ALSO BY KRIS MICHAELS

Kings of the Guardian Series

Jacob: Kings of the Guardian Book 1

Joseph: Kings of the Guardian Book 2

Adam: Kings of the Guardian Book 3

Jason: Kings of the Guardian Book 4

Jared: Kings of the Guardian Book 5

Jasmine: Kings of the Guardian Book 6

Chief: The Kings of Guardian Book 7

Jewell: Kings of the Guardian Book 8

Jade: Kings of the Guardian Book 9

Justin: Kings of the Guardian Book 10

Christmas with the Kings

Drake: Kings of the Guardian Book 11

Dixon: Kings of the Guardian Book 12

Passages: The Kings of Guardian Book 13

Promises: The Kings of Guardian Book 14

A Backwater Blessing: A Kings of Guardian Crossover Novella

Montana Guardian: A Kings of Guardian Novella

Guardian Defenders Series

Gabriel

Maliki

John

Jeremiah

Guardian Security Shadow World

Anubis (Guardian Shadow World Book 1)

Asp (Guardian Shadow World Book 2)

Lycos (Guardian Shadow World Book 3)

Thanatos (Guardian Shadow World Book 4)

Tempest (Guardian Shadow World Book 5)

Smoke (Guardian Shadow World Book 6)

Reaper (Guardian Shadow World Book 7)

Hope City

Hope City - Brock

HOPE CITY - Brody- Book 3

Hope City - Ryker - Book 5

Hope City - Killian - Book 8

STAND ALONE NOVELS

SEAL Forever - Silver SEALs

A Heart's Desire - Stand Alone

Hot SEAL, Single Malt (SEALs in Paradise)

Hot SEAL, Savannah Nights (SEALs in Paradise)

ABOUT THE AUTHOR

USA Today and Amazon Bestselling Author, Kris Michaels is the alter ego of a happily married wife and mother. She writes romance, usually with characters from military and law enforcement backgrounds.

Printed in Great Britain
by Amazon